Emi Yusa

Suzuno Kamazuki

THE DEVIL IS A PART-TIMER!

6

SATOSHI WAGAHARA

ILLUSTRATION BY
029 (ONIKU)

MgRonald

CONTENTS

**SATOSHI
WAGAHARA**
ILLUSTRATED BY ■ **029
(ONIKU)**

YEN
ON

NEW YORK

THE DEVIL IS A PART-TIMER!, Volume 6
SATOSHI WAGAHARA, ILLUSTRATION BY 029 (ONIKU)

Translation by Kevin Gifford
Cover art by 029 (oniku)

HATARAKU MAOUSAMA!, Volume 6
© SATOSHI WAGAHARA 2012
Edited by ASCII MEDIA WORKS

First published in 2012 by KADOKAWA CORPORATION, Tokyo.
English translation rights arranged with KADOKAWA CORPORATION,
Tokyo, through Tuttle-Mori Agency, Inc., Tokyo.

English translation © 2016 by Yen Press, LLC

Yen On
1290 Avenue of the Americas
New York, NY 10104

Visit us at yenpress.com
facebook.com/yenpress
twitter.com/yenpress
yenpress.tumblr.com
yenpress.com/yenpress
instagram.com/yenpress

First Yen On Edition: December 2016

Yen On is an imprint of Yen Press, LLC.
The Yen On name and logo are trademarks of Yen Press,
LLC.

The publisher is not responsible for websites (or their
content) that are not owned by the publisher.

Library of Congress Cataloging-in-Publication Data
Names: Wagahara, Satoshi. | 029 (Light novel
illustrator) illustrator. | Gifford, Kevin, translator.
Title: The devil is a part-timer! / Satoshi Wagahara ;
illustration by 029 (oniku) : translation by Kevin
Gifford.
Other titles: Hataraku Maousama! English
Description: First Yen On edition. | New York, NY :
Yen On, 2015–
Identifiers: LCCN 2015028390|
ISBN 9780316383127 (v. 1 ; pbk.) |
ISBN 9780316385015 (v. 2 ; pbk.) |
ISBN 9780316385022 (v. 3 ; pbk.) |
ISBN 9780316385039 (v. 4 ; pbk.) |
ISBN 9780316385046 (v. 5 ; pbk.) |
ISBN 9780316385060 (v. 6 ; pbk.)
Subjects: | CYAC: Fantasy.
Classification: LCC PZ7.1.W34 Ha 2015 | DDC
[Fic]—dc23
LC record available at
http://lccn.loc.gov/2015028390
ISBNs: 978-0-316-38506-0 (paperback)
978-0-316-39808-4 (ebook)

10 9 8 7 6 5 4 3 2 1

LSC-C

Printed in the United States of America

PROLOGUE

The red sky grew blurred and bleary above him.

It was a short life. And, in his young mind, he was ready to give it up.

Lacking even the strength to move his fingertips, his indistinct view of the world around him was enough to make him realize his life would disappear before long. There was no fear. He was so young that there wasn't any capacity to dread it yet.

In terms of life expectancy, he should have had a while to go. His parents had each lived for a thousand years, he was told. But that meant little compared to the whirlwind of violence he was faced with. Everything around him was stained in red, red, red, making an already scarlet-tinted world even bloodier as it began to consume him.

There was no despair, no sadness; but there was *something*...

"..."

...He was bitter.

Was this soul infused within this body just so someone else could squeeze it out? Did time march on to this point just so that his entire tribe could die in pools of blood?

Just when he began to consciously recognize himself and the paths he had taken in life, that life of his was about to be lost, valueless, like a cloud dissipating into the air. Like a passing breeze, like the loose earth, soaking up the blood around him.

Why did my soul have to take up residence in a place like this?

If a soul being born, then fading away, is the natural order of things, why did mine have to find itself in a body like this?

The red sky blurred a little more, growing further indistinct. Then from his eyes, a strange, clear liquid, different from the red puddle around him, fell downward. At that moment, there was something else ruling over his soul, pushing away the red sky, red ground, red wind, and red-stained body that was at the brink of death.

Within the vast, dark sky above him, untold hundreds of points of light twinkled. Among them were two spheres, much larger and distinct than the rest. Two places that untold numbers of souls called home, or so it seemed to him. And, he felt, lands he might find himself traveling to very soon.

They had an attraction that was difficult to define, their unknown colors alluring and comforting. It was a far cry from the red that now enveloped him, and it called him closer.

But he could not reach them; his body and soul refused to move. And yet they seemed so close, within arm's reach—these spheres where both could finally find solace.

The lights floating in the emptiness grew indistinct once more.

"...Well, not to disappoint you or anything, but it's not exactly a lovefest all day up there, either. If you asked me, there isn't a word out there used and abused more than *paradise*."

The crimson quickly returned to his vision.

His consciousness was buffeted by the jolts of pain that ran across his body. But he had definitely heard it.

"A lot of things change when you have a different perspective, I guess you could say. In fact, I'd say all the red around here is a lot prettier."

"But...I'm scared. Of red."

"Oh? Scared, huh? Well, that's a surprise. Seeing a demon cry is one thing, but I didn't think you'd start whining about the one color that defines the entire demon realms, too."

The existence of a voice meant that someone was nearby. The life was almost vacant from his body, but the fact he was now lying on the ground, defenseless, filled him with a new sensation: fear. And a fearful heart is a heart that wants to live, a heart that thinks it wants to keep muddling forward.

He furtively searched for the enemy with his blurred eyesight, only to find an unknown someone looking down upon him. Its form was not much different from his own young body—even thinner, if anything. It was a foe like none he'd seen before, and now its lips were curled upward in a smile.

"Would you like to know the name of that color you just saw?"

He found himself nodding without hesitation at the query. Enough spiritual force had found itself back inside his soul to make it happen.

The enemy's hair seemed to shine, its aura reminiscent of the color he was now so curious about.

"Once you do, you'll learn more about the world itself. That, and you'll learn about a new aspect of the red that you fear so much."

He found himself bathed in a dim light, the pain palpably easing away from his body.

"What's your name?"

"…Satan."

It was an extremely common name, where he came from. But the enemy still gave it a grandiose nod.

"That's a nice name."

What was so nice about it? It came from some great emperor who united this land at some point in the ancient past. Too regal a name for some kid from one of the bog-level tribes, all but ready to give up the ghost right here. He never had a chance to even try living up to it.

"I'm going to impart to you the knowledge you need in order to learn about the world. The knowledge you need to make that fear-tinged red seem beautiful to you."

The smile seemed to etch itself within his soul.

"The color you saw was—"

THE
DEVIL
CLOCKS
BACK
IN

From the outside, things didn't look too terribly different. Not that it would have been. Despite the extensive renovation work inside, as rent-paying tenants, they weren't allowed to change all that much with the externals. They didn't even apply a new coat of paint to the outer walls. One look at the cornerstone, and it was clear to anyone that the building already had a good twenty years or so of age on it.

"You look disappointed."

His boss gave him a self-satisfied smile as she crossed her arms. The shoulder bag dangling at her side was packed to the gills with paperwork and other necessities.

"Well, I dunno. You said there were all these upgrades we were gonna do, so I figured it'd look a bit newer on the outside, kinda."

As he spoke, Sadao Maou parked Dullahan II, his trusty fixed-gear steed, in the all-too-familiar employee parking area. Today was the day his workplace, the MgRonald in front of Hatagaya rail station, opened its doors once more.

The nonslip construction flooring and antidust covers were all peeled off the building, a sign advertising the new services (the whole reason for the renovation work) was attached to the front, and most of the external fixtures and such were shiny and new. But none of the changes seemed particularly drastic to him.

Still, taking in the new sign, he realized that the red paint on the old one—one of the official corporate colors—must have faded a fair bit over time. Exposed to the city air and the sun's UV rays, that kind of aging process was inevitable.

On that note, the newly installed sign and its vibrant red hue definitely exuded an air of newness.

The large windows facing the door had some new tint work done on them, making it hard to see inside. But the windows themselves were still in the same frames, the automatic doors in the same position, and the interior doubtlessly not all that different, either.

If the kitchen and customer-entrance locations were the same, traffic flow around the dining space couldn't be much different, either. Maou doubted that corporate did much with the seating arrangements and such.

"Well, let's not judge a book by its cover too quickly, shall we?"

Mayumi Kisaki, store manager and Maou's boss, looked supremely confident as she strode up to the door, using a key to release the lock on the bottom—the same as always with that, too. She pushed the door open as she continued, fumbling anxiously through a key ring she'd fished out of her shoulder bag.

"Give me just one minute. Once I open the door, I have to turn this other key on the new alarm panel within forty seconds or else the security company will automatically call the authorities. Um, which key was it…? This one?"

Maou took his first step into the dim dining space as she briskly walked inside, noticing a constant electronic beep from the security panel deeper within. He waited patiently, the still-sweltering heat making him wish summer would end already. Then, after half a minute or so:

"!!"

The lights suddenly turned on.

It was a kind of light Maou had never experienced before in his daily life. Certainly not the fluorescent-tube illumination he had grown so used to. Investigating the ceiling revealed that it was lined with countless lights, each one a tiny yet powerful bulb. They seemed to stab into his eyes with their sharpness, but the rows of alternating white and orange worked together to fill the place with a soft sort of radiance neither too dim nor too bright.

"Whoa!" The shock ejected itself out from his lips. "This must be the LED lighting I've heard so much about!"

And everything it illuminated was a marked departure from what came before it. The plush seating that lined the walls, their plastic pastel colors faded through years of use, were now a uniform, refined brown, modeled after high-priced leather seating.

The swivel seats that once lined the bar counter, which grated annoyingly against the hard tile floor and were a pain to keep neat and orderly, had been replaced with high-seated chairs mounted against the wall. And those walls, whose color had morphed over time from pink to a vaguely sort of Caucasian skin tone, now boasted a line of yellow tiles with patterns in them, their relaxed tone a refreshing match with the lights and fixtures.

Kisaki spun the key ring around her finger as she came back. "What do you think? Still disappointed now?"

Maou firmly shook his head.

"The kitchen equipment got an upgrade, too, though it mostly works the same as before. But we finally got a three-plate grill in, so that oughta make the rushes a bit easier."

"Ooh, I appreciate that!"

Maou wasn't lying. It honestly put a sparkle in his eye.

MgRonald burgers could be divided into several core components—the buns, the patty, then the cheese, vegetables, sauce, and so forth. The kitchen used what was known as a clamshell grill, an industrial skillet featuring movable platens that allowed the operator to cook patties on both sides simultaneously. Their previous grill had only two platens, reflecting the small size of the original business setup.

Since every order had its own ingredients and flavorings, these platens would need to be cleaned after cooking things like fish and teriyaki chicken sandwiches to keep any rogue flavors from bleeding through to the next order. That cleaning process, if it came during the lunch or dinner rush, would inevitably generate what was called "wait time" in MgRonald corporate speak—in other words, customers would need to wait longer than strictly necessary, messing up the store's order rhythm. The availability (or lack thereof) of a single platen made a night-and-day difference in work time and stress.

"Hey, is the wash basin bigger, too?"

"Yep. Plus, the faucet's automatic now."

"Wow!!"

Admiration and wonderment oozed out of every pore of Maou's body. Although, really, the universal presence in Japan of porcelain basins with metallic spigots that spat out fresh water with a simple turn of a handle had been an enormous culture shock to him when he first showed up. Nowhere in the demon realms—and certainly nowhere among the five continents that made up the land of Ente Isla—was there a water system robust enough to bring clean water to individual homes whenever you needed it. The "water system" in Maou's old domain was whatever stream you happened to be nearby, running from the source to wherever it drained to, with maybe a few magically operated valve systems in the manors of nobility.

To someone like Maou, for whom the presence of a water source you could shut off at will was already exciting enough, the first sight of an auto-flushing public toilet left him astonished. *You don't even have to* turn a handle *anymore?!* was his honest thought. But now, he understood their purpose. Faucet handles in public facilities could be crawling with germs. And considering MgRonald's standard rule of one thorough handwashing per hour, having an automatic faucet seemed like a godsend.

"This all is a really big step forward!"

Kisaki looked graciously, if a tad suspiciously, at the astounded Maou.

"You know, I love how…I dunno, rustic you act sometimes."

"Huh?"

"Oh, never mind. It's nothing big. By the way, Number Ten's around this corner. There's three of them across the two floors."

"Number Ten" was semiofficial corporate code for the public

bathrooms. Maou stepped inside the one nearby, only to find himself stopped cold for a moment.

"Something wrong?"

"N-no, i-it seems like something's missing. Did it get smaller?"

A toilet sat inside the room, but it was one wholly beyond Maou's ken.

"Oh, that's one of the new heated-seat models, the kind that doesn't need a separate water tank. And also…"

Kisaki pointed out a panel lined with buttons, a sort of remote control bolted to the wall.

"You can push a button to lift the lid up."

"Whaaaaa?!"

The amazement was deep-rooted and profound. He could see the advantage of an automatic faucet, but what possible need could there be for a remotely operated toilet seat lid? His slack-jawed reaction drew a bemused smile from Kisaki.

"And if you're a guy doing a number one, this button lifts the whole thing up, too."

To Maou, this seemed like taking a simple, instinctive routine and making it needlessly complex. He could understand if someone was leery to use a john touched, rubbed, and/or soiled by God-knows-who before them, but didn't this just mean the germs were on the control panel now instead?

"Um…so what do the buttons with one water drop and a lot of them mean?"

"Right, that's how you flush."

Kisaki motioned Maou to press the single-droplet button. Maou obliged, and a trickle of water—much less than he expected—began to flow along the inner surface.

"Bet I could save on my water bill if I had *this* at home…"

The Japanese-style floor toilet at the Devil's Castle in Villa Rosa Sasazuka, a sixty-year-old wooden apartment building five minutes from Sasazuka rail station, didn't differentiate between little and big flushes. There was a lever, and that was that.

Letting only a little trickle go through was supposedly bad for the water tank, but indulging in a full flush with every trip to the little demon's room caused both a huge racket at night and a fair amount of concern for their utility bills.

Maou put his home affairs aside for a moment in his mind. "Um... so is this kind of thing normal now? I mean, I know my place was pretty much built in the Stone Age, but most public bathrooms still have the regular kind, right? Do you think our older customers will know how to use this?"

"Hmm..." Kisaki nodded. "You might have a point. We should probably post up some instructions. But anyway, this is still just for starters. The *real* show isn't until you see the brand-new space upstairs."

There was no point jaw-dropping in the crapper all day. Kisaki guided Maou toward the stairway to one side of the order counter. "This'll probably be a whole new world to you, up here. A new battlefield, I guess you could say. It'll be a test for all of us. Just remember: outside of myself, you're the first member of the Hatagaya crew to set foot up here, all right?"

Maou swallowed nervously as he followed, holding on to the handrail as he followed the stairs—the same color as the floor—upward. There, at the top, he found...

✳

For Sadao Maou—aka the Devil King Satan, assuming human form in this alien world called Japan, as he worked an hourly job to keep the lights on—it had proven difficult to take much of any action during the first half of August.

Once he and his cohorts returned from their stint at a beachside snack shop in Choshi, they were quickly greeted by the seeds of a new and sinister concern. The winds of war had begun to blow over in Ente Isla—and what was more, the powers that be over there had begun to extend their reach to Japan in a more physical manner than before.

While the three demon cast-outs living in Japan—Sadao Maou, Shirou Ashiya, and Hanzou Urushihara—were away, a new would-be overlord attempted to seize power in their realm, rebelling against the system Satan created and attempting to form a New Devil King's Army. It was enough to put any tyrant ruler on the defensive.

Meanwhile, the human forces of Ente Isla that chased Maou and gang to Earth—Emilia the Hero, now known as Emi Yusa; and Church cleric Crestia Bell, doing human business as Suzuno Kamazuki—were still an ominous presence in his mind.

While ostensibly tasked with the job of defeating the Devil King once and for all, due to the minor family drama of Alas Ramus treating Satan as her father and fusing herself with the Hero's holy sword, these human Ente Islans were unable to act upon their mission with any great sense of urgency. At the moment, the two of them were more concerned that Maou and his generals would be kidnapped by this New Devil King's Army, appointing Satan as its figurehead as it launched a brand-new demon assault on their homeland. Thus, they found themselves in the unenviable position of essentially running guard duty for the Devil King they swore to defeat, making sure he wasn't whisked anywhere they didn't want him to go.

And just when it seemed like things couldn't get more complicated between the Hero and Devil King, a bunch of angels stepped in from heaven to make everything thornier. *Their* plans, however, seemed to have less to do with Maou and Emi and more to do with Chiho Sasaki, mild-mannered high schooler and the only girl on Earth who knew about Ente Isla and the drama involved with it.

It was enough to make Maou and Emi, enraged at how the angels put Chiho in the hospital with a serious case of dark-magic poisoning, voluntarily join forces for the first time in order to drive the angels away from Japan.

But in the midst of *that*, they discovered that Emi's father, thought to be dead at the hands of Maou's old demon hordes, was alive after all. Not to mention some mystery person had lent a carload of holy force to Chiho so she could help dispatch the angel Raguel, making Maou and Emi realize that yet another faction was now trying to make its presence known.

Chiho was right as rain now, though. And even though things

were even more twisted and tangled than ever before, the entire gang still had the mental wherewithal to enjoy the ever-so-light, but still unmistakable, early suggestions of autumn in the late August air.

And meanwhile, in the midst of all this devastating cross-world conflict, the MgRonald location Maou worked at in Hatagaya was due to open tomorrow.

✳

"I dunno, it's like… It's the Mag, but it's *not* the Mag, too—but in a good way. It's still friendly and approachable, but it's all *refined* and stuff, too!"

It wasn't even noon, but Maou already had a towel around his head and gloves on his hands as he tried to resist the pressure of the unrelenting sun in his white T-shirt.

"The second floor overlooks the street by the rail station, but you actually get a pretty good view of the whole area. They've got blinds on the windows so the sunlight doesn't get too rough, but it's like… *Man*, it's gonna be really exciting working there!"

"Aw, that's no fair, Maou! You went all by yourself?!"

The voice complaining about Maou's passionate review belonged to Chiho Sasaki, decked out in a workout jacket and pants, an identical pair of cotton work gloves as he had, and a broad-brimmed hat.

"Hey, you'll be back in the shift rotation too pretty soon, Chi!"

"Well, yeah, but it's still not fair!"

Chiho, who worked on the Hatagaya MgRonald's part-time crew alongside Maou, must have had as healthy of a curiosity about the place as he did.

"So it is called a…MagCafé, yes? How does it differ from a regular MgRonald?"

Shirou Ashiya, aka Maou's Great Demon General Alciel, interjected this question as he wiped at the sweat pouring down his face with the hem of his T-shirt. The towel-bandanna and gloves were a match for Maou's.

"Well, it's a café and all, so there's a buncha different kinds of coffee!

Like, café au lait, caffe latte, espresso, you name it! It usedta be MgRo-nald Platinum Roast or nothing, but not anymore. We got more café-type things on the menu, too, like hot dogs and pancakes and stuff...!"

Maou breathed deeply through his nose, clearly unable to wait another moment to man the counter.

"Alciel, do *not* disrobe and reveal your chest in front of Chiho while she is trying to help us out! The very *nerve*! And *you*, Devil King—stop your jabbering and put in more of an actual work effort!"

These orders came from Maou's next-door neighbor, the cleric Crestia Bell, better known these days as Suzuno Kamazuki.

She had a sash over the kimono she usually wore around the house, a washcloth wrapped tight around her forehead as, with engloved hands, she wielded a broom about the same height as herself.

They were all sweating it out in the backyard of Villa Rosa Sasa-zuka, the apartment building that currently housed the multidi-mensional demon headquarters known as the Devil's Castle.

Whenever summer rolled around, the lone evergreen tree within the apartment grounds played host to several million cicadas and locusts of all kinds. The resulting din of scratchy insect cries made it difficult to make yourself heard without raising your voice.

"Yeah, yeah..."

"M-my apologies!"

Ashiya hurriedly slipped his shirt back down as Maou returned to work.

"No, um... I wasn't offended or anything..." Chiho turned a little red with embarrassment herself before she put it behind her. "Hey! Hey, what's the difference between a café au lait and a caffe latte?!"

Maou sighed deeply.

"...Um."

He stopped his work and looked up into the air, perhaps calling upon the blazing sun to jog his memory.

"Like, a café au lait has milk in it, and a caffe latte has...um, milk in it? They both got milk in it, right, but it's, like, bubbly and stuff in a latte...I think?"

"Yes! Wonderful! Coffee with milk in it! Now, can you stop using your head and start using your hands a little?!"

"Well, I mean, it's not like the cartons of coffee milk they have in the coolers at supermarkets and bathhouses and stuff… *Man*, I could go for a bath."

The sweat that covered his body confirmed that much. Once he was done, the first thing he'd do was march straight over to the bathhouse, no matter how much Suzuno yelled at him about it.

The two of them, alongside Ashiya and Chiho, were in the midst of cleaning up Villa Rosa's yard. This wouldn't be their job as tenants, normally—to say nothing of Chiho, who didn't even live there. But if payment was involved, that was another story.

This time, it all began with another letter from their landlord—one who, now that Maou was fresh off spending a couple days with a relative of hers, was even more of a mystery to him.

Said landlord had forced them out of their homes a while back, thanks to the enormous, cartoonlike hole punched in the Devil's Castle living room wall. It was only temporary while the repairs were made, and she promised to credit them for the time they were out of the place—or so she had informed them. But in the end, they were displaced for only a little more than four days.

Which she could have compensated for easily enough. But Miki Shiba, their landlord—despite her clearly nonhuman physical characteristics, her weird relatives, and the general air of creepiness that surrounded her—brandished an odd sense of duty at times like these.

"I do terribly apologize for breaking my promise," she wrote. "I asked you to travel to my niece to work, but I understand circumstances prevented that from lasting very long."

In other words, she was sorry the demons couldn't work at Ohguro-ya, the seaside snack bar and souvenir shop Miki's niece ran, for as long as they'd planned.

To make up for it, she continued, she was willing to up the discount on their rent, and thus make up the difference from what she had promised, if they were willing to tackle some of the yard work Miki was ignoring so far this summer. To be exact, she offered a fifteen-thousand-yen discount on the rent for August if they cleaned the place up for her. It would bring the figure down to an eye-wateringly low thirty thousand.

Maou and Ashiya had immediately leapt at the offer—as anyone in their position would. Not only was their Ohguro-ya paycheck a fair amount less than anticipated, they had only just purchased a television—an enormous investment by their standards. And while Maou had minimized that financial hit well enough already, there was no way they'd refuse a further discount.

Suzuno, the apartment building's only other resident, had a far less pressing need for such an offer. But she still willingly volunteered her help. "It is only natural," she said, "that a domicile's residents should keep their housing neat and tidy."

Since money was involved, Maou and Suzuno made sure to check in with the real-estate office before officially getting down to work. Today, the day before Maou's job at MgRonald started up again, was the date they picked. Yet, oddly enough, one of the apartment's permanent residents was nowhere to be seen on the big day. Instead there was Chiho, who didn't even live here, pulling up weeds and picking up rocks and pebbles with all her might.

Maou hardly noticed the backyard unless he was parking his bicycle there, but thanks to an extended period of neglect, the grass was up to his knees. As he tromped through it, he noticed that the edge of the yard facing the street was lined with empty cans and bottles, tossed by passersby over his concrete-block fence. Ashiya was just tying up a full garbage bag of the results when the conclusion to Maou's previous explanation rang in from out of nowhere.

"So *café au lait* is French and *caffe latte* comes from Italian, right? And both terms basically mean 'milk coffee.' Both of them are about half milk and half coffee, but with a latte, they generally use espresso as the coffee base!"

Maou looked up from his toil.

"If you're gonna pretend you work at a café, you have to have *that* answer ready when you're asked, at the very least!" the voice added.

There, under the punishing sun, was the Hero Emilia, better

known to most as Emi Yusa, her face squinting in the light as she watched the quartet at work. In her arms was a child, Alas Ramus, smiling broadly, unfazed by the heat that made the grown-ups around her struggle to stay upright.

"Daddyyy!"

"Ooh! Alas Ramus!"

Maou approached Emi and the child, both poised under what shade the cicada-infested tree offered. Emi instinctively swung Alas Ramus away from him.

"Whoa! Don't get her clothes all dirty! I just bought these!"

"Oh, sorry, sorry." He fell back a little. Despite the sweat-soaked shirt and mud-stained gloves he'd just attempted to grab the child with, Maou cared deeply for the little girl.

"Good afternoon, Yusa!"

"I am sorry, Emilia. Is it time already?"

Emi raised her hand in response. "No, I came here a little early..." She stopped and glared at the demons, finding herself having to shout to make herself heard over the cicadas. "Guys, why're you having Chiho weed for you? I swear, you're all *really* abusing her kindness these days, aren't you? How come one of you is missing, anyway? He isn't having Chiho help you so he can weasel out of this, is he?"

The "one of you" Emi referred to was, of course, the third and final denizen of Devil's Castle—the fallen angel Lucifer, although he wrote "Hanzou Urushihara" on any social networks that required him to give his real name. Given his dedication to laziness and complete disinterest in responsibility, Urushihara's absence inherently meant to anyone with a brain that he was trying to avoid work again.

Unexpectedly, it was Suzuno who stepped up to bat to defend Chiho, her voice grim. "From a purely impartial point of view, Lucifer is most certainly *not* weaseling his way out of anything. It was simply a matter of him not being up to the task."

"Huh?"

Chiho giggled a bit at Suzuno's wording. "Urushihara got heat exhaustion."

"Mm. Indeed," Suzuno replied.

"He fainted, eyes rolling into his head, not thirty minutes after we began," Ashiya interjected, his voice as grim as Suzuno's as he looked toward the upstairs Devil's Castle. "It would hardly do to have him die on us, so he is resting inside, under the fan."

Emi followed his line of sight upward, exasperated at the thought of it all. The very idea of a fallen angel who tried to obliterate an entire continent letting the August sun get to him! One would think all the spiky leather armor they liked wearing would make a native demon stronger against the heat.

"All right, but still, why are you having Chiho help you?"

"Oh, this is fine." Chiho fanned herself with a hand, the warm conditions reddening her cheeks a little. "I'm doing this because I want to. And besides"—a quick glance at Suzuno—"I owe her a lot more than just this."

"Owe her?" This seemed to be news to Maou. He looked quizzically at Emi. "Hey, though, why're you and Chi here today, anyway? Like, I'm totally happy Chi came over to help and all, but..."

Chiho had arrived at the apartment at almost the same time as Maou returned home. Judging by how she'd brought her own hat and gloves, Suzuno must have tipped her off about today in advance. But Emi, too...? Maou couldn't hide his suspicion any longer.

"......"

Emi and Suzuno remained silent, faces hesitant. It was Chiho who piped up.

"That's...that's still a secret!"

"A seek-rit! Ssshh!"

There was no saying whether Alas Ramus was in on it or not.

"Right! Better get back to work! Don't want to keep Yusa and Alas Ramus waiting for too long!"

Chiho took another broom propped up against the wall and started evening out the bare earth she'd just finished weeding. Maou continued to look on, quizzically...

"You! Devil King! Alciel!"

...only to have Suzuno's scolding snap him back to reality, forcing him and Alciel to join the cleanup job.

Here, in this little backyard—just a speck in the boiling city, really—the Church cleric, the teenage girl, the Devil King, and the Great Demon General were making surprisingly quick work of the weeding job. Something about it struck Emi as she watched in the shade.

"It'd be so easy…"

"Mommy?"

She whispered it to herself, so softly that not even the child in her arms could hear it among the cacophony from the cicadas above.

"If I could just run him through right now from behind, it'd make everything so easy… Ugghh."

Her eyes were transfixed on the back of his cotton T-shirt, now stained with sweat halfway down his body.

"Wow, there's a public bathhouse here? I live right by here, and I had no idea."

Chiho looked impressed as she took in the front of the building.

Sasanoyu, read the sign on the door. It was the public bath of choice among the Devil's Castle residents, located about ten minutes away on foot from Villa Rosa Sasazuka.

It looked like just another dusty mixed-use office building from the front, but the inside retained the old-fashioned, homespun feel of a Japan-style communal bathhouse from decades ago, complete with the tile artwork of Mount Fuji on the wall.

But this wasn't a relic, either—the bath took pains to adapt its business model to attract modern customers. The selection of bath types available was more than ample, the ticket system offered great deals for regular customers, the mixed-gender rest area in front of the bath entrances had a machine vending cold milk (a staple among any Japanese bathhouse worth its salt), and they even sold soap and other in-house merchandise.

"They're open pretty long hours, too. They start in the early afternoon, and they keep going *juuuust* late enough that I can squeak in after the closing shift at MgRonald."

Maou stood next to Chiho, basket of bath accoutrements in hand. He had changed his T-shirt from his weeding session, but nothing else.

"Sasanoyu offers a remarkable variety of bath types, you know." There was a twinge of local pride in Suzuno's voice. "There are even shower booths, allowing one to enjoy the assorted waters while standing up, and I imagine that would be the best for you today, Chiho. I will gladly pay your admission for helping us out, by the way."

Something sounded fishy about this to Maou. "The shower? Whaddaya mean, that'd be best for her?"

"Yeah, yeah," Emi butted in from behind. "Let's just get inside!"

"Bath! Splish splish!"

Maou didn't appreciate how the Hero accompanied them as if it were her birthright—and, even worse, brought all her own bath stuff with her, like she had been anticipating this. In addition to her usual shoulder bag, she carried another plastic one with a towel and change of clothes for Alas Ramus—so presumably *she* was going in, too.

It seemed like the women were all expecting each other from the get-go today. Maybe they were having a girls' night out later on. Wondering about it only made the suspense worse.

"Hey, we're here, Urushihara. Move it. You are being *such* a pain today..."

"Ugh... Dude, I'm still dizzy."

Urushihara staggered in from behind. The worst of the heatstroke was behind him, but he still had to rely on Ashiya for support. He might not have contributed much to any of the demons' lives in a positive manner, but the gang leaving the apartment for a bath and returning to find his desiccated corpse on the floor would've really bummed out the rest of the evening. Stuffing some water into him and tossing him into a cold bath would help him perk up.

Maou fished a bath ticket out of his basket.

"Well, whatever you guys're up to, keep it legal, okay?"

"Heh. *You've* got it easy," Emi muttered. Maou turned around in response, but she wasn't even looking at him, apparently figuring he didn't hear her. Instead, behind Emi's shoulder, Alas Ramus was staring daggers at him.

"Daddy's not coming?"

"Hmm?"

"Huh?"

Emi and Maou spoke in unison.

"Mommy 'n' Daddy go to different baths?"

"Uh."

It was a simple, innocent question, but it made everyone freeze in place. Maou managed to recover first, trying to muster the most authentic-looking smile he could.

"Um, so listen, Alas Ramus, you'll be heading in with Mommy and the other girls..."

"Yeh! You too, Daddy!"

She refused to budge. Emi, still frozen, was offering no further help, so Chiho decided to try her luck.

"Well, no, Alas Ramus... You see, your mommy and daddy aren't allowed to go in the same bath."

"But I-I went with Daddy! Al-shell 'n' Lush-ferr, too."

She remained steadfast. Suzuno was up next.

"Alas Ramus, grown-ups need to go into either the men's bath or the women's bath. You needn't be so difficult."

"But...with Daddy..."

The child's lips formed a disapproving pout. She looked downward, seemingly ready to burst into tears at any moment, as Emi finally found it in her to speak up.

"...You've brought Alas Ramus here before?"

"Well, sure, when she was staying with us. They got a bath here they keep at midlevel heat for the kiddos, so..."

Before her unexpected fusion with Emi's holy sword, Alas Ramus had spent a short time in Devil's Castle, relying on trips to Sasanoyu with the rest of the gang to keep clean. Sometimes Maou brought her along; when he was busy with work, Ashiya took over. Even Suzuno lent a hand sometimes, which meant Alas Ramus should have had some recollection of how the gender system worked.

But she was still pouting, her eyes moister than before, so Chiho said, "It's just that you haven't had a bath with Maou for a while, isn't it, little Alas Ramas?"

"Really?" Now Emi was pouting, too.

Alas Ramus wiped her eyes and nodded. "...Oon."

"Listen, Alas Ramus..."

"Yehh, Daddy?"

Maou's calm, collected voice kept a tear from popping out at the last moment.

"Do you take baths with Mommy most of the time?"

"...Yeh."

"Really? Great. So how 'bout we take a break from that, just for tonight, and you can go take a bath with me?"

"Wif you?"

"......"

Emi focused silently on the top of Maou's head. He was bent over slightly, on eye level with Alas Ramus.

"Do you know how to get clean all by yourself yet, over at Mommy's house?"

"Snif... Yeh. All by myself!"

"Oh, that's great to hear! Your hair, too?"

"Nuh-uh."

Well, it was honest of her, at least. Although given the length of her hair, it was going to be a while before she could wrangle all of that alone. Maou gave it a pat or two anyway.

"Well, if we practice, I'm sure Mommy will be really surprised when you get back!"

Snatched back from the brink of tears, Alas Ramus turned her head toward Emi, who was a tad despondent.

"Yeah! Let's practice!"

Emi wore a tight-lipped frown.

"Oh, don't look at us like that," Maou shot back. "Trust me. We've done this a few times before, you know. It beats dealing with a crying child. You girls're all doing something later tonight anyway, right? I could babysit for you all if you want."

"......"

Emi's eyes darted between Maou and the child, as Chiho and Suzuno looked on with bated breath from behind her.

"It's not that I have a…*trust* problem with it…"

"Mm?"

Maou had trouble making her out. The words seemed to tumble around behind her teeth, an indecipherable muddle. She grimaced as Maou extended a hand to her.

"Can I, Mommy?"

The three words made her give up all hope.

"Don't *look* at me like that. Ugh…"

She couldn't say no. She just wasn't in the habit of disappointing her girl.

"…All right. I'd appreciate it if you could do that for me."

"Huh?"

"Huh?"

"Huh?"

"Huh?"

"Huh?"

Everyone simultaneously grunted their shock, all but demanding confirmation from her. Not even Maou was expecting this.

The reaction made Emi instinctively add to the chorus:

"…Huh? What's with you people…?"

Despite her doubts, she handed Alas Ramus to the frozen, out-stretched arms of Maou.

"Yay! Bath with Daddy!"

"……"

"Daddy?"

"Like…Emi…?"

"What?"

Jostling Alas Ramus into place with an arm, he brought his other hand to Emi's forehead and touched his palm to it.

"Whoa!"

"Ah!" Chiho joined Emi in abject surprise.

"You'll 'appreciate' it? You're acting *way* too cooperative today. You got a fever or something?"

"What? Of course not! Don't touch me!"

Judging by the way she ruthlessly slapped Maou's hand away, it looked like the same old Emi in front of them. But:

"S-S-S-Suzuno, did…did, did you see that?"

"I did. There is no doubting it."

Chiho and Suzuno huddled together behind her. Even Ashiya and Urushihara were dubious.

"Curse you, Emilia… You had best not be planning some nefarious deed!"

"……"

This exaggerated reaction was doubtlessly justified. Even a few moments ago, it would be impossible to even imagine Emi allowing Maou to touch her. Sure, they weren't seeking to kill each other every waking moment—the fact they were now sharing a public bathhouse was proof enough of that—but Emi had never "appreciated" anything Maou did before, and she *certainly* didn't allow any touchy-feely stuff.

Even Maou noticed how awkward this was. He recalled how, not all that long ago, she had steadfastly refused to let him even help patch up her scrapes after falling down the stairs leading up to his place.

"Wh-what's the big deal, everyone? Am I…am I acting weird, or what?"

"Or what" wasn't the half of it. And Chiho noticed something else unnerving about this defense. The "everyone." Emi had shown a willingness to work with the demons in the past, when they all had a common goal to work for. But in terms of personal relationships, she *never* considered Maou, Ashiya, or Urushihara part of her own social circle—in other words, someone to address as part of the "everyone" she'd just pleaded to. It was always "us"—Suzuno, Chiho, and the other Ente Islans—and "them"—the demons and angels she was pitted against.

"Not at all, no," Chiho lied through her teeth as she attempted a soft smile.

"Chiho?" Suzuno saw through it.

"I'm sorry, Maou. Actually, Yusa and I have a little something we have to do, so could you take care of Alas Ramus in the meantime?"

"S-sure... You, um, got it?" Maou couldn't help but phrase it as a question.

"All right. See you later, Alas Ramus!"

"Byeee!" The girl batted a tiny hand at the waving Chiho. Maou joined in out of habit as he watched the highly suspect group file into the women's bath. Once the door shut behind them, he turned to his Demon General confidant.

"What was *that* about?"

"Perhaps...the sun has gotten to more than one of us?"

"I dunno about *that*, but...maybe. I was pretty damn sure she had a fever or something, too."

"...You think she's still got some baggage from before?" Urushihara butted in. He was still pale, but well enough to return to his usual flippant self. It didn't cheer Maou's mood.

"Before" referred to early August, when two angels from Ente Isla's take on heaven had hijacked TV signals across Tokyo for assorted devious purposes. Ashiya, an active participant against them, was aware of that. And he was also aware that along the way, the archangel Gabriel had revealed something to Emi that made her question her entire identity as Hero.

Emi's father, thought to be killed at the hands of the advancing Devil King's Army, was alive. To Emi—who had shouted in Maou's face that she'd avenge her father with Maou's head—that revelation made things suddenly very complex.

Maou felt no subsequent obligation to worry himself much about Emi. But he couldn't help but wonder if she was aware of another fact, this one obtained by Chiho. A message for Maou and Emi, to be exact, one obtained alongside a vast store of power donated by a new, and heretofore unseen, third party. Chiho never mentioned whether she relayed the message to Emi, and Maou sure wasn't going to tell her, so he wouldn't be asking.

But it still might explain the not-so-subtle changes in Emi's attitude.

"Even if she did, I highly doubt it would cause her to soften her stance against us."

"...Well, if she keeps acting weird like this, I guess I could ask Chi later."

Maou provided a ticket for himself and the money for Alas Ramus to Toyo Murata, the Sasanoyu bath attendant and a woman well north of eighty, and proceeded to the men's changing room.

"Maou?"

"Hmm? What's up, Toyo?"

Toyo rarely spoke much, especially if it meant stopping a paying customer in his tracks.

"'Zat yer wife, there?"

She nodded toward the women's side of the house. Maou snickered to himself and shook his head.

"Nah, nah. Just the mom."

"...Mm. Well, keep the child happy, an' I won't complain." Then Toyo fell silent, returning to her corner of the front room and closing her eyes as she listened to the radio. This was usually how Maou's conversations went with her. It was never easy to tell what she thought of him. He brushed it off, adjusting Alas Ramus's position in his arms.

"Okay, Alas Ramus! Ready to hop in the bath?"

"Yehhh!"

"Dude, quit shouting. I still got a headache."

"Yeah, don't wade into the hot bath, okay, Urushihara? We're not gonna drag you back home, too."

The seemingly worry-free father, daughter, and minions entered the men's bath.

✳

"Wow! Are we the first ones here?"

Chiho's surprise was evident as they filed into the deserted changing room, quite a bit larger than it looked from the outside.

With practiced hands, Suzuno grabbed a clothes basket from the stack and took position in front of the lockers.

"Indeed. Though I imagine not too many people would seek a bath in the middle of the afternoon like this. A stroke of luck!"

"Which is great and all, but what about the men's side?" Emi pointed at the tall partition separating them from the men's section.

"Oh, I imagine we have little to worry about. While it might depend on Chiho to some extent, we can adjust our strategy when the times call for it. Besides"—Suzuno giggled at Chiho a bit—"it *is* Chiho of whom we speak. We cannot hide it from the Devil King and his cohorts forever. It is always far easier to beg for forgiveness than to ask for permission, as they say. Those demons are hardly fools. They can listen to reason."

She began to remove her kimono, Emi's concern obviously not bothering her much. Chiho, meanwhile, seemed far more pensive.

"Um...Suzuno? And Yusa, too...thanks again for all your help, okay?"

Considering the day of work was behind them, this uncharacteristic formality seemed very out of place. Eyes deadly serious, Chiho nodded at her companions as she stood next to Suzuno and began disrobing. Emi began to regret bringing it up. If *this* was how self-conscious she was already, there was no need to make it worse.

"Listen to reason, huh...?"

Now Emi's eyes were on her right arm, the one that held Alas Ramus not long ago.

"I'm really starting to feel like an idiot..."

"...Um, Yusa?" Chiho paused midway through removing her shirt, eyeing Emi with concern. "You think maybe we...shouldn't, after all?"

Oh. Was *that* her question? Emi immediately shook her head, the gloom quickly draining away. "Sorry! No, it's not that. Just something else I was thinking about. If I wasn't up for this, I wouldn't be here. And I wouldn't have brought *this*, either."

She took pains to sound more cheerful as she took something

out of her shoulder bag. At first glance, it looked like the kind of energy shot sold at almost every retail location in the universe. Inside, though, was something that, theoretically, should never have existed on Earth.

"All right, Chiho...this is the source of our powers here on Earth. It's called 5-Holy Energy β."

Chiho grasped the tiny bottle firmly and gave a stout nod.

"Bell and I are gonna be right here the whole time for you, all right? ...Are you ready?"

"Ready!" The affirmation practically burst out of her.

"I still don't know what Bell's gonna do in the bath, but let's get started. Chiho, welcome to Holy Magic 101."

It all began the day after they had defeated Gabriel and Raguel. Coincidentally, it was also the day before Chiho had been discharged from the hospital:

After wrapping up work for the day, Emi had paid a visit to Chiho's hospital room. All the medical tests confirmed that Chiho was a perfectly healthy teenager, but it didn't make the situation any less serious. Not too long before, Chiho had been placed in a coma by a magical force beyond all Japanese medical comprehension. Now, she was champing at the bit to leave.

"This is really erring too much on the side of caution, don't you think, Yusa?"

"That's what every patient in the world thinks, Chiho. Plus, you've put your body through a lot. You need to rest more."

Chiho's powers, which she'd generously showed off at no less than three venues—the Dokodemo Tower, Tokyo Skytree, and Tokyo Tower landmarks—couldn't have been anything that had just appeared within her overnight.

There was a great number of things Emi wanted to ask about these newfound abilities, but from Chiho's perspective, there wasn't much she could say that she hadn't already told Maou—how she had obtained these untold powers, what kind of exchange she'd had with her benefactor, and what Chiho had been up to before Emi saw her. And as for this mystery patron:

"I'm sorry, but I really just don't know, in the end..." Chiho looked up apologetically from her bed.

Emi shook her head in reply. "No. it's okay. Thanks. You've been a big help to me."

"Um, have I? Oh, but there was one thing I needed to relay...I mean, to talk to you about, Yusa. I think, anyway."

"Why're you so vague about it? You 'think' you need to tell me?"

"Um...well, I had another message for Maou, too, but..."

Then she explained to her what she had told Maou—that she had memories of the Devil King's younger days, something she couldn't possibly have experienced herself.

"I just feel like...I dunno, like it's important you knew about that, so..."

And there was something else.

"I saw this big, muscular man. He had a beard, and his hair wasn't that long but he still had it in a ponytail down the back of his neck. He was dressed kind of like a medieval farmer from Europe or something. He seemed nice. Where was he...? I saw something that looked like a really big rice field, except the stalks were all gold, lit up by the sunset..."

"!!"

Emi's heart skipped a beat.

"...Do you think that was actually wheat, maybe?" Emi asked. "Rice plants droop down when they're ready for harvest, but wheat stalks would still be standing straight up."

"Yeah, that might be the case, then. But I couldn't really make out what was in the background. The guy was holding a sword, and he was looking at me...or, I guess, he was looking toward my view-point, anyway."

"A sword?" Emi's pulse shifted from a quick staccato to an oppressive drone of thumping. "For real?"

"Yeah, but..." Chiho paused a moment, unsure of what attracted

Emi's attention. "But that's really it, though. That's all the memory that I have. That, and..."

Chiho found herself pausing again, gauging Emi's clear disappointment.

"Assieth-arra."

"...What?"

"Assieth-arra. That's what that man said."

"Assieth-arra...? Acieth... Maybe it's something in the Centurient language." Emi filed the unfamiliar term into her memory. "I'll ask Bell about it later."

"I just felt like I had to tell you that for some reason, Yusa...but I don't really know what any of it means myself."

Chiho's anxious expression didn't escape Emi's notice as she pondered over this. Not having met the woman in white at Tokyo Big-Egg Town, Chiho had no way of knowing what her memories meant. But to Emi, that all but confirmed her long-held suspicions. She had no idea what was driving her to hide her true identity like this, but only one person in the universe would have a reason to give Chiho a Yesod fragment, toss vast amounts of holy energy around, completely ignore Urushihara, fight against Gabriel and Raguel, *and* plant memories of a man in a wheat field into Chiho.

Emi forged a smile—it took a conscious effort—and showed it off.

"Well, thanks for telling me. It's a big help."

"Um...Yusa?"

"Yes?"

Emi attempted to give an even brighter smile to Chiho, but for some reason she shrugged instead, as if under pressure.

"Are you, like, really angry, maybe?"

"Huh?"

"Um, I mean...I'm sorry. I apologized about it to Maou, too, but...I don't know, just going out there in battle without any training. I thought I might be getting in the way a little, but, um...you know, making people worry about me and all..."

The words of apology came in rapid-fire fashion as tears began to form in Chiho's eyes. Emi put a hand to her face.

"...Is it showing?"

"Oh, I *knew* it!"

The response only unnerved her even more. Emi wrangled her expression back to something more normal for her than a smile in order to calm her down.

"I'm sorry. I'm not angry at you or anything, Chiho."

"...Eh?"

Emi sighed. "Maybe this would be considered kind of passé in modern Japan, but I really think children need to pay respect to their parents. Unconditionally, even, to some extent."

"Um...yeah. I mean, I guess so."

"They feed you, they give you a home you can be safe in, they send you to school...you know? And the older you get, I think, the more you truly realize how much of a blessing all of that is."

"Uh-huh..."

Chiho nodded her agreement, not having much clue what inspired Emi's reflections on life.

"But...I mean, don't you think there has to be a limit to that sooner or later?"

"A limit to what...?"

Emi smiled darkly. She was hardly an ugly woman, but the sight still made Chiho shiver.

"I mean, I have no idea where she's bumping around, she's painstakingly engineering all these headaches for me, she lets everybody else clean up the messes she makes, she scrounges off her daughter's friends, she leaves these stupid cryptic messages that never tell me anything I actually need to know, and *now* she's causing all this trouble in another world, too... It's driving me crazy!"

"Y-Yusa, you need to keep your voice down..."

They weren't alone in the hospital room. Chiho tried her best to assuage the Hero from another world as she shook her head and ranted.

"Why...? If she's watching me, why won't she *come* to me...?"

The soft question from the crouched-over Emi made Chiho freeze. There was an unquestionable twinge of loneliness to the words.

"...Sorry. I'm getting too worked up."

"Oh, no, I..."

Chiho hung her head down awkwardly, unable to find the right words.

"I apologize. This isn't something you'd know about anyway." Emi sighed deeply to collect herself, then picked up the paper bag at her feet. "I got you a little get-well gift. It was Alas Ramus's idea, so it's not exactly a traditional one, but..."

Inside the bag was a pack of fried *senbei* crackers from a top-end candy store. The sight made Chiho finally relax a little. Thanks to the child remaining awake inside her head during work, Alas Ramus was currently enjoying a nap, still ensconced in Emi's body.

"Thank you, though," Emi continued, tying to guide the subject toward more pleasant lands. "This has helped me understand a lot, actually. And I'm glad to see you're doing fine in here, too."

Chiho nodded, crackers in hand.

"Um, Yusa?"

"Hmm?"

"I really want to apologize about all this. It was incredibly rash of me..."

It was out of character for Chiho, apologizing so profusely about something already done and over with.

"Oh, that's fine, Chiho," Emi calmly replied. "You're safe now, and that's what matters. Plus, you helped save *us*, a little..."

"That's the thing!" (Emi's eyes widened as Chiho's tone grew sharper.) "It turned out okay this time, but what about next time? There's no telling what might happen then."

"Wh-what're you trying to say?"

This restlessness on Chiho's part was giving Emi pause. Chiho's eyes turned to the ring on her left hand.

"That power I had is all gone now. Next time I try jumping out of the hospital window, I'm sure it'd kill me. We're on the third floor."

I don't think that's really the problem, Emi thought as Chiho fell silent.

"The way Maou put it, I don't have that much...capacity, I guess?

For that kind of holy magic. That's why I wound up getting poisoned by demon force—it was a reaction to that. So that really wasn't my power at all, I don't think. I just borrowed it for a little bit."

This line of conversation was starting to unnerve Emi more and more.

"But after all the stuff I did to Gabriel and Raguel…well, it's not like I can just stay away from Maou's apartment if something happens any longer…"

"Whoa! Stop right there! I *thought* you'd say that!" Emi put a finger to her temple and groaned. "Lemme try to guess what you're gonna say next. It's something like 'Teach me some skills so I can defend myself,' right?"

"Huh? H-how did you…" Chiho's eyes widened at how easily her intentions were guessed.

"You just said it yourself, Chiho. You worked on borrowed power, and it's not the sort of thing you were ever supposed to use. I really don't want you thinking that holy force is some kind of handy magic trick to have lying around. Acquiring the power to attack and defend with it requires years of careful training and study. It's literally playing with fire."

The only way to fend off Chiho's upcoming defense was with a preemptive offense. The pace of Emi's voice quickened.

"You should know what I'm talking about. Your father's a police officer, right? You wouldn't give a service pistol to a teenager who's never been trained to use it. You wouldn't be able to defend yourself with it, much less fight crime or whatever. And even if you knew how to fire it safely, you're dealing with goons who aren't gonna listen to reason. The only rule is that there *are* no rules. They're gonna go at you with everything they've got, and they're not gonna stop until they take your life. Can you imagine yourself in that situation?"

"That…"

The extra tone of authority to Emi's voice paid off. Chiho fell silent.

"There's no way to tell what'll happen on the battlefield. It's on a whole different dimension from someplace as peaceful as Japan. You learning how to use holy force would be like taking a handgun to a minefield with bullets flying all over the place. You'd be surrounded by people who see your gun as a weapon and you as the enemy. They'll attack you relentlessly until you're dead, all right? They'll never go easy on you."

Emi took a breath before continuing.

"As far as heaven, the demon realms, and Ente Isla go, you're still just a casual observer, Chiho. Neither Gabriel nor Raguel think that power you busted out at Tokyo Tower was actually your own. But if you actually picked up your own weapons and appeared on the battlefield, somebody out there's gonna see you as a target to eliminate. And once you cross that threshold, we might not be able to swoop in to rescue you any longer."

She took a glance next to Chiho's bed. Lying on the floor was a large paper bag with Chiho's personal belongings. It was brought in by her mother Riho, who had written "Separate your dirty laundry for me, please" on it in marker.

"Listen, your mother was seriously worried about you. I can't help it that you're involved in this now, but we can't have people start seeing you as 'the enemy,' all right? And I'm pretty sure this is one of the few things me and the Devil King agree on."

Emi figured invoking Maou's name would help make her argument more convincing. But, when Chiho lifted her head back up after a few moments, she found her eyes imbued with a very different type of force.

"Thank you very much. You're right. I think I see what I have to do now!"

"Huh?"

Emi had been trying to scold Chiho into submission. Apparently Chiho took it quite differently than intended.

"My dad says that sort of thing a lot, too. Like, when he sees an ad in a magazine or whatever for self-defense courses. He's always like, 'If you just copy those moves without any training, all you'll do is hurt yourself.' I guess that's what you're talking about, huh?"

"Um...well, yeah, pretty much. Kind of on a larger scale, though."

Emi found herself puzzled, unable to guess what Chiho would say next.

"But...I mean, if I can, I'd like to use holy magic like you guys, Yusa."

"But I just told you that—"

"When Sariel kidnapped me, Suzuno took my cell phone."

"What?" Emi's eyes darted back to Chiho at this unexpected turn.

"But I wasn't hurt, and my life wasn't put in danger or anything. That was because I was an 'observer' instead of an 'enemy,' wasn't it?"

"...Yeah, maybe so. I think Sariel maybe had some dirty thoughts about you and me, but..."

Emi, kidnapped herself at the time, felt fairly sure about this point.

"Maou managed to save me then, thanks to Urushihara getting the word out to him in time. But what if Gabriel or someone else kidnaps me and takes me someplace where you and Suzuno and Maou aren't looking and I can't use my phone? You wouldn't have any way of knowing where I am."

"...Yeah. True."

Chiho balled both of her hands into fists. "My dad always tells me: 'If you think a crime's taking place, don't try to get involved. You have to call the authorities instead!'"

"Call...?"

Something about the declaration made Emi parrot a certain word of it.

"So...if I get caught up in some kind of Ente Isla trouble or I think I'm about to, I definitely *won't* try to do something about it myself. What I *want* to do"—Chiho tightened her face up, eyes locked on Emi—"is be able to make contact with you and Maou as quickly as I can. I want you to teach me how to use that telepathy thing that lets you talk to people far away... I want to know how Idea Links work!!"

"Th-the Idea Link?!"

"Yes!"

Thus...

"Wh-where'd you learn *that* name?"

"Albert mentioned it. Remember? Back when we were all in Maou's room?"

…Chiho's debating skill overwhelmed Emi's.

"Nhh…"

Emi had nothing to dispel Chiho's argument with. It *could* make everyone safer, she had to admit. She did, however, refrain from giving an answer until she could stop by Suzuno's apartment in Sasazuka on the way home and discuss it.

Suzuno, as expected, had been pretty leery of Chiho's idea, but something about the way she described it as "calling the authorities" was oddly persuasive to both of them. A long, heavy silence pervaded over Room 202 of Villa Rosa Sasazuka before Suzuno spoke.

"The Devil King said it himself. If we continue to whine about not wanting to involve the people of Japan in Ente Islan affairs, why have we not erased Chiho's memories?"

"What're you talking about? That's…"

Emi recalled the argument Chiho and Suzuno had not long after the latter arrived on Earth. Suzuno was ready to erase her memories on the spot for the sake of her own safety, but Chiho refused, stating that she didn't want to forget about all of them. Emi had stepped in as well, professing that seeing sacrifices like wiping Chiho's brain as a necessary evil—closing your eyes to the fact you made your friends cry—was, as she put it, not the kind of peace she was fighting for.

Suzuno chuckled softly, likely remembering the same exchange. "If safety was our only concern," she reasoned, "we should erase Chiho's memories, torch the Devil's Castle, and return to Ente Isla. And yet, neither of us has done that. And we have many reasons for that, but one powerful one is that Chiho has become a friend to us, someone we feel safe in revealing everything to."

Emi nodded. "You're saying that that's how we…want her to be?"

"Indeed. Thus, we have a duty to take whatever measures we deem necessary to protect our friend."

With that, Suzuno stood up and took out a 5-Holy Energy β from the refrigerator.

"This may be presumptuous of me." She smiled, holding the

chilled bottle in her hand. "But seeing Chiho take such a strong stand… It pleases me."

"…Yeah."

Emi, following Suzuno's lead, slowly cracked a smile.

The smile on Chiho's own face when she left the hospital and was formally granted permission to study holy magic was like a spring sunflower in full bloom. She thanked Emi over and over again, to the point where Emi was starting to feel self-conscious about it.

They decided to begin her training on the first day Emi and Suzuno both had ample free time to work with—in other words, today. The morning yard work was, in a way, Chiho's first tuition payment.

"Very well, Chiho. Before you disrobe, we should begin by instilling some holy force within you."

Holy energy drink in hand, Suzuno tied the belt back on to her kimono and sat Chiho down in a changing-room seat. Then she opened the cap and handed the bottle to her, placing her free hand on top of Chiho's.

"Now, drink just a tiny amount at a time. If anything feels strange to you, I want you to stop immediately."

"Okay…"

This was Chiho's request, but something about coming into contact with an unknown force like this still unnerved her. Taking her hand, Suzuno used her magical-sonar probing abilities to keep tabs on Chiho's internals as she slowly drank the 5-Holy Energy β, taking care not to overload her body with the magical force it held.

Once her capacity for the force was filled to maximum, it was time to begin training.

An Idea Link, as the name implied, allowed two or more people to link together on the same wavelength and communicate over vast distances, as well as gain an innate understanding of people speaking foreign languages without any lost-in-translation mishaps. Maou and Emi were fluent in Japanese now, but when they first arrived, they had little choice but to use Idea Links to convert speech to and from Japanese for the sake of the locals.

In a way, the whole reason Chiho was caught up in the angels' conspiracy and sent to the hospital in the first place was due to an extremely long-distance Idea Link sent by Emi's friend, Albert. But if Chiho could master it for herself, it could serve as a kind of insurance in case she needed to contact Emi, Maou, or Suzuno about an Ente Islan issue and couldn't do it on her cell phone.

"Given that there is no one on Earth with holy-magic abilities, you will not have a very large capacity for this energy, Chiho. Take due care not to imbibe too much."

Emi gauged both of them from the side. "She had a ton of power at her fingertips at Tokyo Tower, though. How did that work?"

Chiho raised an eyebrow, apparently wondering the same thing.

"Likely in the same manner as the procedure I am conducting now," Suzuno explained. "In addition to the holy energy we are trying to infuse in her, Chiho's body is being probed by my holy-magic sonar. However, that is run off *my* holy energy, which has nothing to do with her total capacity for it."

The hand Chiho held the bottle with had a magical ring on it, and Suzuno examined it. Afterward, she nodded to herself.

"I imagine the caster actually used that ring as a medium to refract the holy energy into Chiho. To put it in a more brusque manner, one could say that Chiho formed a part of the caster's body at that time."

Emi and Chiho furrowed their brows at this explanation, each for their own reasons.

"Just using people like that... Who does she think she is?"

Emi, for one, was complaining at someone not in the room.

"So I guess I was being manipulated that whole time after all...?"

Chiho, for her part, frowned at herself as she realized the full danger of exposing her body to such a powerful, unknown force.

"Well, I suppose the fact you were not used for nefarious purposes is the silver lining to that cloud, yes. ...Halt, Chiho. Drink no more."

Suzuno stopped Chiho's hand. Emi took a glance at the bottle on the table. "Wow, she drank a lot," she observed. "That's about a third of the bottle."

Suzuno took a look for herself as she kept her hand around Chiho's.

"To put it another way, one could say that 5-Holy Energy β is not so terribly concentrated a supply of holy force. An entire bottle is not enough to restore your energy to what it was in your heyday, is it, Emilia?"

"Well, no, but..."

But Emeralda still had warned her never to drink more than two bottles a day. At first, Emi had thought this was because more than two would overload her body's energy capacity. Drink enough *regular* energy shots at once, after all, and you might be seeing the inside of an ER before the night was through.

"Guess it's kind of like medicine, then, huh?" Chiho said. "Isn't your supply of energy naturally replenished on Ente Isla anyway? It's kind of like how the label on a bottle of supplements still tells you to eat a good diet and exercise and stuff."

"...Maybe so, yeah," Emi agreed. It'd be one thing if they could generate their own holy energy like back at home, but instead they were storing it in liquid form in their refrigerators. Taking too much of it this way might affect their natural ability to replenish it in assorted ways.

After a moment, Suzuno finally removed her hand from Chiho.

"All right. Your body has stabilized itself, Chiho. Do you feel unwell at all?"

Chiho scanned her body visually for a moment.

"No... It doesn't feel like anything's changed, really."

"Likely not. Regardless, we've completed the basic preparations for wielding holy power. Now, off to the bath with us."

"S-sure!"

Chiho sat up straight and bowed her head to Emi and Suzuno.

"Th-thanks in advance for this!"

The two of them exchanged glances. Chiho couldn't be acting nicer toward them. Emi still had no idea what taking a bath had to do with holy-magic training, but Suzuno *was* a highly trained cleric—she must have had her reasons. No point asking questions that would put a damper on Chiho's spirits.

"So now what? You aren't gonna lecture her on the basics of a public bath, are you?"

"No, now is no time for a long-winded treatise on the fundamentals. Plus, not that I distrust Chiho, but such a comprehensive approach might accidentally open her mind to other abilities apart from the Idea Link. For now, we must take the time to focus on keeping her stable and working her through the basic skill set."

"Wow. Sounds kinda tough. But exciting!"

Chiho's voice was starting to sound a tad strained. Emi gave her a pat on the back. "Don't get too nervous. It's important that you stay relaxed at the start. I'm sure that's why Bell brought us to the bathhouse."

"Precisely. Now, while we still have the bath to ourselves, I say we bask in the water and relieve some of the fatigue from the morning's work."

"Sure thing!"

Just a bit of the burden lifted from her shoulders, Chiho eagerly brought her hands to the bottom of her T-shirt.

Several minutes later:

"……"

"……"

"Um… Yusa? Suzuno?"

On the seating in front of the well-polished tile wall, Chiho carefully eyed Emi and Suzuno as they washed their hair and bodies. Their faces looked oddly tormented, and they had looked that way since the moment she'd removed her top in the changing room.

Both of them kept their heads down as water poured from the showerheads mounted on the wall. That way, she wouldn't have to see their tears of jealous frustration.

"I wondered about this at our inn while in Choshi, too, but… man, what did she do to get so, um, big?"

"Uhmm…"

"I am certain that we received just as much nutrition as she has, growing up…but why…?"

"Ehmm…"

"But think about it, Bell. Those *have* to get in the way in battle."

"Would they? Well. A pity for her, then…I suppose…"

A heavy sigh echoed across the otherwise empty bath chamber. Chiho, who wrapped up her washing first due to her short hair but felt odd leaving the other two to themselves, tentatively asked a question.

"Um…is something up?"

The way she was so oblivious made it impossible for them to envy or tease her about it. All they could do was look at her, shampoo bubbles in their hair, and mutter to themselves:

"Best not to keep abreast of it."

"Huh?!"

Chiho, oblivious as she was, looked at the two of them with concern in her eyes.

The Hero and Church cleric, watching Chiho act confused in the most darling of ways in front of them, silently apologized for their behavior over the past few seconds. They knew Chiho wasn't at fault for this.

"…Nothing is more embarrassing for a cleric than letting her feelings turn to jealousy…"

"And she won't even let us do *that*… Man, Chiho can be scary sometimes."

They washed their hair in silence before rinsing the rest of their bodies. In the duration, Suzuno attempted to put the issue behind her. Because:

"Now, Chiho! It is time to begin training!"

"Huh? Oh, uh, okay, but… Huh?"

"It's fine, Chiho," Emi soothed the dubious Chiho with a smile of resignation. Emi and Suzuno had towels wrapped around their bodies, and although they had just finished washing their hair, Chiho noticed that Suzuno had her hairpin in her hand. She wondered idly if the humidity in the air might damage it.

"First, I'd like you to go into the shower booth over there and put the showerhead up as high as it'll go."

"A-all right."

The booths at the far end of the chamber, as opposed to the showers lining the tiled wall, were the regular kind one saw in home

bathrooms, featuring handheld showerheads attached by hoses to the tap. Suzuno had Chiho put the head up to the highest position on the wall, then stood her under it.

"Why that shower, though?"

The casual question lobbed by Emi from behind was greeted with a clear answer from Suzuno.

"All of the best training involves silent meditation seated under a waterfall at some point, does it not?"

"......Huh?"

Chiho and Emi froze for a moment.

Fwooooosssshhhh...

As Chiho stood rigid, eyes closed, feeling the hot water against her skin, she began to kindle a few doubts about Suzuno's training methods. Emi, relaxing in a semiwarm bath in front of the shower booth, had the same concern, eyeing Suzuno with clear suspicion on her face. Suzuno had a habit of using her admittedly vast knowledge of Japanese culture, making terribly wrong assumptions with it, and taking it to the looniest of extremes.

Chiho had mixed feelings about this. She had seen Buddhist monks praying underneath waterfalls on TV as a child, and she had often pretended to do the same thing at bathhouses or hot springs. It wasn't unfamiliar to her, in other words, but it wasn't something she thought had much purpose.

Suzuno adjusted the nozzle so that it wasn't going full blast but instead dribbled a thick stream of water directly on top of Chiho's head in an earnest attempt to simulate a gushing cliffside torrent.

Adding to the worry were the voices they heard over the wall on the men's side of the bath.

"Hah-hah! Hey, Alas Ramus! It's time for your ninja training!"

"Your Demonic Highness! That shower is far too hot for her! If you want to pretend it's a waterfall, use the adjacent one instead!"

It began to make Chiho wonder what she was doing with her life.

"Now," Suzuno intoned, "I want you to stay in that position and listen to me. How confident are you in your strength, Chiho?"

Chiho kept her eyes shut, taking pains to ensure water didn't enter her mouth.

"Well, I guess I'm about as strong as anyone else… I play a few sports at school."

"In Ente Isla, those who wield holy power are known as casters. This power is fundamentally different from what this world would call 'magic.' I have the impression that in Japan and elsewhere in the world, magic wielders are often seen as elderly, bearded, and rather physically weak."

"…I suppose, yeah. I don't play them too much, but wizards in video games and stuff usually don't have swords or anything—agphh!"

Chiho swayed a bit to keep from aspirating water through her nose.

"That is not the case with a caster. If a strong caster and a weak one cast the same spell, the one cast by the stronger will be both more powerful and more effective on a greater variety of targets. Thus, no matter how much natural talent one may have, a child caster would never have a chance at being more capable than the equivalent adult caster."

"Uh, were you watching the *Movie of the Week* yesterday, Bell?"

Emi recalled that Suzuno bought a flat-screen TV at the same time Maou did. Last night, a station was playing the first in a certain series of films starring a young, bespectacled wizard in training.

"They were carrying on about it next door, so I turned it on to see what the fuss was about and wound up watching the entire film. I slept in a bit this morning as a result."

Chiho, eyes still closed, chuckled to herself. She knew Maou was something of a closet film buff.

"But there are many cases of elderly casters attempting a spell they could easily weave during their prime, but dying as a result because the stress was too great on their frail bodies. Assuming one begins at fifteen, devotes oneself fully to training, and is willing to abstain from unhealthy habits for the sake of it, one's holy force stays at its peak only until the age of forty, it is said."

"Wow… Sounds kind of like being a professional athlete."

"Indeed. If someone over fifty can fully wield holy force without the aid of an amplifying device, that would be considered a once-in-a-generation talent. I know this is not a name you two enjoy hearing, but Olba is approaching sixty and still has full control over his holy powers. A practically inhuman feat, that!"

"Yeah… He was a fairly even match for Alciel in demon form, too."

Emi stretched in the bath as she recalled fighting Olba and Lucifer underneath the collapsing Shuto Expressway. The fact that Olba still felt obliged to arm himself with a handgun in Japan was an indicator, perhaps, that he didn't want to overexert himself with casting beyond what was safe.

"Most of who are called the Six Archbishops are cut from the same cloth—elderly casters who still wield considerable powers. But they are the exception that proves the rule. Your sports analogy was expertly stated, Chiho. Think of the ability to cast holy magic as directly proportional to one's core strength and musculature. As for why that is… Emilia, after you imbue your body with holy energy, where is it stored?"

Emi provided a concise answer.

"The heart."

"Huhh?!"

Chiho had assumed that the power just sort of spread itself around her body, not just to a single internal organ.

"The reasoning is simple. The oxygen taken in by one's lungs is transported via the bloodstream across the body, and the heart is the pump that circulates this blood around. In order to cast holy magic, one must transport the energy to either one's entire body or to the necessary region. Just like oxygen, this energy, too, is taken into the bloodstream. To be more exact, the heart acts as a sort of terminal for holy energy as it is circulated around. Now do you see why casting is so intricately connected to physical strength?"

Suzuno paused for a moment before continuing.

"To put it in rather a brash manner, if there is enough holy force transmitted across one's body, even if the resulting burden causes the terminal—the heart—to explode, it is theoretically possible to focus all the circulating force in the body back to its core to reconstruct the heart."

The concept made Chiho freeze in the shower.

"Not that one would dare attempt to brave such undulating waves of force within their own body—it would have to be desperate times in battle indeed to attempt it. You certainly need never worry about that, Chiho, with the power circulating through you right now. Your body's metabolism breaks down only a tiny amount of it at a time; only through actually casting holy energy can one consume it very quickly. It was something we never noticed on Ente Isla, since we regenerated it naturally—only in Japan did it become an issue. Thanks to that, I have made a fascinating discovery..."

Suzuno used a finger to scratch the back of her hand.

"When one has a great capacity for holy force and that capacity grows full, it helps make your skin shinier and less dry."

"Huhh?!"

This even surprised Emi.

"So that—agh!" Chiho, too, was surprised, judging by how she opened her eyes and promptly had them stung by the hot water. "So—Suzuno, that's why your skin's always in such good shape? Like, without any makeup or anything?"

"That, of course, plus a well-balanced diet. Sweets and snacks at a minimum, coupled with regular exercise. And early to bed, early to rise, as they say."

"......"

Whether she intended it to sound like a lecture or not, Suzuno's lifestyle was something neither the chocoholic night-owl teenager nor the call-center rep who split her meals between microwaved junk and take-out junk (and, sometimes, microwaved take-out junk) could hope to emulate. Emi began scratching the back of her own hand, perhaps not as confident of her own skin's quality.

"W-well...I've been cooking more for Alas Ramus lately, so I'm trying, at least..."

"Unless your metabolism has changed greatly," Suzuno said, "I would say you have Alas Ramus to thank for your skin more than anything else. She has fused with you, and the Holy Silver that forms your sword cannot be removed from your body. If there are any gaps in your holy-force quotient, I would imagine Alas Ramus more than makes up for them."

"Huh… Y'know, I think my appetite's gotten healthier lately, actually…"

"Yusa! Can we get back on topic?"

"Regardless," Suzuno said, taking Chiho's cue to free Emi from her trip into the halls of self-pity. "The point is that one's physical strength directly correlates to their casting strength. Or, to put it another way, casting holy spells can have an exhausting effect."

"A-all right," said Chiho. It was a fairly circuitous route to that conclusion, but it seemed sensible enough.

"Emilia and I may seem to be casting our holy force around willy-nilly, but that is because we have the physical strength to back that up. Even if we are injured, we can consume the holy force spread across our body to speed up our healing abilities. Thus, for example, if you and I sustained the same wound, Chiho, that would not restrict me quite as much as it would you."

"Wow. So that's why you guys can keep fighting if you get shot in the shoulder or slashed in the arm with a sword and stuff…?"

"Uh, that still hurts a lot for us, Chiho. We're not action-movie heroes."

From Chiho's experience, at least, it had certainly seemed that way during the battles she'd witnessed.

"Indeed. And when you are still a neophyte in the realm of holy power, harnessing it will sap your energy beyond imagination. We will need to begin by teaching you how to activate this power, move on to casting procedures, then finish up with how to use the force in as efficient a manner as possible. …That should be long enough of a shower. Next, I will have you enter this lukewarm bath."

"S-sure!"

Chiho left the shower booth, shaking off the excess moisture from her hair and wrapping it up with her towel.

"No doing up your hair, Chiho. Just wipe it down and enter the bath."

"Oh, uh, okay." Giving it a few decent rubs, Chiho entered the bath, taking care not to let her hair touch the water.

"Place the back of your head against the edge of the bath... Good. Now, loosen your body up, just enough so that you can feel your body floating. Next, I want you to picture the holy force running across your upper body, from the top of your head to the ends of your fingertips."

This reminded Chiho well enough of the Zen focusing exercises she was taught in her *kyudo* archery club at high school. She followed Suzuno's instructions, letting the tension flow away from her body. The warmth felt good against her skin, and she found herself naturally floating upward.

The back of her head, previously beaten upon by the narrowed shower flow, gradually began to feel like it existed *above* her instead, a sensation difficult to experience elsewhere. That must have been what the "waterfall" bit was for. Chiho apologized internally for doubting Suzuno for a moment.

There was still no sense of some otherworldly power teeming across her body, yet the excitement of taking a journey into an unknown realm of consciousness made Chiho reflexively smile to herself. She had a serious reason for wanting to harness this force, but there was no resisting the pride that came from being able to do something she couldn't before.

"Right... It is flowing healthily, yes. No bottlenecks."

"Yeah, it couldn't be smoother. Stable, too."

The next thing Chiho knew, Suzuno and Emi were each holding one of her hands in place, no doubt monitoring her internals.

"All right. Now it is time to activate it. As a beginner, I would not expect you capable of unleashing strictly the amount of holy force your spell requires. For now, just give each casting everything you have within you. We can focus on eliminating waste after that. I suppose athletics are somewhat similar in this respect as well, yes?"

They were. In terms of physical performance, at least. The mental game was another matter.

"Now, I want you to take deep breaths. Breathe in slowly, through your nose, then exhale slowly through your mouth. I want you to feel the air and the blood that courses through your body."

"All right." Chiho followed her command for the next little while. By the end of it, she was sweating.

"Yes. Very good. Now, Chiho, open your eyes and sit up."

She did. The exercise, plus the heating effect of the bath, made her feel pleasantly warm all over.

"Now, Emilia, if you could, I want you to show us a spell. One that does not require some manner of amplifying device, please."

Emi blinked, not expecting to be called upon. "No amplifier? Most of what I knew is powered either by my sword or the Cloth of the Dispeller, but—"

"Um, I'm sorry," Chiho said, cutting her off, "but what do you mean by an 'amplifier'?"

"Ah. Yes. My apologies. It is, to put it simply, a tool required to cast spells. In my case, for example..."

Suzuno sat up, taking the hairpin sitting on the lip of the tub, and held it in the air.

"Whoa!"

The pin began to shine, transforming into an enormous war hammer in the blink of an eye.

Chiho tensed. A hammer of this size, inside a public bath. If anyone decided to blunder in for an afternoon soak right now, it'd be hard to provide a coherent excuse.

"I use my hairpin as an agent to conjure this spell. I will gloss over the details for now, but having an agent, or an amplifier, handy makes it much easier to conceptualize what you are trying to use your holy power for. This means less power wasted. The amplifier itself does not need to be any particularly special device."

Suzuno's hairpin was an exquisite piece of Asian fashion, but it was neither holy nor magical in nature. It was just one of the many purchases she made during the glitzy shopping spree that marked her first few days in Japan.

"Okay. Well, I really oughta be casting this with my Cloth, but... Heavenly Fleet Feet!"

There was a clear exclamation point on the end, but Emi's voice was soft as she remained seated in the bath. Then, on the floor of the tub, her legs began to light up as she literally floated into the air, legs still crossed.

"Y-Yusa?!"

In the space of seconds, her entire body cleared the water's surface, drifting ever upward.

So, here in the midafternoon hours, the neighborhood bathhouse was now being patronized by a naked woman with a war hammer and another naked woman levitating over the bath. Anyone walking in *now* would certainly have enough material to write a tabloid cover story.

"This is really meant for casting with the Cloth, so I'm cutting a few corners, but you can cast this well enough without an amplifier."

"Oh...um, cutting corners how, exactly?"

Chiho's eyes darted between the entrance doorway and the boots of light over Emi's feet, something that seemed as beautiful as CGI-driven magic from an adventure film. Suzuno's eyes, however, were much more critical as she pointed them out.

"Look at that. The edge of the light. It is undulating, can you see? Like a campfire's flame."

"Oh, you're right!"

Chiho compared the sight with Suzuno's hammer. The weapon was emitting a light of its own, but not the unstable, wavering light of Emi's boots. This struck her as a more well-regulated, uniform flame, like a gas cooktop's burner.

"That undulation shows that the outgoing flow of holy force is unstable. While it depends on the exact type of spell being cast, having an amplifier always lets you more efficiently, and more effectively, unleash one's spell."

"Whew... Yeah, casting solo really tires you out."

Emi gingerly brought herself back down into the water as Suzuno returned the hammer to her hairpin, letting Chiho breathe a well-deserved sigh of relief.

"Now, Chiho, a question for you. What was the difference between my spell and Emilia's just now?"

"The difference...?" Chiho rewound her memory back a few moments. "...Your spell didn't have a name, Suzuno?"

The response made Suzuno lift an approving eyebrow. "Very good. Heavens, on the first try, no less! Although the spell *type* has a name, of course. We call it the Light of Iron."

"But you still cast it anyway, right? Is that because you could visualize it a lot easier with that amplifier thingy?"

"Correct." Suzuno nodded, satisfied. "Executing a spell is, in a way, taking an image and embodying it in real life. In order to use holy force to create the effect you wish, it is vital that you have a refined knowledge of holy activation and the consummate ability to visualize it. A bit like kneading a pile of clay into a work of art, one could say. Thus, in the case of a spell without an amplifier, it becomes more important to do things like state the name of the spell or effect out loud, in order to make it easier to conceive the results in your mind. It can make a surprising difference in the spell's effect and power usage."

This seminar, along with all the visual aids, reminded Chiho all over again that the two women she shared this bath with were no natives of this planet.

"The challenge is activing this power in the first place. It can be rather difficult to visualize at first, given how it has no comparison in the physical realm. Thus, instead of studying the mechanics of ferrying holy force around, it would be quickest to learn instinctively how to activate and process it within your body."

Suzuno motioned with her head toward Emi.

"I apologize for bothering you, Emilia, but could you return to the changing room and provide a distraction for us? I want to deploy a barrier over the entrance and the skylight."

Emi nodded and walked out of the bath.

"Huh? Wh-what for?" Chiho stuttered.

"This is something any student in the holy arts has to go through," Emi replied over her shoulder. "But if we carry it out unprepared in Japan, that could attract some…attention."

Her vague answer did little to allay Chiho's fears.

"Right, but…what is it?"

"Simple. I want you to scream for me."

"Huh?"

Chiho took a couple of dubious looks at her companions.

"It can be anything you like. Just shout it as loud as you can."

"Yeah, but…scream? Here?"

Suzuno nodded, as if someone just asked whether she'd like some noodles for lunch.

"Oh, but don't tense up your body too much when you do," Emi blithely added. "That won't make it come out as much. Stay loose, okay?"

"Um, do I…?"

Thinking about the pair's request made Chiho feel like a giant snake of embarrassment was rearing up to strike at her heart with its venom of shame. This was a *public* bath, after all. Whether they were the only customers or not, the elderly bathkeeper was still at the far end of the changing room—and, more important to her, Maou and gang were just on the other side of the partition.

Suzuno, sensing this hesitation, cleared her throat. "Call it a war cry, if you will," she said. "The effect of such a shout has been scientifically proven in Ente Isla as well as in Japan. Even with a simple punch, the difference between throwing it silently and shouting from the pit of your stomach as you do is vast. It elevates your emotions, energizing your body cells and giving you a psychological sense of release, making it a highly effective battle tactic."

Then, without warning, Suzuno drew her face close to Chiho, making her edge back a bit.

"*However!* Like any manner of training, approaching it with a negative attitude will result in little to no improvement. Shouting here will do nothing to activate your holy force if you are too preoccupied about what the Devil King may think of the noise."

Chiho's face turned red. Anyone's would after being so easily read like an open book.

"But why here, though? Wouldn't it be better if we went in a karaoke booth or something...?"

Suzuno shook her head at the reluctant, non-Chiho-like request. "The psychological release that stems from overcoming your internal conflict and shame is far more potent than any regular type of emotion. That makes it all the more possible for us to achieve great advances in a short time. *Especially* if the Devil King lies on the other side."

Emi, watching Suzuno advance upon Chiho, raised an eyebrow.

"You know, with that logic, one misstep and things could get really dangerous."

Suzuno, witnessing how red and almost teary-eyed Chiho still was, shook her head. "It is an excellent virtue of the Japanese race, avoiding loud commotions in public places, but we are working under different circumstances. Allow me to provide a demonstration. You can follow my lead."

"Oh, but you—"

Chiho could no longer hide her apprehension. For all they knew, there were other male bathers apart from Maou and friends. But Suzuno showed her no mercy.

"When I speak, I want you to reply as loudly as possible!"

"Y-yeahhh...!" Chiho made a token effort.

"...Um, all right. I'll make sure the coast is clear out front, so..."

Emi hurriedly exited the room before she had to watch Suzuno get even more intense with her training.

"Now, let us begin!"

"Okaaaay!!"

Suzuno, satisfied with Chiho's reply, did her best imitation of a vacuum cleaner as she inhaled.

"Now! As loudly as you can! Hyaaaaaaaaaaaaahhhhhhhhhhhh!!!!"

"Whoa whoa whoa whoa... Owww!!!"

Urushihara, washing his hair on the other side, flew to his feet at the volume of Suzuno's voice, dropping the showerhead on his little toe in the process.

"D-dude, what was *that*?!"

"Are we under attack?!"

Neither Maou nor Ashiya were laughing.

The tiled environment made the scream echo time and time again, the war cry expanding to an entire order of knights galloping across the countryside, thoroughly creeping out the demons as it did.

Then, out of nowhere, Alas Ramus—lying on Maou's knee as he washed her hair—opened her eyes and decided to join in at full blast.

"Ohhhhhhhhhh!"

"Agh!"

The resulting bolt of holy force the child unleashed almost blew Maou against the wall.

Then, the next instant, they heard Chiho's scream, a shriek that could've broken a pro basketball backboard.

"Waaaaaaaaaaaaaaaaaaaaaaaaaaaaaaaaaaaahhhhhhhhhhhhhh hhhhhh!!!!"

"?!?!?!"

Maou's eyes bugged out of their sockets as he tried and failed to parse the situation. Sensing Chiho was in some sort of danger, he left the bubble-bath-laden Alas Ramus in Ashiya's hands, took a few moments to wrap a towel around his waist, then flew out to the common platform past the changing rooms with the speed of a tornado.

There he was greeted by Emi, in her postbath shirt, her face burning red as she held Toyo the bath keeper's hand.

"Hey! Why're you looking like *that*?!"

It was hard to tell whether Toyo was sleeping or not most of the time, but there was no way she could have missed all that shouting. Emi had to have used some kind of holy-power spell on her, he realized.

"E-Emi?! What the hell're you girls doing over there?!"

"None of it's escaping the walls of this place, all right? I put the bath keeper to sleep just in case, but there's nothing dangerous about... Whoa, your towel's gonna fall off!"

Emi tried her best to keep Maou from wandering into her line of sight. Only then did he notice how far down the nether regions his towel had wandered. But it was odd. Despite the sheer volume of the screaming—especially that last one—it was like all the sound had shut off the moment he left the bath.

"Look, can you just tell me what—whoa!"

"—raaaaaaaaaaaaaaaaaaahhhhhhhhhhhhhhhhhhhhhhhhhhhhhhhh hhhh!!"

Just as Maou stuck his head back into the men's bath to investigate further, another scream thudded against his eardrums, scaring him enough that he slipped on the changing-room tile floor and fell on his rear end.

"Y-Your Demonic Highness, are you all right?! B-Bell, what in all of creation are you *doing*?! You're being a nuisance to the entire neighbor—"

"Whooooooooooooooaaaaaaaaaaaaaaahhhhhhhhhhhhhhhhhhh hhhh!!!!"

Ashiya, on his way to lodge a formal complaint against the girls on the other side, was cut off by Suzuno's shrill battle cry. It startled him enough to take a few furtive steps backward—right over the bar of soap Urushihara left on the floor, sending him flying.

"L-look out!"

Urushihara, still nursing his little toe, watched Ashiya's large frame swivel precariously in the air…

"Yaaaaaahhhhhhhhhhhhhh!"

…and managed to catch Alas Ramus, screaming in perfect harmony with the ladies as she flew through the air…

"Gehh!"

…as he let Ashiya hit the floor, missing the opposite wall with his head by a few inches.

As Maou attempted to help Ashiya back up, he heard a knock on the sliding door to the men's bath from Emi.

"Hey, that sounded pretty rough. Are you okay?"

"*You're* sounding pretty rough, man! What the hell's up with Suzuno and—"

"Waaaaaaaaaaaaaaaaaaaaaaaaaaaaaaaaaaaaaaaaaaaaaaaaaaaaaaa aaa!!"

"Does it have to do with Alas—"

"Lower! From your stomaaaaaaaaaaaaaaaaaaaaaaaaaaaaaaaaaaaa aaaach!!"

"Emi, you *better* explain this to—"

"One, two, three, *yeeeeeeeeaaaaaaaaaaaaaaaaaaaaaaggggggggggggg hhhhhhh!!*"

"Yes! Yes! Keep it *hiiiiiiiiiiiiiiiiiiiiiiiiiiiiiiigggggggggggghhhhhhhhhh!!*"

"Shut *uuuuuuuuuuuuuuuppppppppp!!*"

The continued rapid-fire screaming contest between Suzuno and Chiho made it impossible for Maou to even talk to Emi across the door.

"Daaaaaaaaaaaaaaaaaddddddyyyyyyyyyyyyyyyyyyyyy!!"

"Don't *you* join in, Alas Ramus!" Maou reached for the child, trying his hardest to shrug off the holy force radiating from her. "Emi, come *on*! I don't know what you're up to, but make them stop! You're driving the whole town crazy!"

"It's fine! We put up a barrier to keep other customers from coming in!"

"What's fine about that?! Now you're interfering with their business!"

"I'll explain once we're done, okay? Don't worry about it so much!"

Emi turned on her heels, refusing to answer the question.

"H-hey! Get back here!!"

Maou gave chase, all but flinging himself out from the bath. But the sliding door to the front area refused to budge. Emi must have been holding it shut.

"How can I *help* youuuuuuuuuuuuuuuuuuuuuuuuuuuuuuuuuuuuuuuu uuuuu?!"

"Right *away*, sirrrrrrrrrrrrrrrrrrrrrrrrrrrrrrrrrrrrrrrrrrrrrrrrrrrrrr!!"

"Oh, now you're waitresses?! Seriously! What're you *doing*?! Emi! Open the door! Come on!"

The unusual scene of the Hero keeping the Devil King locked inside a Japanese-style public bath lasted for less than five minutes. But then:

"Waaaaaaaaaaaaaaaaahhhhhhhhhhhhhhhhhh… Aigh?!"

Amid the droning wail, Maou picked up on Chiho screaming for quite a different reason. *This* called for action.

"Ugh! I don't *care* if someone reports me! Ashiya! Give me a leg up! I'm climbing up into the women's bath!"

"M-my liege, take hold of your senses! If you do something so sordid, your very position in society might be placed at risk!!"

"Okay then, Urushihara! Like *you* care about that crap! Get up there!"

"Dude, I *refuse* to have you treat my social life like it's a piece of garbage!"

Just as the argument between the three arch-demons over who would commit perhaps the most classical example of sexual harassment in Japan reached its fevered peak, they noticed Emi's exasperated voice.

"...Uh, hey, this is open now."

Coming to their senses, they found that the echoing of Chiho's and Suzuno's wicked keening had subsided. Even Alas Ramus, still in Urushihara's arms, had settled back to her usual quiet self.

"What *was* that?!"

Ashiya, finally fishing himself up off the floor, looked up at the partition separating the men's and women's sides.

"Did you not notice, my liege? Perhaps not. It was just for a moment."

"Hmm?"

"Uh, hang on... Emilia was over there, Alas Ramus was over here, and Bell was—huhh?"

Urushihara was the first to notice. Eyebrows pressed flat against his lashes, he stared down Emi from the men's changing room, back turned to the other demons.

"Dude, what're you thinking? Don't do that in, like, real *life*, man. Why're you devoting your frontline resources to add in someone who's gonna be useless to you anyway? You got *that* much free power rolling around?"

Urushihara sounded gruffer than usual. Emi was having none of it.

"That's not what we're doing at all. She's fully aware of that."

Emi couldn't help but feel conflicted. Ideally, in her opinion, this whole situation should have been avoidable.

"She just wants the power to report back to you or me in case of emergency."

"Report...? Whoa! For real?!"

Maou, finally picking up the gist, looked up at the partition.

"She knows exactly what she can and can't do, all right? We put our trust in that. But I think the biggest reason..."

Emi turned her face to the confused Maou.

"...I think it comes down to the fact she doesn't want you expending more resources than you absolutely need to if she's caught up in something. I mean, whether she keeps her memories or not, she's definitely *involved* with us now."

Maou paid only a modicum of attention to Emi as he clumsily wiped himself dry, put his clothes back on, and tore into the front area, Ashiya and Urushihara following behind. There, they found Suzuno, cooling herself with one of the bathhouse's rigid hand fans.

"I will explain why later, but trust me when I say that Chiho is not approaching this lightly. That, at least, I hope you are willing to accept."

With Suzuno was Chiho, lying on a wicker seat, her chest heaving up and down underneath her shirt as she caught her breath. Even considering she was straight from the bath, her face was far too reddened.

"M...Maou..."

Maou stood there, baffled. Urushihara, next to him, pointed at Chiho's hand.

"Dude, don't blame *me* if this goes south on us."

He looked scornfully at her hand, lain limply on the table.

"Wait... Ms. Sasaki..."

Ashiya was just as confused as Maou, his face betraying his utter amazement at the sight.

There, in her hand, was a shining gold ball of pure holy power. It flickered like a sputtering flame, clearly not under her full control.

However, it wasn't the unreal, otherworldly kind of force she'd wielded at Tokyo Tower—no, this ball of holy light came from the corpus of Chiho herself.

"I-I...I didn't want to get in the way, or be a drag on you, or anything..."

Still fighting for breath, Chiho tried her best to give Maou a smile.

"But now I can do it, Suzuno... I can run from danger if I need to; I can have you guys help me if I need to. Next...I'll try...an Idea..."

That was her limit. Her eyelids slowly fell as her consciousness sank into the world of dreams.

"Oh, for..." Maou, watching an exhausted but immensely satisfied smile cross Chiho's face, scratched his head in surrender. "She's getting *way* too worried about this. Like, we're monsters from another world! Why can't she just let us handle all that crap? *We're* the ones who got her caught up in this."

Emi chuckled. "Chiho can't do that. She doesn't want to run screaming if something happens, so she wanted something she could use to either escape or get help more reliably. It's almost too touching, isn't it?"

She sized up Maou with her eyes, her voice dropping so only he could hear.

"I bet there were a lot of kids like Chiho among the lives you trampled over on Ente Isla."

"......"

Maou turned around, but Emi had already let the words melt into the air. Now her attention was on Chiho, wiping the sweat beading on her forehead. She was acting amiably enough, but what she just said seemed even more acrid and hard-hitting than anything that came before it.

"...*You're* making no sense to me, either."

The words rolled out of Maou's mouth and into nobody's ears.

THE
HERO
AND
THE DEVIL
WONDER
WHAT
THE HELL
THEY'RE
DOING
WITH
THEIR
LIVES

"Helloooooo! Welcome!!"

Chiho's booming voice echoed across the restaurant.

Several customers looked up to see what her deal was. The couple just walking through the door stopped for a moment. Maou and the rest of the crew, meanwhile, froze on the spot and cautiously turned her way.

Kisaki, the only person not thrown by the display, patted Chiho's shoulder from her position next to her. "Right. Good. I don't know where you learned that, but the more energy, the better. Make sure you know how to maintain a certain distance, though. You don't have to scream that loud for customers to hear you."

"Oh. Um, sorry..."

Chiho, her face reddened at her unintended prank on the entire store, quickly focused on helping the next customer at the register. As she did, Maou watched her with nervous eyes.

A week had passed since Chiho unlocked the secret to activating holy force from Emi and Suzuno. As a part-time student employee, today was her first day at the newly renovated MgRonald in front of Hatagaya rail station. She arrived, for reasons only she knew, as a girl possessed. If she wasn't shouting in abject glee at customers, she was sticking out from the rest of the crew in other not-so-positive ways.

Chiho was sensible enough to pick up on this, of course, but something about the earlier screaming contest must have put her decibel limiter out of whack, all but cowing her paying customers into submission on several occasions.

"I really appreciate her eagerness," a disappointed-looking Kisaki said, "but I'm not sure I can let Chi up into the café space quite yet if she's acting like that. We're short-staffed up there, so I'd really love to, but…"

Maou stewed in agony, unable to say anything in her defense. That shouting was thanks to her holy-force training, of course. The problem, though, was that there aren't too many places in modern urban Japan where you can keep shouting at people all the time and not have them be a tad leery about sharing personal space with you.

Her parents couldn' t have been appreciating that much, either, to say nothing of the local neighborhood. The sound of a girl Chiho's age screaming in a public park would be enough to summon several patrol cars all by itself. To say nothing of shrieking in a public bath. Everybody was *already* on edge enough in those.

She couldn't just test out her pipes every single day at the karaoke joint, though. So now, apparently, she was trying to get in a little practice wherever she could, at odd parts of the day. At this rate, though, it couldn't last. Stories would get around.

Maou accepted her efforts well enough, however, once Emi and Suzuno sat him down and talked it over. They had a good point. Whether they wiped her memories or not, at this point, Chiho was a collective Achilles' heel to them—especially since Olba Meiyer, lurking behind the scenes in both Ente Isla and the demon realms, was liable to stab at them without warning. If and when that happened, having a way for Chiho to send out an SOS to Maou and crew while making sure her own memories stayed intact would be extremely beneficial to all of them.

Still, Chiho also had her own social life. School, part-time job, the works. She couldn't let her training mess that up.

Once the stream of customers died down, Maou beckoned to her.

"Hey, Chi, you got a moment?"

"...I'm sorry. It's about my voice, isn't it?" Chiho turned her eyes downward.

"Uhh..."

This was awkward already. Maou didn't need her to be *this* self-conscious about it. This was all part of an effort to keep her from becoming excess baggage for him and Emi, besides.

"Well, I'm glad you know, at least. But just make sure you stay focused on your day-to-day life, okay? These are important times for you."

Chiho smiled, a few fatigue lines under her eyes. "Sure."

"'Cause, I mean, if that keeps up, Ms. Kisaki's not gonna let you go upstairs, you know?"

"Yeah... I guess, just make sure I have an on-off switch in my mind, huh?"

"That'd be perfect." Maou nodded broadly, spotting Kisaki signaling her approval out of the corner of his eye. "Go with that."

"But...ooh, I dunno. Even if I do, I'm not sure I'm gonna get up there anyway."

It was unusual, seeing Chiho have so little confidence in herself. Maou rolled his eyeballs down and to the right.

"Welllll...yeah. I get where you're comin' from."

He scratched a cheek as he reluctantly agreed.

"Up there," in the context of this chat, meant the café space on the second floor. It was one week after the grand reopening, and if you accommodated for the fact that the local office-worker clientele was keeping tight reins on their spending after the August Obon holidays, the location was faring decently enough. Given their normal customer base, coupled with the fact that their prices were just that little bit lower than competing coffee chains, they were seeing noticeably more families and single women than usual.

The location didn't make a big deal of separating the regular MgRonald space from the MagCafé upstairs, so some customers would order downstairs and bring their food up to eat. As a result, the café's customer turnover rate was one issue they'd have to tackle going forward. Still, between being the first day after a lengthy closure and the sheer confidence oozing from every pore of Kisaki's body, the regulars were quickly coming back. More than a few were closeted (or not-so-closeted) fans of Kisaki. You could tell because they were the ones snapping cell phone pics of Kisaki's portrait in the corporate "Store Manager" display hung by the café counter upstairs.

So while the MagCafé launch was hardly any disaster, most of the crew—including Maou and Chiho—doubted they had the confidence to dare a shift up there yet.

Why?

"Boy, what do you have to do to make coffee *that* good, huh…?"

Chiho could be excused for muttering it to herself from afar. Something about the coffee Kisaki herself poured up there made it seem to absolutely sparkle.

The Platinum Roast coffee on the regular menu was one thing, but no matter what the crew was asked to prepare from the MagCafé menu, there was a world of difference between Kisaki's work and anyone else's.

MagCafé made a point of giving customers actual coffee mugs for their java purchases, not the paper cups and plastic tops you were rewarded with downstairs. Otherwise, while still technically a café, it operated under fast-food principles—keep things fast and consistent while at a certain level of quality.

To aid in that, MagCafé had its own dedicated coffee server, separate from the one serving up Platinum Roast. This wasn't the kind where a fry jockey brews up a batch and dumps it once its shelf life expires, nor the sort you see in hotel breakfast buffets capable of grinding up a ton of beans in one go. The grinding might've been done with a machine instead of a hand-operated artisan thing, but since employees ground the beans for each individual order, there was room for differences in technical skill from one crewmember to the next.

Kisaki was instructing each shift in how to use the server as they punched in, but somehow or another, no matter what MagCafé menu item Kisaki whipped up, it was either just as good as a tradi-tional café's offerings or better.

"I mean, she's grinding the coffee the same way we are, the hot water comes out at the same temperature, and we're using the same milk for everything, aren't we? What's making it so different…?"

Neither Maou nor Chiho were avid coffee drinkers, but even they could tell the difference in quality between the stuff they tried to make and Kisaki's.

Everyone on staff who tried it agreed: If they wanted their coffee to match Kisaki's, that required a little extra *something* that wasn't mentioned in the training manuals.

"Yeah…well, we're gonna have to work up there sometime, or we ain't gonna be too useful."

Kisaki was on staff nearly the whole day today to make sure the grand opening didn't see any huge disasters. But, being a salaried employee, MgRonald couldn't keep her in the store forever. And it wasn't like they could shut down MagCafé when her magic touch wasn't on hand.

"I guess my question is, what kind of taste is corporate aiming for—Kisaki's, or ours?"

"Corporate?" Chiho said, not catching the aim of Maou's observation.

"Y'know, MgRonald is a chain and everything, so it's got a vested interest in making sure the drink experience is the same no matter which location you visit. You think you can get Ms. Kisaki's coffee anywhere else in Tokyo?"

"Well, that's not a bad thing, is it? It would be if it tasted bad, but hers tastes a lot better than normal coffee, even."

Maou's eyes turned to a stack of fliers next to a nearby cash regis-ter. The back of them had a rundown of the MagCafé menu, clearly showing the 250-yen price point for the café au lait and caffe latte.

"Maybe, but if you put it another way, if customers can't have Kisaki's coffee, we'd be asking them to pay the same price for an inferior product."

"…Oh." Chiho got the gist after a moment.

"When you're a chain the size of MgRonald, there's kind of a quality bottom line every location needs to abide by. If they don't, that goes against the concept of offering the same quality menu nationwide. If it was just a matter of making the best coffee you can at the same price, then some employee could just bring in some gourmet Red Valley beans or whatever to make their location the best coffee place in town. If every location went their own way like that, it wouldn't really be a MgRonald menu they're offering any longer."

There were many restaurant chains that used their regionalism as a weapon to appeal to customers. MgRonald was not one of them. A fact that Kisaki seemed to be freely ignoring.

"Right, but Ms. Kisaki's using the same machine, the same beans, the same milk, and the same mugs, isn't she?"

Maou scratched his head. "Yeah, that's the thing. That's what I don't get."

On the surface, it meant that Maou's coffee wasn't making the grade yet. But if doing it like the manual said wasn't enough, what was?

"It's not really my field of training," Chiho mused, "but maybe you have to put more feeling into it, huh? Like, 'Come on, coffee, get more *flavorful*,' that kind of thing?"

"I don't think saying that out loud in the *kitchen's* gonna help much. It's not like we're farming the beans ourselves."

"Or, like, maybe Kisaki deliberately makes coffee only when Mozart's playing on the PA system?"

"Nah. Also, that whole 'play Mozart to make plants grow more' thing isn't scientifically proven."

They could debate this until the cows came home, but no ready conclusion sprang to mind. What made Kisaki's coffee so *good*?

The stream of customers remained fairly steady until the postdinner hour. Soon the clock struck ten, Chiho's mandatory clock-out time as a minor. She passed by Maou as she left the staff room in her street clothes.

"Well, careful walking home."

"Sure thing. Thanks."

She gave a grateful nod to the remaining staff on hand.

"If anything comes up, give me one of those well-trained screams of yours, 'kay?"

"Huh? …Oh. Um, sure. Dunno how to answer *that*, really, but…"

It took Chiho a few moments to realize Maou was poking fun at her. She turned red in the face, clutching at her cell phone.

"Ahh, no worries. Just watch yourself. Also…"

"Yes?" Chiho pouted.

"I didn't mention it yet, but thanks for working so hard at it."

Maou's voice was just low enough so that only Chiho could hear. She turned red again, this time for reasons that had nothing to do with anger.

"It-it's not just for *you*, though!"

She walked briskly out of the store, still a bit put off by Maou's picking on her. On one shoulder was a large bag, a rarity to see Chiho carrying. It seemed doubtful that she was headed anywhere else tonight, since it was late; maybe she'd had practice for a school activity earlier. Maou shrugged, sighed, and decided to start on the store's closing procedures for the day. But before he could get very far, he was interrupted by Kisaki, who was heading down from the second floor.

"Oh… Did Chi leave already?"

This confused Maou. She almost certainly would've checked with her before changing and clocking out.

"How'd it go with her…shouting, then?"

"Hey, um, are you feeling all right?"

No one could blame Maou for asking his question first. Kisaki, for a change of pace, sounded spent, almost bereft of energy. Which was unusual, because the Devil King had never met a living creature with such seemingly boundless stores of endurance as she had. The nature of Kisaki's job meant she might either get the whole day off or have to stay on-site from open 'til close, but—as if under a spell of some sort—her tempo never wavered for a moment around the crew.

Seeing a woman like that with small rings under her eyes, a finger to her left temple, and a voice one could charitably describe as "zombified" would make anyone worry about her health.

"Yeah, I am… Sorry."

The question made Kisaki come to attention. She quickly scanned the dining area, demonstrating a sense of panic that was also rare for her, and breathed a sigh of relief for reasons Maou didn't follow.

The regular MgRonald space was mostly empty, save for two pairs of what looked to be college students chatting with each other.

"I guess I put in a little more effort than I should've. But, man, at this rate, this is gonna be seriously rough."

A further shock for Maou to hear. These sorts of complaints, Kisaki *never* gave out.

She raised her head and looked at a brand-new LCD monitor on one corner of the register counter. It was set up so employees on the first floor could keep track of the free seating upstairs, but as far as Maou could see, things were empty up there.

"What was the…um…deal?"

Seeing Kisaki grumble to herself and rub her sore shoulders right in front of him was a sight Maou had never seen in all his time at MgRonald. It made his voice a little shaky. Kisaki, looking at him quizzically, didn't answer.

"So, what about Chi?"

"Oh, erm… Well, after we had that talk, she was back to normal. A few danger spots before then, though, huh?"

"…Huh." Kisaki nodded solemnly, a hand kneading one of her shoulders. "You think she's found a new goal for herself, too?"

"Wha?"

Maou focused his gaze more closely on her. Chiho had, of course, and she was vigorously pushing herself toward it. That shouting was part of it.

It was just an offhand remark from Kisaki as she brought up the first-floor daily totals on a register screen, but Maou wondered what made her notice it.

After that moment of concern, something else struck Maou's mind.

"What do you mean by 'too'?"

"…?"

Maou noticed Kisaki gasping a little. The next moment, she shook her head, as if regretting the whole thing.

"Ah, I'm just tired," she said in a low voice. "Don't worry about it."

That reaction was enough to make Maou's curiosity do an about-face. Maybe Kisaki was facing more delicate issues than he thought. He wasn't close enough to her to wade in further.

"All right. Could I ask you about something else, though?"

"Hmm?"

"Me and Chi were wondering… Like, we're using the same server and all, but how come your coffee tastes so much, uhhh—"

"Ahhh?"

"—different from ours…and stuff…"

A wave of terror overcame Maou for a moment. Kisaki seemed to prey upon the exact thing that unnerved him the most today. He asked the question in hopes of improving himself, but now there was something more sinister to her voice than ever before. She glared at him with a gaze so powerful that even the Devil King cowered under it. The entire exchange lasted no longer than a second, but to Maou, it may as well have been forever.

Then, the next moment, Kisaki's eyes immediately widened and looked off into the distance.

Maou began to wonder if any day in his future would be as full of surprises as this one proved to be. Having Kisaki glare at him, then stare into space for a second or two, then lock right back onto his face left him in awe. He wondered if, for an instant, he had seen Kisaki at her most unguarded and vulnerable just then.

"…I'm sorry. Gimme one sec."

Then she closed the results screen and marched into the staff room. *She must've noticed that I noticed*, Maou thought. But Kisaki was never one to dodge confrontation like that. It spooked Maou, seeing so much unfamiliar behavior from his manager in the span of five minutes.

He found himself staring at the staff-room door as he heard the whine of an old printer. Kisaki came right out once it stopped, a sheet of paper in her hand. Their eyes met as she did, and she looked a bit awkwardly at him when he noticed yet another odd reaction.

"Wanna take a look at this?"

Kisaki handed the sheet to Maou, the look of awkward concern still on her face. Maou ran his eyes across it. The title immediately gave him pause.

"MgRonald Barista?"

Barista wasn't a term he was familiar with. *Ballistas*, he knew all about. Large, arrow-launching installations placed on top of forts and bulwarks. He oversaw many a ballista post in his time. The image of one of them propelling hamburgers at high speed, splattering them against a castle parapet, made him snicker.

"Do you know what a barista is?"

"Um...nothing to do with arrows?"

"*What?*"

"N-no...um, I guess I don't." Maou just barely squeaked out the reply.

"Yeah, the term hasn't gone around in Japan much yet. Just think of it as someone with a lot of expert knowledge about coffee."

"Expert knowledge?" Maou parroted back as he stared at the sheet.

The printout turned out to be a clipping from MgRonald's internal newsletter. For Japanese franchisees, the main office was holding a special workshop to help employees handle MagCafé products and provide them more experience and knowledge to serve customers with. This was chiefly reserved for managers and other full-timers, but the MgRonald Barista program was also open to the hourly crew, assuming they had chalked up enough hours on duty and were willing to pay a class fee.

The workshop was mainly about MagCafé's new coffee items. The daylong program went over handling the machinery, working with coffee beans, and the other fine particulars of everyone's favorite deliverance of caffeine.

"Internal company rules state that there has to be at least one person with MgRonald Barista credentials in each MagCafé location."

"Oh," Maou replied. But he remained dubious. What was with this workshop that made it so different from the training manual he and the crew had at hand? He doubted a single day of instruction could make such a dramatic difference in taste—but even without the proven traffic record of Kisaki's coffee, Maou could never turn down a potential chance at career advancement.

"The thing about being a barista, though, is that it's not just coffee you have to focus on."

"Huh?" Maou said, looking up from the course description.

"The word *barista* comes from Italian. What the Italians call 'bars' are really more like lunch cafés, and while bartenders specialize in alcoholic beverages, baristas at these places mostly deal in coffee and other nonalcoholic drinks. They're kind of treated as masters of their craft, the same way chefs or sommeliers might be, although that way of thinking hasn't really permeated Japan yet."

The unexpected lecture piqued Maou's interest.

"But not everyone who works behind a bar in Italy call themselves baristas. That's because some are expected to run pretty much the whole place—drinks, food, restaurant equipment, customer service, the whole bit. Those people get called *barman* in Italy—they borrowed the English word for it. The idea's that they're totally versed in everything the bar offers, they're totally focused on what they're doing, and they can provide the best service possible to customers for any situation."

"Uh-huh…"

Something about this speech seemed to impassion Kisaki. The previous fatigue was long gone. Maou couldn't do much beyond nod at these freewheeling mood swings, but it was her rousing conclusion that made him gasp.

"That's what I want to be someday. A true barman."

"!!"

As far as Maou could recall, these were the first words he ever heard from Mayumi Kisaki as a person—not Ms. Kisaki, manager of the MgRonald in front of Hatagaya station. These were emotions from the heart that beat a rhythm behind her name tag. The fact that this shout from the heart was *still* about work reassured Maou that she hadn't changed that much.

"Well, once you move up the ladder at the Mag, I bet you're gonna accomplish a lot, Ms. Kisaki."

She would, too. Her daily figures were consistently up from the same time last year. Maou understood, or thought he understood, how astounding a stat that was. There was no way Kisaki's career would dead-end at this single location.

He always thought that she deserved a bigger playing field to shine in. But he had no idea that Kisaki—his primary role model, as he strove to attain the seemingly faraway goal of a full-time gig—was aiming for such incredibly lofty heights. It impressed him, despite the fact that his dreams of world domination were quite a bit loftier than that. But Kisaki was surprised at his reaction.

"What're you talking about? I can't accomplish that at MgRo—"

"...Huh?"

"Uh..."

Something told Maou he shouldn't have heard that. His boss undoubtedly noticed, too. She *really* wasn't acting herself today.

"...I'm not setting a good example as a manager, am I?" she intervened. "Chatting on and on about myself like this." Then she fell awkwardly silent, eyes turned toward the paper Maou carried. "But, hey, if you want to get as good as I am, why don't you start by taking that workshop? They'll probably let you in for free, what with your shift-supervisor experience. Lemme know if you're interested."

"Um, certainly..."

"Anyway, I gotta get back upstairs. Hold the fort down here for me, all right?"

Kisaki may have looked no different from before as she whirled around and climbed the stairs, but Maou had the distinct impression she was speaking at a faster pace than usual. And more than that—more than anything—he didn't miss the subtle nuances she dropped into that conversation. He could only pray that he was mistaken about them.

❋

"Huh?"

Back at his apartment building, Maou was puzzled to find a light on in Suzuno's upstairs room. As the ever-humble Church cleric she was, Suzuno always retired early at night. Her being awake after Maou worked the closing shift was unheard of. He decided to bring it up with Ashiya at the front door.

"Hey, what's Suzuno up to?"

"Welcome back, Your Demonic Highness," Ashiya replied with his usual flair. "Ms. Sasaki joined her a few moments ago, so whatever it is, it involves the two of them. More spell training, I presume."

"Chi? I thought she went home after her shift ended. It's past midnight! Why isn't Suzuno letting her leave?"

The Devil King felt obliged to have a word with Suzuno about this. *Letting a teenage girl walk around by herself in the midnight hours? Come on.* Before Ashiya could stop him, Maou tied his shoes back on and knocked on the door to Room 202.

"Helloooo? You in there, Chi? It's already tomorrow, you know. You need to head back hoooome…"

"Silence, Devil King!"

Suzuno stuck her petulant face out the doorway. The design on her kimono was far simpler than her normal wardrobe—leisure wear, or possibly the clothing she wore to bed.

Chiho, seated inside in pajamas, looked toward him, a conflicted look on her face.

"You fancy yourself her guardian, then? I have received permission from Chiho's mother. She is staying overnight in my room."

"…Oh. Is *that* all?"

"Yes." Chiho bowed politely at him. "Sorry."

That explained the large bag she'd been lugging around earlier. She must have planned this sleepover well in advance.

"Oh, not at all. I mean...you know, don't overdo it, okay? Like, for real."

"Of course..."

"I am wholly capable of providing for her safety, thank you. We have completed training and are currently engaged in what I understand is called 'girl talk.' You are *not* welcome."

Suzuno shut the door, not bothering to wait for a reply.

"...Girl talk?" Maou parroted, pouting to himself as he plodded back to his castle.

"Umm," Ashiya sheepishly replied, apparently listening in on their doorside chat. "Ms. Sasaki gave her greetings earlier, actually. She mentioned her mother as well."

Maou brushed him off, focusing his attention on his MgRonald Barista info sheet as Ashiya reluctantly set off to prepare dinner.

"...It's easy to fall into the trap of daily life, isn't it?"

"Dude, what's *that* about?" Urushihara asked, picking up on Maou's passing utterance first.

"Hmm? Well, like, I just think it's funny how everyone changes all the time, whether you notice it or not. It might seem like your life never changes, but it does—time's zooming by, faster than you can perceive it."

"Huh?" Urushihara snorted at the un–Devil King–like observation. "What's with you, man? You gettin' screwy in the head, too? That's the whole reason why life's fun. It'd be weird if stuff *never* changed."

"...Like I need *you* telling me that."

Having an ankle-biting live-in bum sum up his sentiments for him did not make Maou a happy camper. Urushihara stayed on the offensive, chuckling at him.

"I don't think anyone in here knows *that* any better than I do, man."

"Well," Ashiya said, appearing with a plum, a bonito, and a basil rice ball and a bowl of miso soup. "If you care to know more about how life changes, why not prove it by helping out with chores a little? *Hmm?*"

And thus, Maou's sentiments were lost amid his appetite and the usual nighttime squabbling over the division of household duties.

✳

"I *am* impressed, though. Such stable activation in a mere week's time. It may already be time to begin with the basics of the Idea Link."

"You think so?!"

Suzuno and Chiho sat windowside, each with a glass of barley tea in one hand and a fan in the other. A small mosquito coil burned away in one corner of the room, its incenselike scent adding a touch of atmosphere to this rather unorthodox session of girl talk.

"One of my coaches reminded me of that, actually. She said that, like, if you're lifting weights or stretching and you're really focusing on whatever part of the body you're working, that makes a huge difference in the results. So whenever I was shouting, I always tried to focus on whether any changes were taking place within me."

"Perhaps, but this is not something any man on the street can become proficient in. Once one reaches a certain point, after all, one's mental capacities begin to play a larger and larger role. If you were born in Ente Isla, Chiho, I do believe you might have been a gifted spellcaster. Ah..." Suzuno, perhaps sensing this was too much praise, made an effort to harden her face. "But remember, I will teach you the Idea Link and *only* the Idea Link. Do you understand?"

"I do, I do. But thanks for the compliment."

Chiho took a sip of tea and sighed as she looked out at the starry summer sky.

"I'm not trying to hurry things along or anything, but I'd really like to gain that Idea Link ability as soon as I can...I mean, before you and Yusa get too busy."

Suzuno chuckled. "I may not appear as such, but my days grant me *quite* a bit of free time, let me tell you."

On Ente Isla, she was a feared and renowned Church high official; in Japan, to an impartial observer, she was an unemployed young woman with eccentric fashion sense and a mysteriously large bank account. This situation was further exacerbated by the fact that, now that Maou was back at the MgRonald in Hatagaya for most of the day, the archangel Sariel, who worked down the street from him, was serving as a secondary deterrent once more.

Being within Sariel's sphere of influence meant less worrying about rogue demons trying to approach Maou, which in turn meant, for Suzuno, less surveillance of the Devil King and more hours bumping around her apartment instead. There was still Ashiya and Urushihara to surveil / guard / take to task, but that hardly filled enough hours that she couldn't help Chiho with her training.

"Oh, I didn't mean *thaaaat*. It's just, like…"

Chiho stared at the stars for a moment, searching for words.

"It feels like things are…different now. After the whole Tokyo Tower thing."

"Different…?"

Suzuno paused for some tea, eyebrows arched high.

"I mean, we've had tons of trouble with, like, Sariel and Gabriel and the demons at Choshi and stuff, but…Maou and Yusa still haven't fought each other yet, right? Like, mano a mano?"

A dirty look was enough to make them break into fisticuffs. But Chiho was talking about a more…final, potentially lethal, confrontation.

"But don't you think Yusa's been acting kinda…weird since then?"

"……"

Chiho explained the differing sets of memories she discussed with Maou and Emi during their hospital visits.

"Ever since then, it's like Yusa's…well, Maou, too, but…it's like they've both been thinking about a whole bunch of stuff all the time. And…don't get angry, all right, Suzuno?"

Suzuno shrugged, her face serene, as she motioned her to continue.

"Do you remember when all of us ate together in this room after they put that big hole in Maou's wall?"

"Yes. It feels like quite a long time ago, given everything that's transpired...but it hardly was, it's true."

The two of them looked around the room.

"I know this is selfish of me, but I thought back then about how great it'd be if, like, everyone could just forget about all the complicated stuff happening on Ente Isla and just let these days go on forever—Urushihara screwing around, Ashiya yelling at him, you frantically trying to take control of the situation... Then Maou does something to spoil Alas Ramus, and Yusa winds up starting an argument about it... I really don't think you build that kind of chemistry unless you, like, really enjoy each other's company. I know I'm not being realistic, but..."

Chiho shrugged, remembering an argument of her own she'd had with Suzuno once. Suzuno recalled it as well, but she had no intention of chiding her for it now. In fact, Chiho's side of the debate deeply resonated with her now.

"Ah, how the mighty have fallen."

"Hmm?"

"Nothing. You were saying?"

The bladeless fan stationed near the kitchen area circulated the air around the room, lazily sending the smoke from the mosquito coil outside.

"Well...I know Maou and Ashiya and Urushihara are demons who tormented people on Ente Isla, and you and Yusa have a mission to slay all of them...and all it'd take is some kind of trigger to destroy everything we've built up over all these days. It'd be really sad to see it happen, and it'd make all of you leave me...and that anxiety still hasn't gone away."

"......"

"And since Tokyo Tower, I feel like something's really troubling Yusa. I think it's got a lot to do with what I told her about when I was in the hospital. And, like, even when I look at Maou, he'd instantly react to me before, but now it's like he's thinking over whatever he says to me before he says it."

Suzuno silently marveled at Chiho's powers of observation.

Judging by her words, neither Maou nor Emi explained to Chiho herself what the memories implanted into her mind truly meant. But given how much she cared about the two of them, she could obviously tell that the memories had triggered...*something*...that had changed their behavior.

"The war on Ente Isla, and the demon realms splitting into two parts... Yusa and Maou didn't have anything directly to do with that, right? And yet, there's this person who gave me that power; these memories I found in my head; Gabriel; that other angel that I hit... It's like there's something out there, gradually pushing Maou and Yusa and everyone back into the really rough place they started out from."

Now Chiho's face was tilted downward as she started at the tatami-mat floor. She must, Suzuno figured, still be working out all these feelings and thoughts in her mind, asking herself questions out loud and fumbling around for the answers.

"I feel, Chiho, that my sense of faith has greatly weakened since my arrival in Japan."

"Oh?" Chiho raised an eyebrow at this unexpected confession.

"If our god is truly all-powerful and created everything that lives and thrives on our world, why is the land not teeming with people as kind and gentle-hearted as you, Chiho?"

"Oh, I'm really nothing *that* special..."

The sudden out-of-hand compliment almost embarrassed Chiho into spilling her tea.

"There is a story within Church mythology about a relic known as the Scroll of Holocrisus. It is a scroll the gods entrusted to a man named Holocrisus, but so unable was he to contain his curiosity that he eventually opened the scroll. Within the paper was imbued all the negative emotions of the world gathered together, and when he opened it, the emotions turned into words and wriggled their way into the hearts of the people. But, right at the end of the scroll, there was a single word written that could contain those emotions. And that word was *hope*."

"We have something similar here on Earth. About Pandora's Box."

"That story was the very first thing that made me doubt the omnipotence of our god. Why would a truly omnipotent higher being allow the creation of negative emotions in the first place? And why, in a world before negative emotions, would this man Holocrisus's soul be infused with impulses negative enough to make him defy the command of his lord? And the fact that this god is entrusting a mere mortal with the custody of such a vital relic... It honestly disturbs me."

Chiho looked on, eyes filled with kindness, as Suzuno ranted in very non-cleric-like fashion.

"Yeah... I wonder. But when you look at the world... There are a lot of people out there who need a god, or God, in their lives. Religion is an indispensable part of their daily lives, and I certainly can't deny that to them."

"Hmm. Retaining your own sense of self while tolerating others. A rare feat to pull off indeed. Perhaps I should be worshiping you instead, Chiho."

"Wh-what are you...?"

"I simply mean that when the weak lose what they believe in, they need some sort of sign, some sort of path, to lead them forward."

Suzuno finished her barley tea and looked out the window.

"I think, right now, Emilia has lost her way."

"Huh?"

"Tell me what you think of this analogy. You are fervently studying, forgoing food and rest, even, in order to be admitted into your first choice of universities. When the fateful test day arrives, you arrive at the site in triumphant spirits, but at the last moment, they decide to change the test to a flower-arranging competition. What would you think of that?"

"What kind of analogy is *that*?!" Chiho nearly dropped her glass again. The story had turned out to be, literally, too much to swallow.

"Merely an example. But think about it. Everything you have passionately studied in your life, made countless sacrifices for, all for the sake of this 'test' you picture for yourself. And right at the end, you are faced with a seemingly impossible task, one wholly outside of your expertise. What would you do?"

"Me…?"

It was hard for Chiho to connect her situation with Suzuno's whacked-out analogy. She still attempted to give it serious thought, however.

"I-I don't know a thing about flower arranging…and what kind of school would use that for their admission guidelines? I don't think I'd want to join that school too much anymore, maybe."

"But you understand the concept, at least—that one can use flowers to express some sort of emotion or visual sequence. Let's say the test officer presents you your choice of colorful flowers. Would you still attempt it?"

"Well, even if he does, that's still kind of—"

"The university would still offer you a challenging, enriching program in the academic field of your choice. The only difference is, instead of history or English or mathematics, the admission test involves flower arrangement."

"Um, this is still an analogy, right? So, basically, you're saying that you aimed for this thing your whole life, but now you got thrown for this crazy loop and it's making you rethink everything?"

"Indeed. Very observant, Chiho. That is why I was being rather flippant with the topic. It might feel too depressing to discuss otherwise."

Suzuno chuckled to herself and looked at the wall separating her from Devil's Castle.

"I think the Devil King is no longer the target for revenge Emilia originally wanted to slay."

"…Huh?"

Chiho was unable to grasp the portent of the short sentence.

"In fact, the father she thought she lost at the hands of the Devil King's Army is apparently alive and well. That, despite the fact she chased down the Devil King in order to exact revenge for that man."

Emi, the savior of Ente Isla, had fought for most of her short life to defeat the Devil King. That much Chiho knew already.

"Once she killed him, her work would be done, her journey at a final and triumphant end. Yet her father is revealed to be alive. Emilia's path was snatched away from her."

"Wh-what? But all that means is there's no need to kill Maou here in Japan. She can just go search for her father instead!"

"All right. So why are you refusing that flower-arrangement test, Chiho?"

"...................Oh."

Now Chiho understood the crux of Suzuno's argument.

"Everything she had done up to this point, believed up to this point...was all a waste? None of it had any purpose?"

"I imagine that is exactly what she thinks," Suzuno said. "Other people may say there is no such thing as a wasted life, that one's experience will always help out later, and other such banal adages. But that cannot change a person's feelings. The moment you are presented with a table full of flowers, you would be filled with a profound emptiness as you wondered to yourself why you bothered with all of that study. And who could fault you for it?"

"......"

Suzuno's face scrunched up, as if she had drunk something tart.

"And worst of all, Emilia has already been betrayed by Ente Isla once."

Chiho remembered what Emi's friends had told her—right inside Devil's Castle next door, in fact.

"Um, you mean how the Church lied and said Yusa was dead?"

Suzuno nodded. "Precisely. If Ente Isla had offered valid praise for Emilia's efforts as the Hero—if they had showered her with the admiration she so rightly deserves—that would have driven Emilia to carry on. To retain her desire to slay the Devil King and make him pay for his transgressions. But now..." Her face darkened. "We face the exact opposite situation. The Church has announced Emilia's death for their own sinister reasons, and the people believe them. We, the people of Ente Isla—including the very Church that Emilia saved!—have cast away the Hero as obsolete, unnecessary, now that the Devil King's Army is gone. We betrayed her."

But not everyone was duped. Olba, and the denizens of heaven, were after Emi's holy sword, sending assassins to strip her of it, fearful of the power she'd retained after the Devil King's defeat.

"But," Chiho said, fired up, "but Emeralda and Albert are trying to restore Yusa's good name, aren't they? They're both pretty well-known people in Ente Isla, right?"

"Not to great effect, sadly," Suzuno replied, her expression unchanged. "That is how vast and unquestioned the Church's power and belief base is. And it seems to me that Emeralda is so busy dealing with the backlash in her own nation that she lacks the power to directly confront the Church itself. Even before I came here, there were many of the opinion that Emeralda should be branded a heretic for so often taking positions that go against the teachings of the Church."

"Oh, no... But she's not lying or anything..."

"No. *We* are," Suzuno shot back in self-depreciation. "The Church, that is. But it would be unthinkable for the Church to withdraw a statement. That would be admitting they are fallible. If the Church says white is black, or up is down, the people will say it is so. That is the land of Ente Isla...the Western Island portion of it, at least."

She stood up to refill her glass of barley tea. It was clear the Church's stance on this made her physically ill. Closing the refrigerator door, she returned to the window and took a breath, attempting to give the chat a fresh start.

"Emilia was able to fight as the Hero for as long as she did because she had the goal of killing the Devil King, and thereby avenging her father, waiting for her at the very end. But the Devil King was not her father's killer at all. Her indignation at the tyranny of the Devil King's Army was trampled upon by the very people she saved. And yet—"

"—she found out that all the anger and hatred she had bottled up inside was meaningless...but she couldn't just drop it."

"Indeed. But Emilia must, or else it will create a new sadness and hatred within her. Her memory of the tormented people she saw will rekindle her spirit, and then she might strike at the Devil King anew."

It was just a wild guess, but the idea made something twist in Chiho's mind. She imagined what kind of faces Emi and Maou would make at each other, as they squared off.

"With the Devil King dead, Alciel and Lucifer would certainly not stand by idly. But right now, at this moment, none of them could defeat Emilia. Three demons would be dead, gone from the world forever. Could you forgive her, Chiho?"

"I…!"

I couldn't. But being unforgiving is itself unforgivable. But I really, really couldn't forgive…forgive who…?

"Yusa is… She's just as important to me, too…"

"Indeed. Something Emilia is fully aware of. That is why she is at such an impasse right now. Her father remaining alive should be her primary focus, but nothing about it fills her with abject delight…a fact that, in itself, demoralizes her."

"And…Emeralda and Albert could never help, could they?"

"No. She is unable to confide in them. Even *if* they understood where her heart lay and were willing to accept it, do you think Emilia could simply go up to them and say, 'My father is alive, so count me out of this Devil King business'?"

Emi's duty-bound mind would never allow that. Not in a million years.

"Right now, Emilia cannot even figure out which color of flower to pick first. She is stewing, unable to even start on her next project."

That, in a nutshell, summed up Emi's bizarre behavior around Maou as of late. Her internal agitation was making it difficult for her to retain her usual hostile distance from him. That opened her up to moments of inattention, which itself distressed her greatly. She could no longer tell where her heart lay. The paths were all twisty and dark, and there was no guide to lead her.

Suddenly, Suzuno's eyes turned toward Chiho's forehead.

"Perhaps…that is why she decided to help you with this effort, Chiho."

"What do you mean?"

Suzuno used the hand holding her glass to point at Chiho's head. "The memories you tried to relate to Emilia," she said, her face pained. "It only makes sense that the man standing in the wheat field is her father. And this Acieth Alla you spoke of, too. In the Centurient language of Ente Isla, the term means 'blade wing.'"

"'Blade wing'?"

"Yes. It means little by itself, I am afraid...but there is one thing near us with a wing motif."

Chiho gasped, the image clear in her mind as well.

"Alas Ramus... Her name means 'wing branch' or something, right?"

"That is correct." Suzuno nodded solemnly. "I think it safe to assume that this Acieth Alla is a term related to either Alas Ramus or another of the Yesod fragments. Camio did mention there were *two* holy swords, after all."

Chiho nodded her reply.

"Perhaps this Acieth Alla is the name of the second blade...or, perhaps, the presence imbued within it. And think of this from Emilia's standpoint. The fact that her father is alive; having Alas Ramus in the Devil's Castle; the Better Half that she herself wields; and the ring on your finger—to her, it must feel as if someone is deliberately arranging all of these pieces around her. And that person's identity..."

Suzuno didn't bother continuing. Chiho, with her front-row seat to every major battle held in Japan so far, knew the answer well enough.

"Yusa's...mother, isn't it?"

Emi had come close to saying it outright at the hospital: "Why...? If she's watching me, why won't she *come* to me...?"

Chiho could only guess at the swirling emotions behind those choked words.

"Whether it be Sariel, Gabriel, Raguel; Camio or Ciriatto; Barbariccia and even Olba, too—one could say that they are all puppets being played for a show by Emilia's mother. Or, indeed, all of Ente Isla at this point. There is, after all, a cross-nation war about to break out over Emilia's sword. What do you think, Chiho?"

"About what?"

"If your mother went into hiding when you were a young child, never returning home once, then started spreading the seeds of conflict around not just your friends and family, but *everyone*, worldwide—and if she then left you to handle all of the fallout..."

Chiho tried to imagine.

What if her mother were actually a spy for some foreign country who suddenly left her sham marriage and fled from Japan? A woman involved in conflicts across the globe that made her personally responsible for countless lives lost, who then one day texted Chiho along the lines of "The fate of the world is up to you"?

Well then, that would toss Chiho into a struggle against terrorists over some missing nuclear weapons, so that Chiho had to undergo special-forces training to turn her into a cold, emotionless war machine and join the US Navy SEALs; but then she would find out that it was really her *dad* pulling the strings the whole time, and so after a years-long struggle laced with bloody tragedy, Chiho would track down her mom just in time to see her confront her dad in a spectacular, special effects–laden final duel—only to be taken out by an assassin's bullet, at which time she would ask Chiho to carry on her noble mission before dying in her arms. So then—

"Then I'd be the only one left to stop my father...and then they'd both wind up dying!"

"I... Pardon me? Why is your father involved?"

Chiho blinked, then hurriedly walked away from the Hollywood summer blockbuster in her mind. Suzuno, overwhelmed by her friend's flights of imagination, coughed before continuing.

"...Regardless, though. In a situation like that, Emilia's life could no longer be the same. And along those lines, if you can learn how to defend yourself, Chiho, not only would that make you more secure—I think it would help Emi collect herself a little. That is why I did not put up a great deal of resistance to the idea. She might not want to hear it," Suzuno added with a chuckle, "but Emilia was driven purely by revenge and a sense of duty up to now. She never had the time to think, or question, what she was living for. That ultimately led her to Japan, and I think it blessed her with a chance to reconsider her motives."

Suzuno stood up, brought her and Chiho's empty glasses to the sink, and began rinsing them off.

"It would be best for Emilia if she took her eyes off the Devil King for a bit. And fortunately, now that MgRonald is open once more, we no longer have to keep him on such a short leash."

"Huh? What do you mean?"

"Remember the demons who attacked us at Choshi? The force led by Barbariccia that parted ways with Camio were duped into doing Olba's bidding, and apparently are preparing to invade Ente Isla once again."

"What?! That… Is that okay, or…?"

It was turning into a messy state of affairs—demons going away from the Devil King's command and forming their own armies, Olba sowing the seeds of discontent in the background…the works.

"It is cause for concern, it is true. But what worries myself and Emilia is less the current invasion and more the possibility of them kidnapping the Devil King and Alciel and propping them up as the figureheads of the New Devil King's Army. The Devil King does not seem to approve of Barbariccia's behavior, but we must remain vigilant nonetheless."

"Y-yeah…"

Hearing such an ominous tale, Chiho had trouble figuring out how that was related to the MgRonald opening back up.

"Lord Sariel works at the Sentucky across the street, yes? The angels are pulling some very suspicious moves of their own, but they are not at all connected to Barbariccia and his ilk. If they were to attack the Devil King at work, Ms. Kisaki would naturally be caught up in it, and Sariel would hardly allow *that* to happen. I do feel poorly for making Ms. Kisaki into our personal defensive buffer, but so be it."

"Ah…"

"And while Lord Sariel would never come to the Devil King's aid, the amount of holy power within him is more than enough to keep any sensible demon at bay. There is no merit to Olba or the demons taking the risk of stoking an archangel's ire. Barbariccia may very well find the wrath of heaven pointed upon him if he does."

Chiho tried to imagine the position Suzuno painted for Sariel in this. In so many words, the archangel's lack of a direct connection with Olba and Barbariccia made him an effective deterrent—one triggered, in a deep, lizard-brain level, by Kisaki. It sounded convincing for a moment, but then Chiho recalled something.

"Um," she said, "I...I think that might not wind up working out."

"Why not?" Suzuno, in the kitchen, turned around. "How do you mean?"

"Well, the day before we went to Choshi..."

Chiho explained what she had seen in front of MgRonald on that tragic day—Sariel giving her (to say the least) the hard sell, Kisaki banning him from the location until further notice, and the way it all made the archangel melt into mush.

"I spotted Sariel on the street a few times since then, but it's like he's...hollow. Like, his whole face is. I didn't know people could do that kind of thing and be alive still. He walks around in those flashy Sentucky uniforms, but he projects so little of a presence. One time, I saw a dog mistake him for a telephone pole and pee on his leg."

Suzuno's eyes opened wide at the sordid tale. Then, an uneasy memory flashed across her mind—a holy-force reaction, notable mainly due to how weak it was, picked up by the sonar bolt she unleashed from the Dokodemo Tower in Yoyogi.

"Ha-ha-ha! Oh, don't... Enough of that silliness. He *is* an archangel, remember! How could he ever let a—"

Chiho pensively shook her head at Suzuno's nervousness.

"It was a Chihuahua."

It was simultaneously the most damning evidence possible and the least important part of the story.

✳

"Welcome! We've got a large-print menu right here for you, sir!"

The next evening, the crew at Sentucky Fried Chicken in Hatagaya was enjoying a slight lull before the dinner rush; the dining area was about half full. Things were still bright and cheery inside, though, the woman at the register throwing all the sprightliness she could into her voice as she greeted Chiho and her group.

The sight of the freshly cooked chicken tumbling down the

hoppers behind the counter could whet any carnivore's appetite, but the trio of women who approached the register had other things in mind. Chiho, Emi, and Suzuno, freshly ordered iced coffees in hand, set up shop around a table near the registers, taking a quick scan of the dining area as they did.

"I don't see him. Maybe he's in the backyard...or maybe the kitchen or upstairs?"

"Hopefully this doesn't mean he has the day off..."

Chiho's latest bombshell was enough to make Emi hurry right over upon wrapping up work. Given how much she was counting on Sariel to play defense between the Devil King and the forces of Ente Isla, the news that he was now a shell of his former self was something she couldn't ignore.

"No," said Suzuno. "I can feel his presence, albeit only slightly. He may be hiding under the furniture or in the shadows."

This made Sariel sound like a termite, but Emi paid a closer look to her surroundings nonetheless.

"You're right... But if we're this close to him and *this* is all he's letting off, he must be doing pretty bad."

Chiho, meanwhile, had no idea how they picked up on his presence. "Is that another holy-force spell?" she asked.

Her friends gave each other a bemused look. "Not...exactly."

"It is something we can sense, is the only way to put it. ...Well, do you remember how you had difficulty breathing when the Devil King transformed atop the Tokyo Metropolitan Government Building?"

"S-sure."

During that battle against Sariel himself, Chiho felt her breath literally being taken away by the dark force the newly revived Devil King exuded in all directions. She recalled how Suzuno had to erect a magical barrier to keep her from suffocating.

"You might not have felt it, but the dark power had clearly detectable effects on your body, yes? With training and experience, one can hone that sense into something as powerful as smell or sight."

Suddenly, Emi pointed a finger right between Chiho's eyebrows.

"What about that, though? *That's* odd."

Chiho crossed her eyes to follow Emi's fingertip. Then, a moment later, something right there—her skin, her skull bone, some nerve or another—some unknown part of her body began to exert pressure upon her head, as if blood was rushing toward that single spot.

"I-I *do* feel it. It's like something's…being set off right here. Ow." She began rubbing the ridge between her eyebrows, unable to stave off the discomfort.

"Holy force is harmless to the human body, but it *does* form a kind of presence that makes itself known. We can only gain a vague sense of where it is, but…"

Chiho was about to nod distractedly at Emi's explanation before Suzuno's warning made her lift her head up.

"Sssh! He's here!"

She was looking right at the small build of Sariel, clad in a suit. But:

"His skin's gray…"

"Talk about the walking dead."

The shocking transformation in Sariel's countenance made both Chiho and Emi involuntarily tense up. His gaunt face and emaciated, ghostlike form were a far cry from the wannabe playboy of the past. It was hard to picture him having any success with the ladies looking like *that*. Given how he was well on the way to obesity with his thrice-a-day MgRonald habit not long ago, seeing this crash diet of his was honestly disquieting.

"Have a good one, sir!"

Whether he heard another staffer wish him well or not, Sariel barely so much as lifted a hand as he trudged out of the restaurant.

"What do you think?"

"It should be obvious. We must pursue him."

The three girls flew out of their seats and followed behind. The pursuit wasn't exactly a challenge. Sariel's pace was so plodding, so meandering, there was no possible chance he would elude them.

"Okay, but…*then* what?"

"We have to revive his spirits, somehow. Before anything unwelcome happens."

"This is unwelcome enough already, but…we'll see, I guess."

"I would like to accost him someplace without any prying eyes upon us. We will follow him home, then force our way inside."

"Fair enough. Even if it winds up in a fight, Alas Ramus can make short order of that scythe of his."

The conversation between the Hero and Church cleric reminded Chiho of little more than a pair of burglars plotting their heist. She glanced at the time on her phone.

"Ah…it's already six…"

Emi doubled back and took a look at the MgRonald behind them. "Oh, you have work tonight, Chiho?"

"Yeah. Sorry…I probably wouldn't be back in time for my shift if I joined you."

"I totally understand. I have the worst time getting free of work myself, sometimes…"

"Oh, don't worry about it, Yusa! I'm just glad you made it here."

"Yeah. Well, we'll go ahead first, then. Just focus on work for tonight, Chiho."

"Sure thing. Sorry I couldn't be more help."

"You're already more than enough help, Chiho," Emi reassured Chiho. "If it weren't for you, we'd have no idea that idiot angel is in trouble. We can handle the rest."

The three girls parted ways in front of Sentucky Fried Chicken. Emi and Suzuno followed the staggering Sariel to parts unknown.

Smartphone at the ready so they could track their progress on a map, the pursuers followed him down the shopping street, through a walking path, and into a timeworn residential zone. At the far end of it was a condo building.

"Is that it?"

Even before Sariel approached it, the pair could tell the building was almost brand-new. Zoning regulations prevented it from having too many floors, but through the windows, Emi could tell its occupants enjoyed more free space than she did at her place. Its front faced a two-lane road, and like many apartment buildings downtown, the first floor had two spots reserved for business tenants; one was occupied by a convenience store selling fresh produce.

"That would certainly make things easy on rainy days," praised Suzuno, her motherly/housewifery instincts coming to the surface.

The other business space had a FOR RENT sign on it, but judging by what was visible through the window, it was set up to be a café of some sort.

Sariel, paying them no obvious mind, made it through the crosswalk and disappeared into the building's entrance.

"That must be the place. 'Heaven's Chateau,' though? Seriously?"

That was the name on the sign—HEAVEN'S CHATEAU HATAGAYA. Emi sneered at it before something occurred to her.

"Hmm?"

"What is it?"

Emi's eyelids burst open as the duo waited for another walk-signal cycle before crossing. Someone familiar had just exited the convenience store. The figure walked down the opposite sidewalk, not approaching them. Emi watched her walk off, breathing a sigh of relief that she didn't have to pass her by and give her a polite "hello" or the like.

"What is it?"

"Didn't you notice? Maybe the street clothes threw you off. That's the manager at the MgRonald... Kisaki, I think it was."

Suzuno followed Emi's gaze, but the figure was already out of sight, going down the next crosswalk ahead and behind a building.

"Kisaki...? Why was she in *that* building?"

"...I dunno. I'm sure it's just a coincidence, but..."

"But? Do you have your doubts?"

"Well, like... If they *were* speaking to each other, Sariel wouldn't be going around like a zombie, would he?"

"...True."

As they spoke, their eyes drifted back to the signal. The walk sign was already about to tick down to zero.

"Ah...!"

The moment they took a step to cross, the timer stopped and flipped back to red. The two of them resignedly brought their feet back to the curb.

"...No, the very idea is impossible. I could never imagine Kisaki giving Sariel so much as the time of day. Kisaki's dismissal of Sariel is the whole reason for his downtrodden behavior, is it not?"

"One would think... I haven't spoken to Kisaki all that much myself, but from what the Devil King and Chiho tell me, she's not the type of lady to give a crap about some guy who crumbled to dust the moment she dumped him."

Disquieting thoughts crossed Emi's and Suzuno's minds for a moment.

"Well. We can consider this later. Lord Sariel takes precedence."

"Can we get the apartment number from the mailboxes? Oh, but what if it's an auto-lock door?"

Considering the building's newness, that seemed pretty likely. They had no problems with storming Sariel's residence, but not if it meant causing trouble for the other tenants. Emi tried to think of a way to reach his place without causing a ruckus.

Then, both of them gasped out loud.

"Ah!"

To their amazement, Sariel himself walked back out of the building. When he had his suit on, he could just barely manage to maintain an air of decency. But now, in a beat-up jersey and T-shirt, he looked beyond all hope.

"Well," observed Suzuno, as he walked to the convenience store Kisaki had just departed, "clothes certainly make the man after all."

"If *that's* how he's looking, I guess Kisaki didn't just pay him a visit, no."

"Quite true. The light is turning green, Emilia. We had best accost him while we—"

The pair were already halfway across the street when they realized Sariel was stopped in front of the convenience store's automatic door, standing bolt upright.

"?"

Did he notice us? Not that Emi cared. But why didn't he turn around?

Gingerly, Suzuno attempted to engage him verbally.

"Lord...Sariel?"

"My...goddess..."

"Huh?"

"My goddess was *here*?!?!"

"Aghhhh!"

Without warning, he latched on to the shoulders of Suzuno, eyes wide and bloodshot. It caught Emi off guard.

"Wh-what are you doing?! Get your hands off Bell!"

"Answer me, Crestia Bell! She *was*, wasn't she?! She was *here*, my most beloved of goddesses, until mere moments ago!!"

"P-please, Lord Sariel, calm yourself! When, when you say 'goddess,' do you mean Ms. Kisaki from MgRonald?"

"Sh-she was here?!"

Suzuno's revelation clearly took the wind out of Sariel's sails. He turned his pleading eyes toward Suzuno, then Emi.

"Why do you care if she was?! Just let go of Bell already! I'm calling the police!"

The police wouldn't be much comfort in a fight between a Hero and an archangel, but the threat proved surprisingly effective as Sariel removed his hands.

"No. She was... I can tell."

The sadness that dripped from every word made even Suzuno, his victim, feel a twinge of pity. For a moment.

"This...the scent of my goddess...of the coffee brewed to perfection by a goddess's hand..."

"Gross!!"

Emi's one-word evaluation didn't stop Sariel from sliding down to the ground.

"Ahh...she was a mere arm's length away from me... If only I could turn back time...ahh..."

"Bell, what's with this guy?"

"I cannot say. I cannot say, but at this rate, someone may very well call the authorities. Lord Sariel, please, could you stand up for me, at least?"

"…Ah. I am sorry. This has been all too shocking to me. My shopping trip will have to wait. Whenever I think about my goddess, nothing else can occupy my mind."

Emi and Suzuno watched wordlessly as the chagrined Sariel wobbled back toward the apartment entrance. Checking up on his status and confirming his address was probably the most they could hope to accomplish tonight. They had other questions, but Sariel was clearly incapable of conversation as he checked his mail cubby.

"Number three-oh-two."

With Emi nabbing that final piece of vital info, the pair decided to call it a night.

This was even worse than they expected. It'd be one thing if they were in a position to perhaps mend the bridges between Kisaki and Sariel. But Emi and Suzuno knew Kisaki only faintly. Nothing a couple of passing acquaintances could say would make her forgive Sariel, as Chiho put it.

Something had to be done, though. Otherwise, Sariel would cease to function as a defensive net, and any attacking demons would have a truck-sized hole to plow through on the way to their target.

Emi muttered to herself, out of earshot of Suzuno:

"…Why do I have to go through all this headache just to keep the Devil King safe?"

✳

Just as Chiho changed clothes and began her shift, she noticed something was missing.

"Oh? Ms. Kisaki isn't here today?" she asked one of the front-end crew.

"She's out somewhere. Said she was on break. Maou's handling upstairs right now."

"Really? Wow. Wish I could go up there sometime."

Maou seemed less than confident yesterday, but even Chiho wanted to try her hand at some new responsibilities sooner or later.

"Oh?" the crewman said, shaking his head and smiling. "Ever since I drank Ms. Kisaki's coffee, I don't think I have it in me to run second-floor duty. If someone complains that my stuff tastes different from hers, what am I supposed to do then?"

"Yeah, that might be true."

Chiho laughed. She definitely wasn't the only one with that concern. But:

"Ah-*hem*. Who's complaining? They'd be providing vital feedback."

Somewhere along the line, Kisaki came back. Her employee vest and hat were off, and she had a convenience-store bag in one hand and a shawl over her shoulders to prevent sunburn.

"Oh, welcome back. That was quick."

"Hello, Ms. Kisaki. Did you go out somewhere?"

"Just a little errand. I'm sorry; I'm gonna have to hole up in the staff room for a little while. Are things going okay upstairs?"

"Yeah. I think Maou's staying above water up there, anyway."

Kisaki took a peek at an upstairs security-camera screen.

"Great...but I'm gonna have to get all of you working up there sooner or later. It's gonna be tough to schedule you all otherwise."

"Oh, hey, that reminds me—Maou mentioned something about some kinda MagCafé accreditation you can get?" Chiho asked.

"Accreditation?" The crewman sounded surprised by this.

Kisaki nodded casually. "Well, it's not like you need it to work the café or anything. You get a neat little certificate if you take the course, though."

"A certificate...? You mean like the one upstairs with your photo on it, Ms. Kisaki?"

"Yep. Those are meant for showing off in the dining area. That way customers will know if there's a specialist on duty, sort of thing."

Chiho never bothered taking a close look at Kisaki's certificate. She had assumed it was just for showing who the current manager on duty was.

Kisaki handed the two of them a copy of the same printout she gave Maou earlier.

"MgRonald Barista… Is Maou taking this course?"

"Yep. He signed up for the very next one, in fact. You can join him, too, if you like."

"Will that let me make coffee as good as yours, Kisaki?" asked Chiho matter-of-factly, as she perused the printout. Kisaki hesitated a moment before replying.

"You might…come just that bit closer, maybe."

"Man," the other crewman said in a disinterested tone. "Tough competition." He might have seen Kisaki's reply as her lording it over the staff, but after a moment of thought, Chiho nodded and turned her head upward.

"Could I take that workshop, maybe? It says here you need at least some work experience, but…"

"Well, as long as you have the manager sign for you, no problem. I can't waive the course fee for you, since you don't have management experience like Marko does, but if that's all right with you…"

"That's fine. It sounds kind of neat, actually."

"Oh? Well, just fill out that application and give it to me tomorrow, okay? I should be able to put you in the same workshop with Marko if you do."

"All right. Thanks very much."

Chiho neatly folded the sheet, bounded for the staff room, and put it into the bag in her locker.

There was no subterfuge there. As a MgRonald crewmember, she really did want to brush up on her knowledge and technical skill. But there was one other motivation.

"…I wonder what Maou *really* thinks about all this."

She wanted to get Maou's take on current events—in a place with no Emi, no Ashiya, and no Japanese uninitiated to the existence of Ente Isla.

His reply to Chiho's long-ago confession of love was still on the back burner, but she was at least convinced that her presence in Maou's life was something he saw as a net positive. The evening she stayed over at Suzuno's place, learning about how lost at sea Emi felt, she couldn't help but wonder how Maou was grappling with it all.

Looking back, it never seemed like Maou saw Emi as much of an enemy at all. Not even at the very start. There was, of course, that whole past where he tried to destroy an entire world and remake it in his own image, but currently Maou was eking out a living in Japan and not demonstrating much in the way of violent, despotic behavior at all.

She could always go over to Devil's Castle and ask to speak with Maou in private. Suzuno would almost certainly object, though.

With Emi starting to see Maou as something besides just an enemy, and with demons turning against Maou and starting wars in his native realm, and with Chiho attempting to learn a magic spell crafted on another world—with all these changes in his everyday life coming at him all at once, what did *he* think? She wanted to know that—and she wanted to hear it from his mouth. Alone.

Alone...?

"Is that like...like, a da—"

"Something bothering you?"

"Hyah!"

Chiho leaped at the voice, her mind righting itself from its momentary meandering. There, her eyes met Kisaki's, as her manager sat at her desk, munching on a convenience-store sandwich.

"Well, you were kind of talking to yourself after you put that sheet in your bag. Don't forget, you're still on the clock."

"Oh, um, was I spacing out *that* bad?" Chiho blushed, the embarrassment driving her to touch her head in assorted random spots.

"More than you usually do, anyway," Kisaki chuckled as she took a sip from a plastic bottle of tea. "Is there an achievement test you have to take once summer break is over?"

"Huh? Why?" Chiho found the question puzzling.

"Oh, no, I just felt like something's been bothering you lately. Pretty much ever since we opened up again, your face has been telling me that you're up against a wall over something. Right now, even. When you smile, your eyebrows don't even budge."

Oops. She was trying not to let it show on her face, but having the oblivious Kisaki spot it so easily taught her all over again how futile the effort was.

"You're easy to read like that, you know? I'm actually getting kind of frantic over something right now, too. I mean, I try to make sure that what I'm doing isn't making me go down the wrong path, but..."

Kisaki tossed the remainder of her sandwich in to her mouth, then washed it down with a swig of tea.

"I hope you don't mind a thirty-ish woman like me lecturing a teen like you about life, but lemme give you one word of advice. Don't let fear keep you from taking action. A lot of things in life... unless it literally kills you, you'd be amazed how often you get a do-over with them."

"You think so?"

"If you don't take action, then maybe it won't end in failure...but more important, it won't *start* anything, either. If you do, whether you succeed or screw it up, something's gonna change. And if you're afraid of change, you're gonna have a lot of trouble living in this world."

"I...I'm not...afraid of change, exactly...but..."

Kisaki nodded lightly as Chiho lost herself in thought.

"If it doesn't seem like stewing over it's gonna produce an answer anytime soon, just concentrate on the work in front of you instead. Like, right now, during your shift, I think your first priority is MgRonald work, Chi."

"Oh! Yeah! Um...sorry I'm being all lazy."

A glance at the clock revealed that Chiho just spent the last ten minutes tormenting herself in the staff room. The sight of her galloping out the door made Kisaki decide to open a desk drawer and take out a stack of employee résumés.

"Hmm..."

Looking over Chiho's application, Kisaki's thoughts turned to Maou, currently brewing coffee straight above her.

"Oh, Chi's taking that, too?"

After her break ended, Maou discovered Chiho's interest in the MgRonald Barista course from Kisaki.

"Yep. She's scheduled for the same time you are, Marko. You oughta go together."

"Sure. I can do that."

Kisaki swiveled an eye downward at Maou.

"Hey, by the way, Marko, do you know when Chi's birthday is?"

"Uh, no, I don't," Maou instantaneously replied, unsure where this was going—until he saw Kisaki's expression. It was chiding, somehow.

Was that the wrong answer?

"Hmm. Hard to tell if you don't *care*, or if she's too reluctant to tell you."

"Hah?"

Kisaki shook her head, exasperated, at her employee's semicomedic yelp.

"There's a lot of privacy regulations I have to follow when it comes to this sort of thing, but…it's coming up, lemme just say."

"Oh, is it?"

Maou, ever the eager student of Japanese societal customs, knew that a birthday was something to be celebrated. But having it thrust before him like this made him realize that he'd never actually thought about someone else's birthday before.

"Yeah. And looking at you guys… I'm kinda getting the picture that Chi's going through some stuff because of you, Marko. Why don't you man up and show her what she means to you a little?"

"Uhm…"

"I mean, you've got something to do with that, right? The way Chi's been acting all weird lately?"

"!!"

Maou stared at his manager. He doubted Chiho ever told her the *real* truth, but he also had the feeling that not even he, the Devil King himself, could hide anything from this woman.

"I don't exactly need it laid out for me in black and white, you know? Something happened between the two of you during the renovation...and now you're both acting a lot different."

"Are...we?"

"And that's not a bad thing! Everybody's going to feel a little lost every now and then as they age. But if somebody's there next to you, that can really change the entire story."

Kisaki grinned and gave Maou a nudge with her elbow.

"So why don't you solve some of Chi's problems for a change? You could score some major kudos!"

"...You really act like my mom sometimes, Ms. Kisaki."

Kisaki pretended not to hear it.

"It's *called* the art of winning friends and influencing people, you know? Maybe I'm not a mom, but any successful mom's got to have it. Otherwise, who knows how screwed up the kids are gonna be?"

That was hard to counter.

"Anyway. Once you guys get barista accreditation, I can start sending a lot more people upstairs. It's really nothing that tricky, but make sure you get it down cold for me."

"Absolutely."

"I wonder, though," Kisaki continued, apparently reading Maou's thoughts, "what would make a good present for her?"

Even Maou could tell that Chiho was far more mature and disciplined than most her age. Something that screamed "girly" at one glance might not work too well with her.

"In terms of something that'd be useful... I dunno. I can't think of much except, like, a salad-oil set or an economy-sized bag of rice."

"She's not a restaurant, Marko." Kisaki rolled her eyes.

"But it's hard for me to figure out what kinda fashion accessories she might like," Maou protested. "And I'm pretty sure she'd have whatever book's hot right now... But I think flowers would be too... you know, meaningful?"

"Yeah. Given that weird distance you're keeping from each other, flowers could be tough."

It *seemed* that Kisaki was on their side. But she sure wasn't interested in providing direct answers, Maou was noticing.

"Well, at the heart of it, really... As long as it's at 'present' level, anything's fine. Nothing too complex, nothing that'd be too much of a burden on her. To use the cliché, it's the thought that counts. So just pick whatever comes to mind."

A new customer climbed up the stairs, the air-conditioning unit blowing his hair to the side. There were no orders on-screen, so he must've been a MagCafé client. Looking closer, Maou recognized him as a local businessman, a regular from before the renovation, although they didn't particularly know each other.

Despite the August weather, he didn't have a drop of sweat on him—and yet, whenever he asked for a Platinum Roast coffee, he'd always place an odd emphasis on the word "*hot*, please" in his order. Maou had already nicknamed him "Mr. Hotplease" in his mind.

Now he and Kisaki barked out their "Welcome!" in unison to him.

"Um, one medium cappuccino, *hot*, please."

Maou couldn't keep a smirk from erupting across his lips. "Certainly," he said as he tossed the order over to Kisaki. "Do you need anything else? ...That'll be three hundred yen, please. ...Out of five thousand. Ah, can I get a check, please?"

MgRonald policy stated that whenever a cashier received a large bill like this, another crewmember had to run up to double-check that the correct change was being given. The lack of a bill denomination between one thousand and five thousand yen led to a lot of easily confused paper getting shuffled around. Maou was expecting Kisaki to handle the job, but as he turned around, he spotted her running a finger against the bottom of each MagCafé mug in the stock shelf, one after the other.

"All right," she said as she counted out the bills in Maou's hand. He turned to hand it back to the customer.

"Feel free to have a seat. We'll bring it right out to you in a moment."

The businessman took the number card and sat down on a new, pliable café seat. Confirming his location, Maou watched Kisaki spring to action, taking a mug from the middle of the shelf…and, for some reason, washing it with the hot-water line they used to prepare tea and other drinks.

After thoroughly rinsing it in scalding water, she positioned it on the coffee server, loaded it with frothy milk, then crafted the cappuccino just as Maou learned how to in the manual.

"Hm."

Kisaki nodded, satisfied at the job, then went into the café space and traded the mug for the number card. Maou focused his attention on Mr. Hotplease for a moment as he took out his phone, idly scrolling through something on it, eyes locked on the screen as he brought the mug to his lips and took a sip.

"…?"

The mug froze in place, midair, as he was about to place it on the table.

His eyes left the phone screen. Then he brought the mug back up to his lips, taking a longer sip than before, savoring the taste more deeply before placing it back down. Maou had the dim impression that, yet again, this wasn't the cappuccino he'd been serving up earlier tonight.

"What's so *different* about it…?"

Maybe the MgRonald Barista workshop would help answer that question a bit. Hopefully. But Maou, watching Kisaki return to the counter with a triumphant look on her face, couldn't dispel the anxiety from his mind.

✳

Ten PM arrived, and Maou—on duty since the store opened—began preparing to leave alongside Chiho. They both couldn't help but notice how much Kisaki seemed to be enjoying herself as they walked out of the restaurant.

"Heading home?" Chiho asked.

"Uh-huh!" Maou replied.

They usually walked together for a bit on nights like these, their paths diverging midway.

Chiho hadn't known that Maou was free from closing duties today, however. *Too bad*, she thought. *If I had known, I wouldn't have had to wait for the day of that barista thing to talk to him.*

"……"

Just as Maou was taking Dullahan II out from the bicycle lot, he saw something behind Chiho that made him cringe, as if he just took a sip of motor oil while thinking it was cola.

"Ah! Are the two of you free from your work duties?"

"…We weren't waiting for you, so just get *that* idea out of your minds."

It was the completely at-ease Suzuno and Emi. No matter which way you sliced it, they *had* to have been waiting for Maou to leave. To Chiho, though, the fact they were still lurking around Hatagaya indicated Sariel wouldn't be any kind of quick fix.

In other words, they were standing guard—just in case Ente Isla decided to seize the initiative tonight.

Maou, never greatly interested in Emi hanging around him for long periods of time, sighed.

"What do you want?"

"I *told* you, we weren't waiting for you."

"…Yusa?"

Chiho suddenly realized that something was different. Emi was being just as acerbic and harsh toward Maou as she always was. But there was something not quite *her* to it, now.

"It is as Emilia says. We had an errand over at Sentucky Fried Chicken. We completed it long in the past, but we had another exciting round of girl talk in the meantime."

"You really like that phrase, don't you?" Maou replied wearily, as he looked to Emi for confirmation.

"You were thinking we needed something from you?" Emi asked.

"Well…" the Devil King found himself replying, "you pretty much always do, yeah."

Maou expected Emi to tell him to take a hike or get screwed or whatever else she usually did at times like these. Instead, she just said, "...Oh," and turned her back to him.

"Uh?"

"What do you think I want?"

"Uhh?!"

This was certainly a new attack strategy. It successfully floored Maou. Chiho, following his eyes, finally realized what threw him so badly: Tonight, Emi wasn't looking Maou in the eye. Usually, she'd have both her eyes, every bit of her hostility, and usually an index finger, pointed squarely at Maou. Now, all of that was lowered—a physical sign of her emotional insecurity, perhaps.

"I... Well...?" Maou said, scratching his head. "I dunno. You wanna follow us on the way home just in case I pick tonight to finally prey on her or something?"

"Oh, like you could do that. Her mom would kill you, you know."

"...Okay. Maybe you think I'm scheming something up in Mag-Café? What, are you scared 'cause you can't spy on me in there from the bookstore?"

"Not with that manager you adore so much breathing down your neck, you wouldn't."

"Right. So, again: What are you doing here? Just felt like flirting me with a little tonight?"

"Flirting?" Emi sighed and ruefully looked downward, unable to hide her frustration. "Why does the Hero need some kind of reason to go see the Devil King?"

"I don't think 'no particular reason' is gonna cut it with me, Emi."

"Well, what if that's all it is? What if it's more Sariel I'm worried about?"

This was starting to frustrate Maou, too. "Uh, what's *with* you?" he said, lowering his voice. "'Cause you've been acting all kinds of weird lately."

"...!"

There was something to Emi's eyes as she raised her head at his lecturing tone.

"Yusa?"

"Wh-what...?"

"..."

They had tears in them.

How long had it been since the last time anyone saw Emi's tears?

Even Maou had at least an inkling of what Emi was getting emotional about. The truth Gabriel revealed, that her father was apparently alive, was enough to send the young Hero's heart reeling. He knew the lust for revenge kindled by that supposed death was her main driving force in life. As a Hero, he was sure justice and fairness and all that were at least secondary missions for her, but avenging her father's death—one side effect of the invasion he engineered—must have constantly loomed large in her mind.

Then, thinking over that, something else occurred to him. A Hero's tears, presented to the Devil King. When did he see that last? And what did she say back then?

"Why are you kind to me, to other people, to the whole *world*?!"

She was crying.

"Why did you kill my father?!"

The pained shouting, the deep hopelessness impossible to hide within it, played against the back of Maou's mind.

"Hey, Emi?" he said, almost surprising himself with how gentle the voice sounded.

"...What?" she replied, her own voice clearly trying to hold something back.

"Y'know, maybe trying to conquer the world is a better fit for me in the end."

"...Huh?"

"Maou?"

"Devil King...?"

The air was disquieted—enough to agitate even the staid Chiho and Suzuno.

"Maybe this whole human-world thing ain't suited for me after all. I guess I got a lot of people waiting for me. If I felt like it, I bet I could make contact with Camio and have him cart me out of here right now."

"M-Maou?" Chiho said, standing next to the somber young man, her voice quivering.

"You aren't serious, are you?"

"Chi, it's just all been too weird anyway," Maou replied, his voice unchanged. "I united over a hundred different demon tribes. I led a Devil King's Army and sat at the forefront of a good half-million demon fighters. What am I even doing, trying to learn about the human world?"

"……"

A twinge of wary caution began to cross Suzuno's eyes. Like Chiho, she had trouble figuring out Maou's aims.

"I mean, it's not like the Devil King can ever reconcile with the Hero. So instead, I'm gonna go be as cruel and despotic as possible, all right? And once I try taking over the world, you better snap back to it and kill me. That'd be a lot more natural, wouldn't it?"

"Maou…"

"Sorry, Chi."

He gave her a pat on the shoulder, then stepped in between the three women, wheeling Dullahan II along.

"I bet Ashiya's gonna lose his mind when he hears about this. If we can invade before they get done rebuilding, maybe it'll be in the bag this time."

"…that."

"Better make sure Camio brings a pretty big posse with 'im when he shows up, though. It'll be nice to give Japan an appetizer of what's to come."

"…even do that."

Emi's quiet voice began to make itself known above the rambling demon.

"…Yusa?"

"Emilia?"

Emi raised her head, ignoring Chiho's and Suzuno's quizzical stares. She stared Maou down, eyes sharp, then screamed at the top of her lungs at the back of his UniClo T-shirt.

"You can't even *do* that!"

"……"

Maou stopped, turning only his eyes toward Emi.

"You don't even…*want* to do that…!"

"Ms. Kisaki's gonna fly out of the store screaming at us if you keep that up."

"Oh, you're scared of your fast-food manager, but you're gonna take over the *world*? Come on!"

"Hey, some things you just can't fight, y'know?"

"What do you want to do, even?"

"Conquer the world. I told you that."

"No. I mean, what about after that?"

"……"

Emi's question took Suzuno and Chiho aback.

"As long as they have access to their dark force, the demons in *your* realm don't even need to eat. No way are they gonna get used to life in the human world. And what meaning does the human world's land and treasure have to you, anyway? You're settling down in this world where the only attraction for you is killing humans. Once you wrap that up, what next?"

It was just as she'd discussed with Suzuno: The demon realms, and Ente Isla, ran on a whole different set of values from this world.

"Well, how 'bout I start by killing all the humans and plunging the world into despair?"

"Just hearing *that*, I can tell you're not being serious."

There was a searching tone to Emi's voice.

"The Southern Island that Malacoda invaded was cast into a maelstrom of death and suffering. Lucifer's army ran roughshod all over the Western Island, too. But the Northern Island… Unlike his brethren, Adramelech didn't even let his troops touch anyone besides the knights and other fighters who resisted him. And even though the Eastern Island was under your control the longest, the Azure Emperor still reigns over most of it now, just like he did before."

"…Yeah, you sure *did* travel the world, didn't you? Glad to see you were paying attention."

Emi glared at the gloating Devil King, not bothering to hide the tears any longer.

"If… If you were really the bloodthirsty, maniacal Devil King you claim to be, then I…I-I wouldn't be having so much *trouble* with this!"

"Yusa…"

"I should have known something was off the moment you looked me in the face and said, 'Ooh, lookit me, I'm gonna be a salaried employee with all the benefits!' You don't want to conquer the world at all! You just…"

Emi turned toward Chiho for a single passing moment before she continued.

"You just want someone to praise you for being a good little boy in Japan!"

The effect was immediate:

Maou's sneer disappeared from his face.

All three girls could tell that he was about to explode into a violent rage, something that went far beyond mere anger or shame. But when that moment came:

"…?!" Emi asked.

"M-Maou?!" Chiho cried.

Right in front of them, without any warning, Maou and his bicycle disappeared.

"Wh-wha…?"

Emi, the other side of the argument, was at a loss for words. Right there, at that moment, Maou was about to shout back at her. His mouth was open, he had just taken a deep breath, and he was clearly just about to fire back at Emi with everything he had. He showed no sign of unleashing any dark force, but the group still looked into the sky, then on the ground around them, picturing Maou using some kind of supernatural skill to flee. They knew very quickly that he hadn't.

"Um…Maou…?"

With uneasy steps, Chiho approached the spot where Maou was

previously located. Not a single sign of his presence remained on the pavement. Even with Chiho mimicking Maou's exact position, nothing occurred.

"What...just happened?"

The city around them ran along its familiar evening rhythm. They could hear the unending string of cars on the Koshu-Kaido road above, and as the trio grew increasingly frantic, they heard another new customer enter the MgRonald to the side. Only Maou and Dullahan II were gone, as if they were mere phantoms the whole time.

"Maou..."

Chiho instinctively brought a hand to the shoulder Maou had patted just before he vanished.

"E-Emilia... This surely could not be..."

"I thought it could've been for a moment...but how is this even possible?"

Both Emi and Suzuno feared the worst—a Devil King–napping engineered by Barbariccia. But both then and now, there was not a drop of detectable holy or dark force.

"...Is Devil's Castle safe?"

Emi gulped nervously. Suzuno was right. Perhaps the same anomaly had just befallen Ashiya and Urushihara. Maybe not "anomaly," though—if Emi's theory was correct, this was exactly what they had expected from that demon faction. But this was just too confusing. She took out her smartphone and started tapping.

"I have Lucifer's SkyPhone number. Assuming he's screwing around with his computer as usual..."

But no matter how long she waited, there was no ringtone. She looked at the screen, only to find the words "No Service" on the top header.

"Huh? What do you mean, no service?"

"Show me the number! I will try on my—"

Suzuno seized the smartphone from Emi's hand and opened up her own flip model. But:

"*I* have no service...?"

Watching this unfold, Chiho whipped out her own phone, only to find the same result. She swallowed nervously.

"But…this is crazy. I always call my parents right in front of this building to tell them I'm heading home!"

They each stared at their phones for a few moments. All of them refused to change their stance. No service. Then:

"Huh? Hello? Hell—agh!"

A young woman passing right by the trio made a face at the phone in her hand.

"Aw, my reception got cut off…"

They saw the woman wave the phone in the air as she walked off, only to bring it back to her ear after a certain distance.

"Is there reception over there?"

It was around 150 feet away. Emi and Suzuno sprinted over, only to find the bars spring back into life on their phone screens.

"That was weird," a relieved Emi said as she called Urushihara, "but at least we can call people again."

"…?"

Suzuno, for some reason, was looking down at her feet, taking a step back as if she had just stepped on something ominous.

"This is strange."

"Huh?" Emi asked Suzuno, a little annoyed that Urushihara didn't seem to be picking up. Suzuno crouched down and began searching the ground.

"Bell, what're you doing?"

Suzuno didn't answer, taking a pebble from the pavement and placing it on her palm.

"Hngh!"

The stone began to shine dimly, infused with her holy power. She flicked it with a finger.

"Huh?!"

Emi's eyes bulged. The magic-infused pebble bounced off some invisible obstacle, just as something resembling an azure-blue flame flickered in the air before Suzuno's eyes.

"…A barrier."

"A-a barrier?!"

Emi couldn't hide her shock. Suzuno was notably more somber.

"And not a demonic one, either. This…this is holy force! The Devil King's been encased in a barrier of holy force!"

Emi hung up on her still-unanswered call.

"Wait, so that's the edge of it?! Then why can we go in and out of it at will?!"

But before Suzuno could answer:

"………ahhhh."

"Did you say something, Bell?"

"I thought that was you, Emilia."

"……mn……nnnnngh!"

"Huh?!"

The voice was in the air, behind their backs.

"My goddesssssssssss!!!!"

Another voice, the last one they wanted to hear, dropped in from above.

"Eeep!"

It went without saying that it belonged to Sariel, his gaunt, ghoulish face framed by his bloodshot eyes and gnashing teeth.

"I have come to rescue *brghhh*!!"

Suzuno did not hesitate to strike him with the Light of Iron.

"Bn… Gnh… Baagghh!!"

She rained down blows with her giant hammer, sending him down to the ground in a single bounce.

"Bepph!"

He only stopped rolling after he hit the curb.

"……He's not dead, is he?"

Emi couldn't help but ask. That was a textbook display of using an amplifier to enhance one's holy force. The Light of Iron was distinct, powerful looking in Suzuno's hands, even as her breathing was ragged.

"Nragh!"

"He's up!"

Sariel himself, however, did not seem terribly affected as he sprang back to his feet. "What…what is the meaning of this?!" he said as he waved at Emi and Suzuno.

Just then, a blast of holy magic from his arms tore across the area, equally as effective as Suzuno's. It caromed off the barrier, making its boundaries clear to all. It was a dome of holy magic, one that extended across the entire street.

"I'd kind of like to know why *you're* here personally, but…"

"Where is my goddess? Is she unhurt?!"

"Uh, nothing's happened to the MgRonald, so…"

Emi and Suzuno turned back toward Maou's last known location. It remained perfectly empty, normal, and after a quick check, they—

"Wait…"

"Chi…ho?"

Chiho was gone.

She must have been with them, at least up to the point where their phones were out of range.

"Nngh!"

Emi hurriedly ran to where Chiho had been, not bothering to care whether or not she hit Sariel in the back of the head with her shoulder bag. For some reason, only Sariel was blocked by the barrier—neither Emi nor Suzuno were affected.

Just as before, there was not a trace of Chiho left to be found. Emi's phone remained out of service on that spot, but looking inside MgRonald, the scene was serenely normal—crewmembers walking to and fro, customers dipping French fries in little cups of ketchup.

"What is going *on*?! It's just a regular old barrier! Why are people disappearing on us?!"

"I-I don't know! Maybe they're still here, but invisible inside the barrier… But the fact we can travel through this barrier at will is beyond all comprehension!"

"This can't be any regular barrier!"

Sariel, still sprawled out on the ground after that latest strike, glanced to his side. A group of businessmen on their way home from work crossed to the other side of the street to avoid coming near him.

"It's a dimensional-phase barrier! Like the one I used on top of Tokyo's city hall!"

"Dimensional…phase?"

When Sariel had kidnapped Emi and Chiho, he had used a barrier to envelop the entirety of the Tokyo Metropolitan Government Building, one of the tallest skyscrapers in the city. Suzuno saw that for herself. But unlike the barriers Maou built from dark force, Sariel's had no clear boundaries. All it did was ensure other people in the area weren't affected by what happened inside.

"I-I thought this was a plot from heaven to expunge the goddess preventing me from returning to my world. I thought I had to save her very life!"

Emi and Suzuno, shutting out Sariel's half-dazed ravings, placed themselves back to back as they scanned the area.

"We've got…company…"

They were here. But they couldn't be seen.

❋

The MgRonald, the Hatagaya skyline, and the Dullahan II supporting his weight were all the same. But the sound was gone. He could feel the presence of no one else.

Emi, who was just about ready to go trampling all over his heart with her tear-laden eyes, was gone.

Maou had been enraged a moment ago. But the disquiet that now replaced that wasn't out of surprise over the bizarre scene that faced him. It was because, as much as he hated to admit it, her final words had pushed him over the brink.

His palms were sweaty—not because he was hot—and the negative energy pouring out of him made it feel like the blood that surged to his head would form horns for him on the spot.

"I… Look, I'm having trouble making decisions right now."

"……"

"We were having a *pretty* important chat just now, okay? But I kind of lost my cool for a moment. I think I may've said something that I regret."

Maou dropped the kickstand on Dullahan II and removed his hands from the handlebars.

"I think I avoided screwing it up *too* badly, but after all that crap she said to me, it was *really* getting hard for me to digest."

Wiping the sweat from his brow and drying his hands off with the hem of his T-shirt, Maou turned around from his position in the middle of traffic and returned the gaze of the two people looking at him.

"Who're you? Just give me your names and addresses and get outta here, okay? 'Cause I think I still got some steam to blow off."

There were two figures, both human looking. Maou didn't know either of them.

One was a young man in a stuffy-looking business suit, his shiny black hair done with a Clark Kent–style part—the kind of extreme-hold wet look that no young man would be caught dead in today. He wore large and equally out-of-date silver-frame glasses, but even from his vantage point, Maou could tell they were just for show, the lenses just two flat pieces of glass. The young man's suit was a humdrum (if oddly bright) shade of navy blue, and between that and his unadorned black-leather briefcase, he looked like the quintessential Japanese salaryman from the 1970s or so.

That still beat his partner, though. *That* guy was off by a good two hundred years or so, what with his full-body samurai armor. That, and he was a kid. Not just small-sized, like Urushihara or Suzuno—the balance between his shoulders, legs, bone structure, and head all indicated he was still a child. That didn't prevent him from encasing himself in a crimson-red suit of armor, complete with a frightening-looking *hannya* mask to seal the deal. The whole outfit looked hot, heavy, and somewhat lacking in visibility for the wearer.

"Jeez, thanks for going all formal with me, guys. So what is it? You angels, demons, North, South, East, West, what?"

"You seem less than surprised," said the Beatles-era businessman.

"I *am* surprised—at your wacky outfits. Did that get you a free gift certificate at some restaurant for winning their Halloween party, or what?"

"I thought it ample enough to keep from arousing suspicion."

"Uh… You, *maaaaaybe*, but you know that kid ain't doing himself any favors."

"I am afraid we do not always operate in tandem."

Maou glared at the simpering businessman. There was something gratingly gracious to his speech.

"Demons, huh?"

"I will admit this is the first time we have personally met, Devil King Satan. My name is Farfarello. I occupy the junior position in the Malebranche's council of chieftains."

"Ah, I nailed it."

A high-level demon after all. On the same rung of the ladder as Ciriatto, Maou's attacker in the seas off Choshi. The name was unfamiliar, however—and Maou was pretty sure he remembered the names of all of Malacoda's warlords.

"Farfarello… I'm sorry, I haven't heard of you."

"Of course not," the dapper demon said, unoffended. "I attained my chieftain's position *after* you led your army to the glorious invasion of Ente Isla, my liege."

"Aha. So who's the little action figure with you?"

"You may feel free to ignore him. He was merely a pilot of sorts from Ente Isla, and nothing that you need to—"

"I was talking to him. *Not* you." Maou glared at the armored child.

From one slit or another in the armor, a surprisingly meek-sounding voice made itself known.

"…Erone."

"Erone? Okay. Human, demon, or angel?"

"…Human."

"Why are you working together with a demon?"

"…Orders."

"Ah."

Maou decided to pursue other matters for the time being. There was no point worrying over what this boy was doing with his life, and there was no telling what Erone thought of his "orders," or what motivation was driving them.

"Right. So what do you character actors want from me? Uh...Farfarello, right? I'm not sensing any demonic force from you. Has your body devolved into human form like mine?"

"It has, Your Demonic Highness. Ciriatto and the others believe that one reason for their failed invasion of this land was because they were not used to the changes it wreaks upon the body. And I will add..." The eyes beyond Farfarello's spectacles beheld the Hatagaya cityscape. "I have orders from Barbariccia not to cause any damage upon this land unless absolutely necessary."

"Huh. I thought the Malebranche's crew was wilder than that."

"Oh, very much so, my liege. The other chieftains had their... misgivings over whether such an order was necessary, but the one who suggested it to Barbariccia managed to bring them over to his side. He said that the Devil King Satan has a certain affinity for this land... That you may not be so forgiving upon those who attempt to desecrate it."

"Olba?" Maou wrinkled his nose as he intoned the name.

"Yes, my liege."

The only people back on Ente Isla who could correctly surmise the Devil King's feelings were Emeralda, Albert, and Olba. And there was no way the first two would contribute to the cause of Emi's foes.

"Kind of 'im."

"My orders are to provide full disclosure for any and all questions the Devil King asks of me."

Maou's eyes narrowed, a threatening glare. "Good. Honesty is the best policy. Let's cut to the chase. *What* do you want?"

The response Farfarello subsequently offered to Maou's question was expected, at least. He'd seen it coming ever since Camio showed up on Choshi and told him Barbariccia had split the demon realms in two. The demon knelt before him, the fabric of his stuffy suit crinkling in protest.

"I come here both to express our eternal gratitude that our leader,

Satan the Devil King, remains alive and well, and to report that we who serve the Malebranche have risked life and limb to successfully secure a beachhead, a new front for a second invasion of Ente Isla. We also humbly request that our Devil King return and guide—"

"Nooooooope."

"—us to newfound glories as we—*huh*?"

Farfarello's penchant for going on too long was made all too clear in how he handled Maou's response. Once his brain finally caught up with the denial, he completely lost his steam.

"Don't *huh* me. I said, nope. Forget it. Gone. Outta here."

"............."

The creepy armored kid remained silent. *Doesn't speak until spoken to, perhaps.* The mask made it impossible to gauge his expression.

"But…but *why*, Your Demonic Highness?! The Azure Emperor of the Eastern Island has sworn his allegiances to us. I understand, my liege, that you have never given up your great ambition of conquering the entire world—and, indeed, that you plan to place this world under your rule as well, someday."

"Yuh-huh."

"Then please, my liege, come back to us and use us once more as your invincible force! All of us of the Malebranche promise to do whatever it takes to support this great and noble mission!"

"Huh."

"…You are choosing your words carefully because the Hero of the Holy Sword is near, perhaps?"

"Near? She's, like, right there, isn't she? It's not like she's… Okay, maybe she's a *little* involved in this, but not so much that I care what *she* thinks."

"Then, Your Demonic Highness…"

"Then *what*? Hey, you know this expression they have in this country? 'Strike the face of the Buddha three times, and even his anger will be roused'? Well, I'm not giving you a third time. I'm out. Beat it."

"But why, I ask you?" Farfarello looked up at Maou, face ashen. "My liege! Please give me a reason!"

"Look," Maou replied, exasperated that his point still hadn't come across. "Do I, Satan, your one and only Devil King, look like the kinda guy who'd be happy to see my team win the World Series after sitting on the bench all season and letting everyone *else* do the hard work?"

"……"

Maou may have looked all of twenty in human form, but the oppressive sneer on his face made Farfarello instinctively gulp.

"If…if I may, Your Demonic Highness…"

"Yeah?"

"What is this…'World Series' you speak of…?"

"Oh, come on!" The question drained the energy from Maou's mind. "Didn't you study anything about Earth?!"

"I apologize, my liege, but I remain less than fluent in the realm of analogy. I only had so much time to work with—"

"Oh, but you had enough time to learn how to talk like Smithers? Okay…so the World Series is a really important battle in this traditional yearly summer ritual here called 'baseball,' and if you're sitting on the bench, that means you aren't very good, all right?"

"So winning this World Series means…submission of your foes?"

"No! There's no murdering in baseball, okay? It just means you get bragging rights for the year! Look, what I'm saying is that you can't fight with someone else's armor, you get me?"

"Ah. I see. So you establish your position on this 'bench,' then when the time is right, you engage in 'baseball' until your opponent is soundly defeated?"

"That's…kind of close, yeah, but I think you're envisioning something a lot different from what it is. But *uggggh*, why am I even playing this game with you?! This is gonna devolve into 'Who's on First?' in a second, isn't it?"

"Maou! They don't play the World Series here! That's in the U.S.!"

"Huh? Oh. Right. Wait, so what're all the teams over *here* playing for?"

"Wh-who goes there?!"

"Well, there's the World Baseball Classic, too, don't forget about that! I'm, um… I'm kind of Maou's, like, friend from work!"

"Yeah, I taught her how to run things around the............*Huhh hhh???*"

Just as Maou cursed himself for letting an inane argument about pro sports take over the subject:

"Ch-Chi?! Why are *you* here?!"

Chiho, not even visible to Maou before now, descended into existence, as if she had always been there. Farfarello and Erone both tensed up, wary of this new and unexpected presence, but Maou was thrown into disorder for different reasons.

By now it was clear that Farfarello had used some sort of barrier spell to separate Maou away from his physical presence in Japan. He could tell from the way it served to cut him off from Emi, Suzuno—and, of course, Chiho. And now Chiho was here, without any previous warning. If Emi and Suzuno had found a way to break down the barrier, they would've stormed in without bothering to take another breath. Their absence meant that, unbelievably enough, Chiho had found a way in by herself.

After making her triumphant entry, Chiho faced the two mystery figures. "You...you can't bring Maou back to Ente Isla!" she shouted, her voice quivering a little. "He's still got a bunch of stuff left to do in Japan!"

"Ch-Chi, knock it off! Please! Get back a little bit!"

Maou felt obliged to step between them, given how Chiho gave every indication of wanting to slap silly the pair in front of her. Farfarello might be in human form, but as part of the Malebranche force, there was no telling what tricks might be up his sleeve. And this Erone guy, too—between his bizarre dress and the way the Malebranche chieftain called him his "pilot," he must have been far more powerful than any normal human child.

"Why are you attempting to protect that human?"

A dark fire began to burn behind Farfarello's eyes. Maou could sense the danger.

"No 'why' about it, man. You're watching out for that Erone kid yourself, no?"

"I should say not, my liege! This child Erone is working for us. We are not on an equal basis with each other."

Erone betrayed no reaction to this.

"Your Demonic Highness, is what this human claims the truth?"

"What is?"

"She claims you have...unfinished business in Japan, is it? What is it you are doing, exactly, in this land called Japan? I understand you have successfully regained the full brunt of your strength, which led us to believe that you have extended your conquered territory to this planet as well. It greatly excited all of us."

Farfarello paused to size Maou up, from head to toe.

"But what is this great business of yours that remains undone? This...business which requires you to dress in such mundane garments and hide a human girl behind you?"

"......"

Maou valiantly resisted the urge to shout, *You better apologize to UniClo for that!*—something about the current atmosphere suggested it was ill-advised.

"I regret to tell you, my liege, that some among the Malebranche are spreading dark rumors that your will to conquer the world has atrophied. Ciriatto, in particular, has refused to join us in the Eastern Island...and now I find you here, in this country, with only a sliver of your powers intact. Is this part of some great, intricate plan beyond my imagination...?"

Farfarello turned his eyes away from Maou and onto Chiho, behind him.

"Or has my liege decided to abandon us...abandon his own realm...?"

The change in Maou's attitude at that instant was nothing short of dramatic. "Don't give me that BS!" he shouted from the pit of his stomach, loudly enough to startle Chiho. "Never...never for a *moment* have I forgotten about the demon realms. About the subjects who served me and called me their king!"

"But what of—"

"Do *not* try me any further! Why aren't you waiting for my return under the watchful eye of Camio? If it wasn't because you've cast off all loyalty to me, *why*, then?!"

"...!"

Now it was Farfarello's turn to fall silent.

"The whole reason Barbariccia managed to split the demon realms' loyalties was because of that bastard Olba egging him on, right? I left Camio to govern in my stead as I led the Ente Isla invasion force. He is my regent and sole representative in that land! And if you refuse to serve him, what reason would I possibly have to trust you?!"

"But, my liege! Simply deploying a large Devil King's Army force into Ente Isla does not solve the core problems that plague the demon realms! If my liege has been felled in battle, it is vital that we send a second, even a third army as quickly as we can! And yet Lord Camio lacks the mettle to do so!"

"The mettle?! Even with the unexpected element of the Hero, the finest troops of our land, led by the strongest of Great Demon Generals, couldn't even keep their territory safe for three years! Do you guys have some kind of amazing plan to turn the tables *this* time?!"

"We do not, my liege!" Farfarello fired back. "But the more lives at stake...the longer the demon realms may yet survive."

"...Huh?"

Maou's ears didn't fail to notice the voice of a very confused Chiho behind him. But he had bigger fish to fry.

"That's exactly what I'm talking about! You've got no plan whatsoever! No matter how many warriors venture into Ente Isla, what do you think that'll amount to in the end?! It's simply lining them up to be slain! All it will bring to the demon realms is a slow, painful death!"

"That is exactly what the Second Devil King's Army was established to prevent! We of the Malebranche may have seceded from the demon realms, but our pride in our homeland remains ever strong. Olba may be allied with the Hero who decimated the original Devil King's Army, but he is no fool. He listens to reason. And when the time comes, it would be trivial for us to extract all the knowledge and information we can from him, then slay him where he stands! So please, return with us and fulfill your role as king!"

"I'm *telling* you," Maou bellowed back even more loudly, "that whole line of thought is one huge mistake! It takes more than that to save a world ruled by violence and blood! It takes more than that if we want to survive, and thrive, as demons! That's why neither Lucifer, nor Malacoda, nor Adramelech, nor Alciel could retain the land they conquer. That's why *I* lost!"

"But things are different now, my liege. The Eastern Island of Ente Isla is under our control. And thanks to our strategy, the humans are now distracted by a debilitating war against their own kin. Soon, the entire land will be drenched in blood and chaos, and our paradise will be—"

"Are you *that stupid*?!"

There was a new sense of power behind Maou's voice.

"!"

"Agh!"

"......!"

Farfarello reluctantly remained quiet as Chiho squealed in shock. Even Erone, standing bolt upright the whole time, shivered a little. The sheer force behind his voice was all it took for Maou to make the Malebranche chieftain submit to him.

"*This* is the result of all that!" he continued, spreading his arms wide. "We had no idea what conquering the world really meant. All I—your king—thought about was spreading violence and massacre across the land and expanding the demon realms' territory. And *now* look! If I came back with you now and the path you've laid out for me is identical to the highway to hell I took before, what do you think will happen? I'll be reviled once again as the enemy of all mankind, some new Hero will slay me, and that's the end of our realm! We'll simply return to the bad old days of tribal warfare—the sky, the seas, the very ground soaked with our blood!"

"...Why? Why...do you refuse to understand? We will never walk down the same well-trodden pathways of the past!"

"You may think you're avoiding that, attempting some kind of new route, but I'll say it to you again and again! No matter how much we redraw the maps, our ultimate fate's gonna stay the same! Unless we're willing to change the roads themselves, it's never going to be any different!"

"Maou..."

"...Change the roads themselves...?"

Farfarello remained in his kneeling position, but one could see a glint of disappointment to his eyes—a glint that made it clear Maou's words hadn't reached out to him.

"I'll tell you this one more time: Whatever you do, don't listen to Olba, no matter what he says to you. Pull your forces out of the Eastern Island and get them back home. Ciriatto's willing to work with all of you, and I promise you Camio is going to punish no one."

Farfarello slowly rose.

"...I see our conversation is at an end. I could hardly believe my ears when Olba first stated it...but I see, Your Demonic Highness, that this world has defanged you. I hope...you can understand how difficult this is for me, having to grapple with this reality thrust before me."

"What did you...?"

The rage coursing out from Farfarello's body was palpable. Maou tensed himself up, pushing Chiho farther behind him.

"But it is the truth, I see. And if I am not able to restore the will to conquer within you, then—"

"—then what? You'll kill me and make Barbariccia the new Devil King?"

"No. What I see before me is a Devil King who has grown too fond of his human form. One with a changed heart. But, with enough demonic force to restore you to your original form, perhaps the passion will once again return to your soul."

Then Farfarello, with both hands, grabbed the helmet of Erone next to him, lifting it off his head.

"?!"

The helmet, along with Erone's mask, shrunk down into an inky-black sphere.

"I want you to accept this. Accept it, and use it to restore yourself to the proud Devil King Satan all of us once knew."

He threw the tennis ball–sized sphere at Maou. Maou dodged it, sending it rolling until it came to rest against a streetside tree.

"……"

With his helmet and mask gone, Erone's face was finally exposed. He was a boy, no doubt about it, likely not even ten years old. His face had a childlike innocence to it, but its expression was flat, emotionless. He was looking at Maou, but his red eyes refused to meet his own.

"…?"

Yet, Maou couldn't shake the feeling that he had seen Erone's face before.

"You look…kind of familiar…"

Chiho, apparently, had the same thought. She craned her head out from behind Maou's back for a closer look. From his shiny black mane, there was a single shock of red, the same red as his eyes.

"Whoa, is that…?"

Maou motioned toward the sphere that used to be Erone's helmet.

"It is a concentrated ball of demonic force. This land has a custom of balling up its staple crop and consuming it in cooked form, does it not? This should be far less conspicuous than carrying a helmet around with you."

"Uh, are you talking about a rice ball?" Chiho whispered. "And since when was dark power a 'staple crop'?"

Maou's eyes remained focused on Farfarello. "So you intend to have your king eat something off the street?"

"These are trying times, Your Demonic Highness. And even if you are our leader, I cannot have you refuse to recover your force."

"……"

So was all the armor Erone had on him the same way? And perhaps that explained why Farfarello was in human form—he extracted as much of his own power as he could to form it into that armor. Which meant that if he wanted to, he could release the power he had infused in Erone and turn himself back into a demon at any time.

Thus, much as Ciriatto did, Farfarello could tap into his demonic powers whenever he wanted while in Japan. But what did Erone himself have to do with that?

"...All right. I'll keep it. But this ain't gonna change my mind."

"You will *keep* it? What are you saying, my liege? Please, you must ingest it right this moment. How long has it been since you have been able to savor demonic force in its purest form?"

"...I'll eat it once I take it home and wash it, okay?"

"...But not here? If you find it unappetizing, you may slay me on the spot, my liege! You may do whatever you wish with me!"

"What's the big hurry?"

"......"

"You had no idea what happened to me for over a year," Maou continued. "What difference is a day or two gonna make?"

"It..."

The frustration on Farfarello's face was starkly clear. But just as he opened his mouth to say something:

"?!"

Suddenly, Erone looked upward.

"It's breaking."

"Mmh?"

The warning made Farfarello shudder as Maou and Chiho followed his gaze.

"Wh-what...?"

There was a crack in the sky. A straight one, in what was otherwise thin air—and as the four of them watched, it raced across the sky.

"Heavenly Fang of Light!!"

With an ear-splitting shout, a golden bolt of lightning descended between Maou and Farfarello.

"E-Emi?!"

"Yusa!"

It was the Hero Emilia, her scarlet eyes wide open beneath her silvery hair as she carried her shining holy sword. The Better Half was teeming with power, and Chiho—who had never really seen it as anything besides a really strong sword that lit up on command before now—now had enough holy-power experience to realize exactly how much of it Emi had at her fingertips. It felt like something from a new and unknown dimension. Perhaps this was what Emi and Suzuno meant when they described it as an overwhelming presence, constantly exerting pressure upon you.

Suzuno followed soon after, her hammer just barely making it through the hole in the barrier. She squared off against Farfarello and Erone, keeping Maou and Chiho behind her.

"E-Emi! Suzuno!"

"...You're both all right?"

Emilia had no intention of looking Maou in the eye, but there was still a sense of relief mixed into the voice. Then Maou found himself looking up at yet another voice—the last one he was expecting here.

"Emilia! Bell! That child built this barrier!"

It was Sariel, wings open and his eyes a shade of purple, who had broken through the barrier for them.

"Guys..." Maou sighed, taking in the sight of Emilia and Sariel exercising the nuclear option and Suzuno swinging her bizarre home-improvement tool around again. "Seriously? In the middle of the city?"

Suzuno turned around and looked toward the hole in the sky.

"It is a full moon. A time when Lord Sariel's powers are at their peak. He was able to destroy the dimensional-phase barrier that exists above the one sheltering us now. Breaking that barrier changes nothing to the outside observer, except perhaps improve their cell phone reception."

"...You disappeared right in the middle of starting a fight with me," Emilia groaned. "I wasn't gonna let it end like *that*."

Oh, right. They *had* been in the middle of an argument just now, hadn't they? Maou was so preoccupied with his debate against Farfarello that he'd completely forgotten.

"But don't overthink it, all right? I'm pretty much over it anyway. I had a pretty good workout getting this barrier out of the way."

"What's *that* mean?"

Maou had no idea why the girl was being so casual about it. But he smiled anyway, glad to see a bit of the old Emi back in action.

"So…if my hunch is correct, you're a Malebranche messenger who's here to bring the Devil King back to the Eastern Island, right?"

Farfarello, in his suit and glasses, placed a hand on Erone as he faced Emi. "Who are you?" he said, tensing up. "Why do *you* know that?"

"Oh, haven't you seen me before?" Emi replied smarmily. "You're a demon, I'm guessing."

It was enough to make Farfarello's eyebrows rise.

"Y-you…! It couldn't be!!"

"I'm not generous enough to allow demons to go running around willy-nilly in the human world. You shall bear my name, Emilia Justina the Hero, upon your heart as you crumble to pieces!"

"Rrgh! No! How could this be…?!"

Farfarello twitched a little, attempting to infuse himself with the demonic force in Erone's armor. But Emi, and the godlike speed she had control over, wasn't about to let that happen. A light leap, and then the next instant, her fist was planted deeply into the pit of his stomach. The force sent the all-too-human Farfarello to the ground, one heel planted squarely on his back.

"Gnngh!"

"If you forget everything you've seen in Japan, run back to the demon realms, and live out the rest of your life in peace, then *maybe* I'll let you go. But if you try anything funny right now, you can say good-bye to your head."

"That's *still* not very heroic-sounding, man," Maou muttered warily to himself. One glance from Emilia's scarlet eyes was enough to silence him back into submission.

Farfarello, meanwhile, had only one word to say:

"Erone!!"

"?!"

The child immediately took action, attempting an unplanned, off-balance bull rush at Emilia.

"H-halt!" Suzuno shouted, trying to stop him from the side. Then:

"?!"

She was blown back, left floating up into the air.

"Suzuno!!"

Stepping between Emilia and this child of no more than nine resulted in her getting tossed back like a bus had just hit her.

"Wh-what…?!"

It did nothing to stop Erone as he continued his advance. Suzuno was a powerful enough warrior to dispatch the Heavenly Regiment if she wanted to. She might have let her guard down, yes, but seeing her so casually blown away was enough to give Emilia severe misgivings. But she couldn't afford to take her foot off Farfarello, either. She opted to form her Cloth of the Dispeller into a shield to ward off whatever force this child was wielding.

Not hesitating for a moment, Erone smashed right into the shield.

"Gah!!"

With a grunt, Emilia found her weight shifted back, forcing her to stagger off of Farfarello's body. This was Emilia in Hero-transformed shape, her Better Half sword and Cloth of the Dispeller both deployed at full power. A Hero who, after seeing Suzuno falter, knew to stay focused on the fight. The shock wave coursed across her body, and out of defensive instinct, she swung her sword at Erone.

Then, something that truly no one in the barrier could have expected, happened:

"Wha?!"

Erone's arm stopped the holy sword's blade cold.

Not the armor Farfarello had formed out of dark energy for him. The sword effortlessly sliced through one of his gauntlets, as well as the cloth sleeve he was wearing under it. The skin below, however, was completely unscathed.

A voice that was not Emilia's coursed across her head.

Erone?!

Alas Ramus voiced her objections at a wholly unexpected time.

Mommy! Erone! Don't! No fighting! Don't hurt Erone!

Emilia, quite against her wishes, found her holy sword disappearing from her hand.

"Huh? What? What're you—?!"

Don't hurt Erone! Please!

"Wh-what do you mean?!"

Outside of her fight against Sariel, Emilia had never seen her holy sword disappear out of its own volition before. Erone, as if cognizant of the voice inside Emilia's mind, retreated a long distance back from the Hero…

"…! Alas Ramus?!"

And even said the name of the child inside her sword to boot.

"Who…*are* you…?"

Then a voice descended from above.

"Enough of this nonsense!"

It was Sariel's.

"Evil Eye of the Fallen!"

With barely any hesitation, Sariel unleashed his holy-force-draining powers directly upon Erone.

"Nnh!!"

The force of Sariel's strike made Erone fall to his knees on the spot. Still, perhaps because of the demonic armor he wore, it didn't seem to affect him as much as it had Emilia, way back when.

Erone glared at Sariel, his face filled with an anger he never betrayed when engaging any of his previous three opponents.

"E-Erone…we must go."

"!"

A single murmur from Farfarello was enough to make his rage vanish. Emilia could feel the barrier they broke through disappear entirely, only to be replaced with the presence of the larger barrier Sariel erected earlier.

"M-my liege… We will pay you another visit, sooner or later."

"Pretty bold words, considering you need a child to cart you outta here."

It was exactly the case. Farfarello, leaning heavily upon Erone's shoulder, bore none of the bravado of a moment ago. As they painfully limped their way away, it was Sariel who had the final word.

"Do you bastards think you can escape my barr—oh, what the *hell*?!"

He probably meant it to sound more arrogant and triumphant than that. It kind of fizzled out when the pair apparently walked right through the edge of his barrier. Once through, Erone, with surprising stamina, took a single leap and carried both himself and his charity case beyond anyone's view.

"...You are so useless," Maou whispered.

"Oh, come *on!*" Sariel replied, the quivering in his voice revealing that not even he was expecting someone to just waltz through the boundary like that.

"Still," Maou continued, "you pretty much saved us, so thanks for that. You okay, Suzuno?"

"Mmh... Whew. All my bones are intact...but that did hit home, yes."

"Well, color me impressed," Emilia said, rubbing her shield arm. "That was one rough head-on strike there."

And if the Hero was willing to admit it, Maou thought, that showed how overwhelming Erone's strength must have been.

"...But look, Alas Ramus, you really shouldn't be putting away my sword like..."

Then Emilia gasped, still in midconversation with her child.

"Wh-what is it?" Chiho asked.

"He's... 'Gebba'? You mean that Erone kid?"

"What's up?" Maou asked. Emilia turned to him, the surprise evident on her face.

"I think...Erone might be the same kind of thing as Alas Ramus."

"Eh?"

Maou wasn't alone in his shock. Suzuno, Chiho, even Sariel—they were all gasping for breath.

"Alas Ramus isn't being too specific, so I can't be sure..."

Despite the summer heat inside Sariel's otherwise isolated barrier, the group could feel a cold wind rush across all of their shoulders.

"But I think Erone...was born from Gevurah, one of the Sephirah."

THE
HERO
AND
THE
DEVIL
TAKE
A STEP
TOWARD
A NEW
DREAM

"Okay, one more time!"

"Um, S-Sariel, I'm sorry, but I don't think I'm strong enough…"

"Don't be silly! Time isn't going to wait for us! Bell! The phone!"

"Ugh… I do hope this will work out…"

"Whoa, whoa, hang on, guys. Chiho just said this is too tough for her. We've been at this for two hours straight! Give her some rest already!"

"Silence, you limp-wristed Devil King! It is not up to *her* to decide what her limits are!"

"Dude, if she can't figure those out for herself, then what *can* she do, huh?"

"Enough! I am finding the limits of my own composure tested *frequently* by your lily-livered whining!"

"Al-cell! No pickin' on Looshifer!"

"Don't spoil Lucifer, Alas Ramus."

"Uh, dude, shouldn't that be the other way around? *I'm* the one being spoiled?"

"Now, Chiho Sasaki! I want you to summon your voice from the bottommost depths of your stomach! Here we go!"

"At, at least let me have some water first…"

"Knock it *off*, you stupid angel! Are you tryin' to kill Chi?!"

"She may be killed indeed if we cannot succeed at this! The pains of today will bear the fruits of tomorrow, before ultimately blossoming into the return of my goddess! Come on! Focus for me!"

"Nobody's talking about *killing* her, man!"

"Erm... Lord Sariel, I think a small break might be advisable..."

Inside the large gymnasium, Chiho was about to falter at the hands of Sariel's Spartan-style training.

They were at the Hatagaya Sports Center, a public gym not far from Sariel's condo—around a fifteen-minute walk from the Hatagaya MgRonald. It boasted a standard-sized indoor track, a heated pool in the basement, and facilities for martial arts, as well as rental space for local events and sports education. Maou and crew had reserved the biggest of the center's public spaces, large enough for two full-sized basketball courts, for six straight hours. Their goal: to beat the full powers of the Idea Link into Chiho's brain, come hell or high water.

"Yaaaaaaagggggggg...*koff*! Hakkh..."

"So be it!" Sariel grumbled dolefully. "Ten-minute break!"

"That's too short! Give her half an hour, at least!"

"Silence, Devil King! What are you, this girl's parental guardian or something?!"

"Well, yeah, I kinda *am* right now! I have a duty to make sure Chi stays safe!"

"If the two of you are going to mindlessly squabble with each other, can you do it over in the corner?" Emi asked. "All right, good... You doing okay, Chiho?"

"Um... I think I... *Hakkk!*"

Chiho had a courageous smile on her face, but it wasn't enough to keep her from choking on the words.

"That is a fine effort, Ms. Sasaki," Ashiya said from next to Emi, offering Chiho a towel and a bottle of water. Chiho accepted them with a groan.

"Hmph. I am running low. Emilia, let me borrow the charger, please."

"Hooph... Oh... Let me borrow it, too *koff koff*!"

With things simmering down, Suzuno and Chiho began charging their phones.

"Hey! You can't charge your phones in ten minutes!"

"Then perhaps we could do some basic concentration training until they are charged..."

"Dude, come on!"

Remarkably, it had been Sariel who'd suggested a gym for this project. Once he learned about Chiho's training efforts, he suggested the site would be the most ideal for them, given how shouting and roughhousing was fairly normal behavior in gyms, and it would give the spellcasters the space to fully devote themselves to their practice. Maou didn't believe him at first, but reluctantly agreed once Suzuno called Sariel's training regimen "sound in principle."

Still, this was late summer. The non-air-conditioned gym was akin to a sauna. Just standing in it made the humans and demons break out in a sweat. Between that and all the physical effort Chiho had to devote to refining her holy force, even a club athlete like her couldn't hide her fatigue.

In a nutshell, Sariel suggested a little mobile-phone–based image training. The core concept of the Idea Link was summed up in its name—the sharing of concepts in one's mind, via a link between two people. For it to work, the caster had to understand, both in body and in soul, that it was actually possible to transmit one's thoughts to another person without opening one's mouth.

The human soul instinctively understood that any regular person could not accurately convey their will to others without the power of speech, or at least some pretty determined gesturing. Breaking down that mental barrier proved surprisingly difficult. Just because you wanted to eliminate a core concept etched into your mind didn't mean you could simply wish it away.

In Ente Isla, overcoming this block began with two casters touching foreheads in order to plant the image of communicating across minds into them. Sariel substituted cell phones for that mnemonic instead. This was because conversing with someone over the phone—with someone whose face you couldn't read—often presented very real obstacles to making one's intentions clear. It shared that in common with the Idea Link, a spell where you linked with any given person too far away to be visible and exchanged information with them. A very compatible core concept, in other words, one every modern Japanese person had etched in their minds.

Thus, they began with Chiho calling Suzuno. Then, they drew farther and farther away until they could no longer physically hear each other's voices. Once they were far enough, they'd attempt to communicate with their minds over the phones, picturing themselves physically linked through the cell signal. The exact way Emi harnessed the Idea Link to converse with Emeralda, in other words.

Chiho was proving to be an apt pupil, one whose holy-force activation skills astonished even Sariel, but using that skill for spellcasting purposes was another challenge entirely. Plain Jane telepathy was one thing, but casting one's own voice into the spell was an even more difficult task. That was why, even with all her activation skills, Chiho struggled to convey her thoughts through an open connection just from one wall of the gym to the other.

"I-I'm fine, Maou. I need to keep working on this..."

"There! See? You heard it from the girl herself! Do not rob this young human of her chance to improve, Devil King. Now, sit over there in the corner and contemplate the depths of your sins for me!"

"Why the hell do I have to sit here and listen to you—*agghh*?!"

"All right, all right, that's enough from you. For once in his life, Sariel's got a point."

"Daddy, Chi-Sis is tryin' real hard! Don't be mean!"

"No, I'm...I'm not angry at Chi or anything... G-get your hands off my collar! You're gonna choke me!"

Chiho inhaled deeply as she watched Emi and Alas Ramus drag Maou away for her. Then, she began to sing.

"Welcome to a new *morrrrrniiiiing*!! A morning filled with *hope for allllll*!!"

"Oh?"

"Hmm... I like it."

Urushihara and Sariel both looked at Chiho, duly impressed.

"Guess it doesn't matter *how* you release your mind, long as you do it, huh?"

"I suppose not. This is quite a surprise."

As she sang, Chiho released a bolt of holy force, one not at all inferior to her physical voice just before. In fact, if anything, the magic seemed a bit more refined than if she had just shouted it out.

"I practiced it with Church hymns, myself," Emi said, fingers still clasped around Maou's collar. "But you didn't teach her that yet, right?"

Suzuno nodded in agreement. "But," she said, her lowered eyebrows tempering her obvious pride in Chiho's creative skills, "why're you singing the song from the morning-calisthenics bit they play on the radio?"

"Oh, you know that one, Suzuno?" came the surprised reply from Chiho.

"I recall hearing it on MHK when I rise in the morning. They have an extended piece in the summer, if I recall."

"Well, I figured it'd be good for this. It always makes me feel better, hearing it. And plus, being on radio's kind of a match for what we're trying to accomplish, right?"

"Oh, is *that* what it is? I never seriously thought much about the lyrics before."

"A new morning, huh…?" the still-bedraggled Maou muttered to himself as he shot a look at Emi.

"Is that all there is to it?"

"No, there's a second verse, I think! Umm…"

Chiho paused as she checked her memory, then began to sing anew. The past two hours of voice training were worth it, after all. Chiho's singing voice echoed attractively across the gym. *Shining trees rustling under the new morning. Stretch your arms and legs high, then stamp down on the ground. Keep your legs limber every morning with MHK Radio 1. Now, touch your toes against the ground, one, two, three…* Something about the joy Chiho put into it made the benign exercise song seem like a love-laden ballad.

"Hmm," Maou reflected. "I like it."

"I know, right?!" Chiho beamed, excited at her new powers. "My friends all say it's lame and embarrassing and stuff, but..."

The thing was, Chiho's acquiring the Idea Link spell was about all that linked Emi and her friends with the Maou contingent. All this was happening only because there was a nonzero chance that the one supreme unwritten law between them—"don't get Chiho involved in Ente Isla drama"—was in danger of being broken. Engaging in this training, and getting Sariel involved in it, was wandering into unexplored and treacherous territory.

But it was also the destination at the end of the path Maou and Emi had chosen for themselves. It clashed against the thanks they had for Chiho, and all the regret and desire to help she felt in her heart, and it made their own hearts waver.

The night of the encounter with Farfarello and Erone, an emergency conference—one that even Sariel received an invite to—was held in Devil's Castle. Having this gaggle of uninvited guests show up at his door late at night all but terrified Ashiya, but he nonetheless reluctantly prepared tea for the whole gang under orders from Maou. His choice of beverages for everyone—cold green tea for Maou and Chiho, blazing hot tea for everyone else, Urushihara included—symbolized, perhaps, his approach to Great Demon General diplomacy.

"Ooh, this is nice!" Chiho said, enjoying the chill of her drink. It was a nice thought, but a token one. Between the heat and the population density around Maou's table, the atmosphere was beyond oppressive. In a space of just over one hundred square feet, after all, there were two demons, one archangel, one fallen angel, a Hero, a Church cleric, and a teenage girl.

In terms of the faces in attendance alone, this was a historical (albeit cramped) summit of intergalactic proportions. In practice, Ashiya, too tall to find space to sit, was forced to lean against the kitchen counter instead.

Maou decided to begin by summarizing the late events around Hatagaya station to Ashiya and Urushihara. Among the highlights, the most noteworthy was undoubtedly the fact that the boy Erone might be born from a Sephirah, albeit a different one from Alas Ramus. What made things so confusing was that this Erone was accompanied by the demon Farfarello—practically his servant, even. This marked the first time in history that a Sephirah, not just a Yesod fragment, was directly involved with events in Ente Isla. Amane Ohguro mentioned something about being a "Binah" of Earth, but despite how much of a total mystery she still remained, it seemed doubtful she was at all involved with this twisty web of Ente Islan intrigue.

The suggestion soon came up that it was all a case of mistaken identity on Alas Ramus's part. "But there's no way she'd make a mistake about something so important to her," Emi shot back, as the girl herself rapidly nodded off in her arms. "I mean, she pulled my holy sword back into her body, like, completely by herself. And besides, if he *wasn't* something like that, then no way could he stop a blade that cut right through Durandal with his bare skin, no matter *how* weak my swipe was."

"True," Suzuno added, one hand placing pressure on the elbow she wrenched on the rebound from Erone's battering-ram blow. "I hesitate to believe it, but if Erone is the Sephirah known as Gevurah, that would explain several things I observed during the battle... Ahh, this will ache for quite a while. Gevurah is associated with the number five, rubies, iron ore, the color red, and the planet of the god of war. It wields the power of the gods, and its guardian angel is known as Camael. Even its hair resembles Alas Ramus's—dull gray, the same color as its associated metal ore, with a single lock of red."

Alas Ramus, by comparison, had silver hair to match Yesod's ore and a purple shock to match her Sephirah's theme color.

"So given that Alas Ramus has taken the form we see here, it is not beyond comprehension to think that the other Sephirah have human forms as well. It would just mean that Erone is the first we have seen beyond the one in your hands, Emilia. The problem, however, is—"

"—that he's a demon lackey, right?"

"Indeed, my lord." Suzuno grimly nodded at Sariel, never forgetting to remain on her best manners around the archangel. Then, with a start, the blood drained from her face.

"W-wait a moment... Lord Sariel, did you know about...Alas Ramus...?"

"!"

He had become such a natural part of these proceedings that it had never occurred to anyone, but Sariel was still theoretically after Emi's holy sword. The infant he saw Kisaki carrying once no doubt scarred him emotionally, but he still shouldn't have known about this Yesod fragment. Maou and Emi stared at him, tense and ready to defend Alas Ramus with their lives, but the archangel puffed out his hollow cheeks and sighed lightly.

"Yeah, I did. Gabriel stopped by my workplace a while back and started whining about how I didn't get the sword from Emilia. He said that baby I thought was my goddess's child had fused itself with Emilia's holy sword, you see?"

Neither Suzuno, who had accepted Sariel's heartfelt confessional inside MgRonald at the time, nor anyone else had told Sariel about Alas Ramus before.

"To be honest with you guys, I really don't care *who* that kid is, as long as my goddess isn't the biological mother. All I need is my goddess at my side, and... Ow! Eesh, did you put this cup on a hot plate before you gave it to me? This isn't winter, you know!"

It took at least a few seconds before Sariel noticed how hot the tea Ashiya presented to him was, as he brought it to his lips midconversation. It still remained difficult to believe this was the archangel who almost brought Emi to her knees.

"Wow," Chiho said, almost moved by how pathetically pained Sariel looked. "Ms. Kisaki really *is* the only person on your mind, isn't she?"

It was hard to say how honest Sariel was being, but given the subject matter at hand, it was impossible to keep Alas Ramus a secret any longer. Maou, Emi, and Suzuno relaxed in their seats a little.

"If we assume that Alas Ramus and Erone are cut from the same cloth," Suzuno continued, "it seems fair to say that Erone was born either from the Sephirah Gevurah or a fragment thereof. But—"

"—but when I came down from heaven," Sariel said, picking up Suzuno's line of thought, "I didn't hear about anything unusual going on with Gevurah, no."

Alas Ramus, at least, was created from the irregular situation of Yesod being split into an untold number of fragments. It seemed hasty to make the same conclusion with Erone.

"Seems to me," Maou stated matter-of-factly, "it'd be easiest to explain this by assuming heaven's getting involved again."

"You're right," Chiho said. "I mean, the angels…" She paused, taking a moment to size up Urushihara and Sariel.

"Yes?"

"Dude, what?"

Chiho hurriedly lowered her eyes. "Umm, uh, never mind. Sorry."

"I know exactly what you mean to say, Ms. Sasaki," Ashiya chimed in, unable to restrain himself. "One hundred percent of the angels *we* have interacted with, at least, have proven to be scoundrels to the last man."

"Well, I guess there's not much I can say to convince you otherwise, but—"

"Lucifer!"

"Oh stop it," he continued. "I can't say I'm completely confident about this, but if we're talking about the angel Camael, I find it, like, *super* hard to picture him caring about this."

"What do you mean?" Emi asked. Instead of answering, Urushihara turned his eyes toward Suzuno.

"Camael…the 'Wrath of God'?"

"Yep." Urushihara nodded. Sariel said nothing to deny it. "Camael's the guardian angel of Gevurah, but he's not like Gabriel or Raguel. He's, like, hard-line, old-school brimstone and fire, and all that crap. Just like his name suggests, he only takes action when God wills it—so, like, if heaven itself is in danger. Otherwise, it's a toss-up whether he'll even get up off his ass if someone's screwing with Gevurah. I mean, when he *does* take action, it makes the other angels look like the Little Rascals, but he's just as aware of that as the rest of us are."

"I agree with Lucifer's take. It takes a lot, after all, for guardian angels to venture away from heaven in the first place."

"So why," Ashiya asked, "is Erone mingling with Barbariccia's demons?"

The question summed up the doubts of everyone in the room. The archangel and his fallen companion answered it with silence. It was beyond their knowledge.

"Um, Ashiya?" Chiho said.

"Yes?" Ashiya replied, far more meekly than what he saved for the angels in the room.

"So maybe this isn't the greatest thing to ask right now...but don't *you* ever think about going back home, Ashiya? I mean, to the demon realm or Ente Isla?"

This sudden query could prove to be a rather devastating land-mine. It aroused Emi's and Suzuno's suspicions at once. But Chiho had a reasonable idea what the reply would be. Ashiya would never agree to side with the Malebranche.

"Well, certainly...if I were to be completely honest, I would gladly return. However..." He paused, face stern, his indignation clear in the way he crossed his arms. "Seeing this pack of ravenous hyenas, the Malebranche, turning their backs to His Demonic Highness, throwing the demon realms' denizens into disarray, and cheerfully seizing the foundations I built as I conquered the Eastern Island distresses me. This may not be something you should hear, Ms. Sasaki, but even if it were not the work of a human provocateur, neither myself nor my liege would ever be at peace with it. Especially considering..."

He then rose to take the ball of demonic force Farfarello gave Maou out from the refrigerator, glaring at it ruefully. Given the summer heat, he had taken the time to wrap it in plastic for safekeeping.

"This baseborn dark power he threw in our faces. Even if asked to, I would never deign to harness it."

"Really...?"

It wasn't quite for the reasons she anticipated, but Maou's distaste for the Malebranche was clearly one shared by Ashiya. At least now she knew neither of them would take up Farfarello's invitation.

Emi and Suzuno took a look at each other, sighed, and peered at the teacups.

"…I almost had goose bumps for a moment."

"Quite so."

"…Pfft."

Suzuno calmly drank her tea, now down to room temperature. Emi, meanwhile, brought a handkerchief to her sweat-caked forehead, reached over to Maou's chilled glass, and emptied it down her throat.

"Wh-whoa! I was drinking that…"

"You want me to get heat stroke?" Emi half-slid, half-tossed the glass down the table at Maou. "That might hurt Alas Ramus, too, you know."

"That-that's not the issue here! I don't—"

"Ashiya!"

"Y-yes?!"

Something about the frozen smile on Chiho's face as she sat opposite from Emi made Ashiya stiffen up from his kitchen position.

"Would you mind making something cold for Yusa, too, please?"

"Erm, yes. Absolutely."

Now Ashiya and Maou were the ones in danger of breaking into hives.

"Wh-what's with you guys…?"

Emi tensed up, not realizing she was the cause of this sudden standoff between her three acquaintances.

"Dude," an exasperated Urushihara said, "I think everyone *but* you knows what." It didn't help clue Emi in too much.

As this charade continued, Ashiya took the glass Emi finished and replaced it with two new ones for both her and Maou, chancing odd glances at Chiho for some reason as he did.

"Wh-what're you…?"

"It's better if you don't notice it," Chiho said, smile still etched onto her face by a force whose depth Emi could only begin to guess at.

"Well, um, anyway," Emi said, trying to get the subject back on track. "That's really constructive, though. Now we know you aren't going to take up Barbariccia's invite, at least."

"Yes. It certainly is."

The lack of emotion to Chiho's reply probably wasn't just in Emi's imagination.

Emi did have a point, at least. But Maou's and Ashiya's ambitions still had little relation to them turning down Farfarello's offer. Maou took a swig of cold tea and picked up the thread for the Hero.

"Y'know, maybe I was a little too quick on the draw, though. I stepped up to keep Chi safe back there. Didn't even think before doing it, either. Assuming Farfarello isn't an idiot, he has to know that Chi's involved somehow. In a way Emi and Suzuno ain't."

"Do you think he knows I don't have the power to fight against him?"

"If I were him," Sariel reflected, "I'd take you hostage in a New York minute."

The observation made everyone in the room except Urushihara shudder a little. Sariel magnanimously accepted their accusatory stares. "What do you want? It worked, right? And if it occurred to *me* back then, why not *him*?"

Sariel had kidnapped the powerless Chiho alongside Emi in order to seize the latter's holy sword. It pained everyone to admit it, but it was certainly a persuasive move.

"But how did Chiho even get into Farfarello's barrier?" Emi asked. "She didn't *do* anything."

Chiho shook her head. "I don't know. I looked up, and the next thing I knew, Maou and everyone else were right there."

"This is just a supposition...but it might have something to do with how Erone so easily slipped through Lord Sariel's barrier. Both Erone himself and Chiho's ring are, at the core, forged from a Sephirah."

"Oh, God, not again," Maou and Emi groaned in unison.

"...What's with you?"

"...Huh?"

The pair found themselves glaring at each other yet again. Then they awkwardly turned away and tried to drink their tea, independently deciding not to let this spark yet another fruitless argument.

"......"

They *tried* to drink their tea, but their glasses were both empty. The synchronized failure to distract themselves only made things more cringeworthy.

"Your glass, my liege."

Ashiya, unable to bear any more, obediently filled Maou's glass from his bottle of chilled tea, then plunked the bottle on the table to let Emi fill her own damn glass, thank you very much.

"But if that is the case...what next, then?"

"What next?"

"You know what I mean. About Chiho."

Suzuno had both Maou and Emilia in her line of sight, but her somewhat peeved expression was pointed straight toward Chiho.

"This is exactly what we feared. If Farfarello sees Chiho as 'one of us,' what are we supposed to do with her now?"

"Why don't you and I just take turns guarding her?" Emi swiftly replied, staring the annoyed Ashiya down as she tilted the bottle to fill up her glass.

Suzuno shook her head. "I am asking the question because you cannot do that."

"Huh? Why not?"

That was Chiho, who wasn't naïve enough to turn down a little extra security at this point. Maou and his demon cohorts had none of their original powers. It only seemed natural that Emi and Suzuno would step up to protect her. But:

"Emilia, how long can you truly escape the responsibilities of work? If we are going to guard Chiho around the clock, it must be at least two people at all times, or else we are doomed to defeat."

"At the hands of Erone, you mean."

Suzuno nodded at Sariel. "Precisely. Erone seems at least as powerful as Farfarello, if not moreso, and yet *he* plays servant to the demon. Their dimensional-phase barrier was holy in origin, not demonic. If Erone were to play a primary role in battle, Emilia or I alone would be unable to stop him. Especially with Alas Ramus demonstrating the reaction she had..."

The pure muscle behind Erone's attacks surpassed any common-sense appraisal. And looking back, even Alas Ramus had the power to flick Gabriel away like a gnat, once she put her mind to it.

Even without her holy sword, Emi could rely on Albert's martial-arts training and her own holy-magic skill well enough. But against a personification of a Sephirah and a Malebranche chieftain? While protecting a noncombatant? It was hard to see how that *wouldn't* pose a problem.

"I fear that should Erone take center stage in the battle, Alas Ramus may choose to interfere with you."

She already had, really, dispelling Emi's Better Half. And even if "interfere" was overstating it, it was clear Emi couldn't necessarily rely on her holy sword. Given how Alas Ramus was fused with it, the Better Half was really no longer Emi's. It was a sentient being of its own.

"Well, if you put it that way..." Maou sighed. "...We're pretty much screwed, aren't we?"

"Is this barrier of theirs that simple to enter from the outside?"

"That's mostly down to what the caster wants." Sariel crossed his arms. "The one I put on the Tokyo Metropolitan Government Building covered such a large space because it was meant to keep what happened inside away from the general public instead of blocking external attack, so I didn't make its boundaries all that strong. That's why *you* wriggled your way in, after all."

"Oh...yeah. True."

Maou had gone inside the Tokyo Metropolitan Government Building knowing full well his enemy was up on the roof. The difference between that and this more recent barrier was clear. Whether one could break through or not depended quite a bit on whether the infiltrator knew it existed in the first place—whether the concept registered at all in one's mind. It was a unique spell, but just like the Idea Link, it took more time to wrap your brain around it than actually cast it.

"But it took a while after I disappeared for you to work your way in, didn't it? If Chiho wound up getting transported in by herself... that would've been it for her, huh?" Maou asked.

"......"

A heavy silence ruled over Devil's Castle.

"Ooh, way to take a hammer right to the core of it, dude ....sorry."

Urushihara's remark failed to lighten the mood. In fact, it darkened it. Ashiya tried again, pointing a finger at Chiho.

"In that case," Ashiya offered the silence, "our only option is to teach Chiho how to protect herself on a rather, I suppose, accelerated schedule."

"What do you mean?"

It surprised Chiho to hear Ashiya, of all people, suggest it.

"This Erone boy... Even when Emilia had her blade on Farfarello's neck, he never took action unless Farfarello ordered him to, no?"

Emi nodded.

"He showed no outward sign of hostility against us otherwise. It might be simpler to think of Erone as just a weapon in Farfarello's arsenal."

"A weapon?"

"Wait," Emi said. "Doesn't that kinda make Alas Ramus the same thing, though?"

"No, just *listen* to him, man," Maou replied.

Emi fell silent as Ashiya continued.

"Erone never makes any move by himself. Even if they are physically far from each other, you could theorize that Farfarello always needs to be within eyeshot of Erone."

"Why is that?" Suzuno asked. "Erone must have his own will, too. As long as his orders are clear enough, he should be able to fulfill them. I hardly see the need to be together like this..."

Ashiya snorted at her. "Perhaps *you* would not. But being stuck in these human bodies is as shameful and embarrassing for us as it would be for you humans to walk down the street in the nude. I must apologize for phrasing it that way to Ms. Sasaki, but..."

"...Your point being?"

Suzuno didn't appreciate Ashiya attempting to walk back his insult of the human race for Chiho's sake alone. Ashiya ignored her.

"My point is that Farfarello was ordered not to hurt any Japanese bystanders—to the point that he willingly devolved himself into a human. That is how faithful he is to his mission. A demon as driven as that would never leave a weapon as powerful as a Sephirah out of his surveillance."

Emi nodded. "I'm not a fan of your treatment of the human race, but okay."

"On the other hand, having a servant who refuses to act without orders, even in life-and-death crises, indicates a severe lack of readiness, or perhaps worse. If Erone were left to his own devices and something unusual happened, he might react in ways Farfarello cannot predict. This suggests to me that Erone will never venture farther than a certain radius from Farfarello."

"All...all right."

This was a demon general—one who held on to his conquered Ente Islan territory longer than anyone else—at work.

"I will also note that this Farfarello became a chieftain after our forces invaded Ente Isla. In other words, he has less battle experience than the other Malebranche chieftains. In a full-on clash of forces, I doubt Emilia would falter against him. And not even a high-grade robot can make its own decisions without a well-trained handler guiding it."

"So we should just ignore Erone and try to beat Farfarello as quickly as possible?"

Ashiya shook his head. "No. Otherwise, there is no point in teaching that spell to Ms. Sasaki."

"Oh, right." Chiho had almost forgotten the original arguing point in the midst of Ashiya's well-organized exposition. "You thought I should learn that, didn't you, Ashiya?"

"If all we did was kill Farfarello, I fully guarantee you that a second force will be knocking on our door sooner rather than later. It would be a never-ending cycle. We need to find a more fundamental solution."

"You really think so, though?" Emi replied instinctively. "If they were going to send another force, wouldn't they have done that after we defeated Ciriatto and his thousand-strong Malebranche army, as opposed to some entry-level chieftain?"

"Fool."

"What?!"

"If Farfarello were to die, Erone would remain here alone. We may not know his origins, but a Sephirah is a Sephirah. Having this force—which, I remind you, only a fragment of which allowed you to dominate an archangel in battle—lie unclaimed in Japan is something Barbariccia would *never* allow."

Ashiya took a moment to survey the others in the room.

"In other words, if we ever want to stop fretting about the future, finding a way to make Farfarello return home, with Erone, in a civilized manner would be best."

"You make it sound so easy," Suzuno replied, poking at Ashiya's theory. "If we allowed Farfarello safe passage back home, the entire demon realm would learn of Chiho's presence. *That* would do far more to attract a second wave of attackers."

"And *that* is why we must teach Ms. Sasaki the ways of holy magic as soon as possible. Why do you fail to understand this, Crestia Bell?"

"What?"

"…Oh. I think I get it." Maou seemed to grasp Ashiya's intent before Suzuno did. "But that's betting on a lot, no? You think he'll be willing to accept that?"

"We will have to make him do so, my liege. However, we must also remember the old adage of 'expect peace, prepare for war.'"

Ashiya turned to Chiho to make his point clear. "We simply need to make them understand that His Demonic Highness is proceeding along with his ambitions for Japan, and that Ms. Sasaki is an integral part of them. The Malebranche on the Eastern Island have not abandoned their loyalty to the Devil King. If Farfarello can return home a convinced demon, that reduces the chance of Barbariccia meddling with us."

"So basically," a distressed Emi said, "you want to drag Chiho into the demons' side?"

Having Chiho become an official ally of the Devil King could have long-standing repercussions. If word leaked out to the human society on Ente Isla, they might very well start seeing Chiho as a traitorous enemy to mankind.

"What're you gonna do," Emi continued, "if we can't take that back later on? There's no telling how much time we have left."

Chiho lifted her head up at the words, but Ashiya's firm voice rang out first.

"I have never been of the philosophy that I should stop what I am doing in life because I cannot predict what the future may bring. It is better to take action than worry about it endlessly. Besides"—taking a glance at Emi, then Suzuno—"who will the people of Ente Isla believe? The Malebranche pouring into the Eastern Island, or a counselor for the Church's Reconciliation Panel? As long as you can keep Ms. Sasaki safe, it would be a simple matter to ensure she is not looked upon with hostility."

Emi and Suzuno found frustratingly little to fire back with.

Suzuno had three overbearing goals in her life: rid the Church of corruption, ensure the Hero Emilia's feats were recognized for what they were, and make Emilia the leader of a post–Devil King's Army world. If achieving that meant protecting Chiho, this human from another planet, from Ente Isla itself, she was ready, willing, and able.

Urushihara watched as both of their faces softened. "Yeah, who knows?" he mused. "Maybe those demons're more gullible than we thought."

Ashiya had a point. Just because the future was murky didn't mean wasting time in circuitous debate would accomplish anything.

"Actions over words… Imagine a demon telling *me* that."

Emi put a final exclamation point on the debate.

"Very well," Suzuno reluctantly said. "In that case, starting tomorrow, we will have Chiho engage in intensive holy-magic training. But if this puts her in danger at all, I will ensure you pay for it."

"Well, not that I really get what's going on, but good luck, guys. I'm heading home." Sariel, watching the proceedings from one side, stood up. "It sounds like you all have a lot on your plate, but as long as my goddess isn't in danger, it's nothing to do with me. I promise I won't meddle in your affairs, so have fun!"

No one tried to stop him. Maou and his cohorts weren't exactly counting on him as a team member in the first place. But as he put on his shoes by the front door, Sariel found himself stopped by a voice.

"Umm...!"

"Hmm?" Sariel asked.

"I... Would you mind helping me out, Sariel? Please?"

It was Chiho.

The unexpected request aroused Emi's concern. "Uhh, Chiho?"

"...Are you insane?" Sariel looked back at Chiho in confused scorn. "Why do *I* have to cooperate with anything you all are doing? We're enemies, aren't we? And even if we weren't, this has absolutely nothing to do with me."

"But that light from your eyes stopped him, didn't it, Sariel?"

"So what? Of course it did. A Sephirah's basically a giant ball of holy energy, so naturally the Evil Eye of the Fallen's gonna work its stuff against it. But why does having *that* mean I'm obliged to work with you?"

"I know that. I'm not asking you to fight for me. Just while I'm learning this skill is fine."

"Chiho, what are you saying? Bell and I are right here for you—"

"Well, we might not have a lot of time before something happens, but depending on what the demons decide to do, we might have more than we think, too. I don't know how much time it'll take, but I can't keep Yusa away from work that whole time."

This sudden concern for her day-to-day life took Emi by surprise. "What're you talking about? This really isn't the time for—"

"Sure it is. Even if we get past this, Yusa, what if you lose your pay-check next month or get fired for being out of the office too long? I'd never be able to make that up to you."

"You are being far too anxious, Chiho. I have more than enough financial freedom to allow for an extra roommate or two, and even if Emilia does lose her job, I am sure she can find another—"

"If her friends in her *next* job get caught up in Ente Isla stuff, too, what then? You can't cover everybody."

"!"

Suzuno, recalling what Maou told her during their TV shopping trip, fell silent.

It was not exactly advisable for Emi and the rest to expand their base of human acquaintances more than necessary right now. She and Maou already had a fairly decent, stable circle of friends in the relatively narrow parts of Tokyo they frequented. The wider a radius this circle covered, though, the better the chance their enemy—whoever they turned out to be—could find a way to strike at it.

"Well...no, but..."

Emi glared mournfully at Sariel. It failed to cross her mind until now, but this archangel had injured both her body and, more deeply, her pride not long ago. The option of leaving Chiho in his hands seemed unthinkable. And Chiho had been there the whole time, too—she must have understood Emi's misgivings.

"And I know you have work, too, Sariel, so I won't count on you the whole time, either. I mean, maybe Yusa or Suzuno could cover for this or that day. And if you *can* help us..."

That was exactly why Chiho chose this moment to break out her most secret of weapons.

"I can't promise it'll happen immediately, but I'll try to find a way for you to make up with Ms. Kisaki."

"Right! Your phone done charging yet? Let's move, Bell! Head for the other side now!"

"Yes, my lord!"

"Ugh…"

And here was the result.

The sheer amount of holy force Sariel unleashed upon the room that evening, so eager he was to mend their friendship (as if they had one in the first place), was enough to knock Ashiya out of his master-strategist speech and straight into unconsciousness.

"So you've been doing this kind of thing in this sweltering gym all afternoon?"

Emi, fresh from work, watched the proceedings with a bored look on her face. She didn't complain about it, though. The theory behind their training was sound enough.

"I keep having to tell 'im to take a break, or else Chi just gets too involved in it."

"Still…if this keeps up, she might just be able to learn a skill before the end of the day, won't she? That's really amazing. It's like Chiho's a born holy-force activator."

"Don't let her hear that. Sariel warned me about it. She might wind up developing a spell by herself, remember."

"Good point… Not that I think it'd be that simple for her."

"Wow, Chi-Sis!"

Alas Ramus must have instinctively picked up on it. Her eyes were transfixed upon Chiho's training.

"So?"

"Hmm?"

"…You really think she can have them make up?"

"…I dunno."

That, in a way, was the anxiety none of them could banish from their hearts, more so than either Farfarello or Erone.

Having them "make up" was a fairly dicey proposal, given that their relationship this far consisted mainly of Sariel falling in love with Kisaki and eating every meal at MgRonald, not even trying to hide the fact he was pursuing her as he wasted his food budget on fattening junk. That was about the extent of it.

"But Ms. Kisaki never stopped treating Sariel like a customer, at least, so…"

In Maou's eyes, "making up" simply meant that Kisaki's blanket ban from allowing Sariel on premises would be lifted. That, at least, seemed sort of within the realm of possibility, but whether Sariel would be content with that was another issue entirely. For now at least, Sariel was playing the part of an eager holy-magic coach—but if they failed to provide the kind of "making up" *he* might be picturing, there was no telling what kind of fallout could result.

"It's always times like *these* when I can't rely on Rika, either..."

"What does Rika Suzuki have to do with this?"

"Well, it's not like they're rekindling some kind of romance or anything, but I thought I'd ask her if she had any tips on helping people mend fences a little. She loves gossiping about stuff like that, you know? But...you know...*him*."

Emi used her eyes to point out Ashiya's back as he watched over Chiho's magic drills. As Emi's coworker and friend, Rika didn't know who she or Maou really were, but she was on at least casual terms with Maou, Chiho, and Suzuno—and, more relevantly, currently crushing on Ashiya like a hydraulic press.

"So I asked her, and she was like, 'Ooh, I don't think I even know *myself* anymore,' so I put an end to the conversation before it descended into pajama-party gossip."

It had become customary for Emi to arrive at her cube and see Maki Shimizu, another work acquaintance, occasionally try to unravel the cause of "don't think I know myself anymore," only to be dodged and verbally beaten away each time.

"...And you're fine with that?"

"With what?"

"That." Maou pointed out Ashiya's back with his eyes.

Emi shrugged as she leered up at Maou. "Bell told me about it. How you've been lording it over her about getting too involved with relationships."

"Not lording it up, really. I may've just said that it'd be arrogant of me to try and get Rika 'way from Ashiya, you know? Like *we're* some kind of saints."

"That's what 'lording it over' is, you know. Not like you care where *I'm* coming from on this."

"I haven't exactly cared about what the Hero thought before now, so..."

Maou shrugged in an attempt to escape Emi's peeved gaze. Emi kept up the effort, peering straight at Maou's chin, but gave up after another moment or two.

"...I'm just like her, though."

"Huh?"

Emi rested her chin on her knees and looked on as Sariel barked his orders at a huffing, puffing Chiho.

"I don't think I know myself any longer, either, I mean. So I don't know if I have the right to judge other people at all."

"......"

Emi was acting remarkably reserved today. Maou had trouble figuring out how to respond.

"Don't know yourself any longer...?"

He dodged the issue by ruminating over Emi's words, then turning his attention away from her and toward Chiho and her trainers.

"Mmm..." Sariel pondered to himself for a moment. "If you've grown this adept at activating holy force, I feel we're just one or two steps away... Right. Let's change our approach. Bell! Send a message from your end this time! Maybe she'll get the knack if she picks up on what it feels like to receive one."

"Yes, my lord!"

Suzuno, on her end of the gym, raised a hand into the air. Suzuno tried to concentrate.

"But what should I send?"

Suzuno considered for a moment. "If I want her to pick up the 'knack,' as you say...perhaps some form of conversation would be more effective than simple sounds." She continued muttering to herself as she called Chiho on her phone. "Some concrete keywords that will create an internal response strong enough that Chiho could pick up on it..."

Something Suzuno could easily pick up on wouldn't be a bad idea, either, just in case she needed to hear Chiho's response.

"…Umm."

"What's the problem, Bell? Move it! The radio-calisthenics song is ending!"

Suzuno failed to respond for a moment. The solution she stumbled upon was, to say the least, distressing.

"Ehm… Ahem!"

She brought the phone to her ear and coughed, a nervous habit whenever she had to ask an inconvenient question. Focusing on Chiho and her phone, unsure what was making this so embarrassing for her, she sent her an Idea Link. Thank heavens Maou wasn't on that side of the gym.

{*"Do you want, perhaps, to mar—um, become the Devil King's lawfully wedded wife?"*}

The shame made her dart around the question a little, but the final result was still more direct than she wanted it to be.

{*"Waaauuuuuooooooooo!!!"*}

But it had the desired effect. The next moment, a flood of powerful emotion, coupled with something like a coyote's howl, thudded through the air and into Suzuno's brain. The sheer force behind the feelings, represented in the volume she perceived, made Suzuno's sight darken as though she were concussed. The resulting dizziness made her drop her phone.

"Whoa! Bell?!"

Emi stood up, realizing something was up with her. Looking toward Chiho, she found that her head now resembled something like an inflated, hyperventilating red balloon.

"H-hey… Is she okay, Emi?!"

The reaction from Suzuno was stark enough to attract even Maou's concern. The cleric was curled up, holding her head with one hand and using the other to occasionally beat against the parquet floor, the phone, and sometimes herself.

"All-all right, I, I-I-I-I apologize! P-please, calm down a—"

"Chi?!"

"Owwwww…"

As if Suzuno's flailing around like a fish on a dock weren't enough, now Chiho's own phone fell out of her hand as she slumped to the floor. Maou hurriedly ran over and grabbed her shoulders.

"Hey, Chi, are you all—"

The moment their eyes met, her irises, already wide open, expanded all the way to their physical limits.

"M-M-M-M-Mao-Mao-Mao-Ma-Ma-Ma-Ma-Maouuuuuuuu-ma-ma-ma-Maou-a-ma-ma-mah, *nyeagggggggghhhhhhhhhhh*!!"

Suzuno writhed in agony, as if being physically struck with every *Ma* the panicked Chiho let out.

"What the hell, man? What's happening?!"

"Bell! Bell, get ahold of yourself!"

As the two girls fell deeper into panic, Sariel sidled up to Maou's side.

"Dahh… Hnh!"

With one fingertip tap on her forehead, Chiho fell limp in Maou's arms, as if fainting. As she did, Suzuno took a deep breath and sat up from Emi's arms, released from whatever tormented her.

"Bell must have knocked on one hell of a door in her heart," Sariel deadpanned, looking down at Chiho in exasperation.

The unconscious Chiho soon began to blink her eyes, still in a daze. The moment she recognized Maou's face, she immediately turned her own aside, ensuring her hateful glare at Suzuno was at an angle no one else could catch.

"Well, I suppose we've broken through the biggest wall there. Bell must have picked up on Chiho Sasaki's Idea Link just then."

"!!"

Chiho was the most surprised out of all of them.

As if to back those words up, Suzuno groggily spoke.

"It was…*impossibly* loud."

The training session continued until seven PM, when their gym reservation time expired. However, given how they had no idea when Farfarello and Erone might decide to strike, they opted to stay

in a group as long as possible, each member leaving in the order of whose home was closest to the complex.

"You all right, Chi?"

"I-I-I'm A-Okay!"

Fresh from successfully casting her own spell (whether out of sheer coincidence or not), Chiho seemed to be keeping an oddly long distance away from Maou, hiding in Emi's shadow ever since they left the building. Suzuno was a bit wobbly herself at first, but was now managing to maintain a decent walking pace by herself.

"So," Sariel asked Chiho in front of his condo door. "Same time tomorrow, then?"

"Um, sure! I have work in the evening, though, so I can't stay around for quite so long."

"And you all?"

"Yeah, I got work in the afternoon, so Ashiya and Urushihara'll join in instead."

"I was kind of hoping Bell could substitute for me tomorrow, but...would you mind?"

Emi's hands were regrettably tied during the weekdays on that front. Suzuno was still slightly dazed at Chiho's mercilessly high-decibel scream bouncing off her cerebral cortex, but she still nodded her approval.

"Great. Let's say one to four PM tomorrow, then. Is that all—"

Is that all right with everyone was what the suddenly bossy Sariel probably intended to say. Instead, something in the evening sky, the stars just beginning to twinkle above the setting sun, made him freeze in place.

"Hm?" Maou followed his gaze. "Hey, what's up, Sarie—uh?"

"Uhh?!"

Chiho and Emi were soon gasping themselves at the figure standing above them.

"Oh, it's you guys? What're you all doing here?"

She had a business outfit and a shoulder bag filled to bursting with files and work tools. Her heels were high enough that even Maou had to turn his head upward to look at her. Mayumi Kisaki, head manager at the MgRonald in front of Hatagaya station, exuded beauty in the dim light, her long hair shining in otherworldly colors. And now she was looking at them in abject surprise.

"What, what about *you*, Ms. Kisaki...?"

Maou and Chiho couldn't hide their alarm at seeing Kisaki *here*, of all places. Meanwhile, Emi and Suzuno gave each other a quick glance. Their previous sighting was no fluke after all.

"I'm not sure I've met all of you before," Kisaki said as she sized up Ashiya and Urushihara. "Friends, maybe?" Urushihara rarely bothered going outside at all, and Ashiya had only visited MgRonald a couple of times since Maou began working there. He couldn't blame Kisaki for not recognizing him. But the moment her eyes settled upon the man between him and Urushihara, her kindly expression turned into one of spiteful scorn.

"...Why are *you* here, Mitsuki Sarue?"

Chiho and Maou attempted to explain, but found themselves wagging their tongues fruitlessly. "This...um, this is just a..." "I... Oooh, I was...um..."

"You aren't messing around with MgRonald customers and crew again, are you...?"

Kisaki pushed the women in the group out of the way to give herself a better position to interrogate Sariel from. Neither Maou nor Chiho could think of any way to stop her. They were both eyewitnesses to the moment Kisaki banned the guy, besides.

Not only would this certainly *not* mend the fences between them—it'd only put more suspicion on Sariel's shoulders, solidifying Kisaki's decision even more. Clearly, it was up to Sariel to step up and do *something*.

"Um," he began shakily, "ummmm, I actually live in this condo building, so—"

"...What? *Here?*"

"Y-yes, erm..."

The overbearing high-school coach act Sariel put on back at the gym was a faint memory now. Sariel was weak at the knees, a wholly unbelievable sight given the daily rose bouquets and burger feasts he was known for. Then Kisaki brought the conversation in an abrupt new direction.

"Since when?"

Sariel, caught off guard, gave the honest answer. "Since they built the Sentucky I manage in Hatagaya, but—"

"You lived in this fancy-pants condo the entire time, you freak?" Maou's grim and resentful aside went unheard.

"Mitsuki Sarue."

"Y-yes?!"

Being called by name like a drill sergeant made Sariel's voice quiver.

"Lemme ask you something. Was that storefront empty when you moved in?"

"Huh?"

Another abrupt zigzag. Sariel had trouble sizing this one up.

"Well?"

The repeated question shot him back to attention.

"Um, I think it was a restaurant when I first showed up. It didn't look that old to me, but it closed less than a month after I moved in…"

Kisaki's eyebrows twitched thoughtfully once or twice. Then:

"Ugghh…"

She sighed. Not out of rage or exasperation, but out of resignation.

"I guess I was figuring as much."

"Um… How do you mean, exactly?" Maou couldn't resist joining the conversation. "I mean, ever since the MagCafé opened up, you've been acting kind of different from before. Like, it feels like you're stretching yourself a lot thinner than usual…"

Kisaki had never betrayed a single millisecond of exhaustion to Maou before. Now she was talking about how "seriously rough" work was and going off manual for the coffee she made Mr. Hotplease.

That's what I want to be someday. A true barman.—She *had* said that, hadn't she? A barman, someone she described as a true service professional. And now she was examining a storefront that used to be a restaurant. It wasn't hard to draw a conclusion from that.

"You were talking about how difficult it was to become a barman back at MgRonald, right?"

"...Yeah."

Maou looked up to Kisaki as an example of what climbing the MgRonald corporate ladder could accomplish for someone with enough ambition. Now she was acting almost...vulnerable. He decided to push the topic.

"Ms. Kisaki, are you...are you actually gonna quit MgRon*gah*!!"

The sentence Maou conceived in his mind was cut off by one of Kisaki's files batting him on the head.

"Don't jump to conclusions, you idiot."

"The-the corners on those files hurt, you know..."

The Devil King who laughed at the face of the Hero's holy sword was nearly brought to tears by something from the stationery aisle. Kisaki sighed, finding herself at an impasse.

"...You know, I do feel bad for not being my normal self around the crew lately. It's just, with all the new stuff we do at MgRonald now, one of my old dreams is starting to make its way back into my head."

"Your old dreams?" Maou looked up at Kisaki as he cradled his head.

"Right. I should probably let Chiho know most of all, shouldn't I? Even grown-ups are allowed to dream about the future, after all."

She smiled.

"I've always posted up better numbers than anyone else hired with me in Tokyo."

Maou knew this well enough by now, but those were the words that suddenly came from her mouth as she lovingly stared not at Sariel, not at Maou, but at the lonely FOR RENT sign on the window.

"But lately, I've started to think...like, maybe I want to see how far I can go by myself."

"So you're thinking about going solo sometime in the future?" Emi gingerly asked. "Not necessarily right now?"

"Pretty much, I suppose," Kisaki quickly replied—so quickly, in fact, that it caught Maou unprepared. "I mean, it's all just kind of a 'wouldn't it be nice' thing in my mind right now. I'm not taking any concrete steps toward it."

"Uh, I'd think that scoping out real estate is a pretty concrete step…"

"Oh, this? This is just playing at it, really. It's like seeing a help-wanted ad on the Net and immediately fantasizing about what you'll do with the first paycheck."

"Ooh."

"Mm…"

"Uhhh…"

Maou, Emi, and Chiho all groaned uncomfortably. They'd all had experience with that. Kisaki smiled at the display.

"Hey, it's nothing to be ashamed of. That's what motivated you to get working."

She approached the empty storefront window, peering into an interior lit only by the dwindling western sun.

"All my fellow managers keep heaping praise on me for the numbers I put up. But I don't really feel like I'm doing anything much different from any of them. The fact that the Hatagaya MgRonald keeps beating its previous sales figures year over year isn't just because of me or anything."

"Oh, of course it is!" Chiho breathlessly replied. "I hear all these stories about evil managers and lazy part-timers, but it feels like our MgRonald's on a totally other level from that. We pretty much never have angry customers, and I think a lot of that comes down to you, Ms. Kisaki!"

Kisaki shook her head, still facing the window. "I'm glad to hear that, but it's really nothing I could do alone. I've only been at that location for a year and a half—that's actually pretty damn long for a manager to stay at one place, but even before I showed up, there was already something there that set up the framework I worked under."

She turned her eyes toward Sariel's reflection.

"What do you think that is?"

"…The previous manager?"

Kisaki bunched her eyebrows at Sariel's reply.

"Wow. Considering how you go around embarrassing yourself,

calling me a goddess and just barely skirting Japan's stalker laws, you really know nothing about me, do you?"

Sariel visibly shrank.

"You probably know the answer by this point, Marko. What is it?"

"The MgRonald Corporation. The brand."

Kisaki nodded her approval at the confident reply.

"I am a single MgRonald employee. I take pride in that, and I couldn't even tell you how much I've learned from them. Even if I make it all the way up the ladder, I'd still just be walking a path trodden by so many people before me. The assorted things I've been doing at that location all came about as part of the MgRonald system that already existed."

"Is that…how it is, then?" Emi asked softly.

Kisaki neither nodded nor shook her head as her smile broadened. "You are… Ms. Yusa, right? Do you use a lint roller to get the junk off the shoulders of your work clothing when you get home?"

"Huh?" Emi instantly turned her head toward one of her shoulders. "N-no, nothing quite like that—"

"When you wash your hands, do you lather up all the way to your elbows and use a brush to polish up and disinfect your nails?"

"Well, I use soap, but—"

"Right, you see? A quick soap and rinse is just fine. There's some great soap out there in Japan."

Then Kisaki took her hands, refined and beautiful enough to feature in a cell phone ad, and thrust them into the evening air.

"Those are two examples of the kinds of things MgRonald's spent years hammering into its store locations. That kind of hygiene isn't something a place besides MgRonald can encourage through just a little education alone. That's what I mean when I say there's nothing about that location I've built up by myself."

She turned around to face the group.

"And, of course, there's still a lot I want to do. A lot of things I could *only* do in MgRonald. I kind of went off script a bit ago, actually. I know what some of my regular customers like in their coffee, and I tried to adjust my procedure for them…but *man*, it's been hard. And now I guess I'm checking out a storefront that's doomed to fail, huh? I've still got a lot to learn. It'll probably be a while before I start talking about any dreams again."

"W-was *that* what you did?!"

It was the day Kisaki had begun whining at Maou. He couldn't believe *that* was what she was doing up there. It wasn't too long after their grand reopening, either; they had to be fairly crowded. Their regulars numbered in the dozens, if not the hundreds. Remembering all of their preferences and crafting the perfect cup of coffee for them…?

"So the coffee you had us drink, Ms. Kisaki…"

"Yeah. Sorry about that." Kisaki winked and gave them a mischievous chuckle. "That was kind of unfair, I know. I just figured it'd be nice to remind everybody who's boss. But I didn't treat you to 'today's special' just for fun, either. You like your coffee bitter and not too hot, right, Marko? And Chi likes hers with no sugar and tons of milk."

Kisaki made a regular habit of treating the crew on duty to free Platinum Roast coffees whenever they exceeded their revenue goal for the day. What this meant was that through the days and weeks, Kisaki grasped how everybody on payroll liked their coffee—their MgRonald coffee, something specifically engineered not to be all that customizable.

"……"

Maou and Chiho were shocked.

"But don't let that make you think the MgRonald Barista workshop is a waste of time," Kisaki said. "Having a broader knowledge of the stuff you're working with creates the foundation for a whole new world of skills and technique. Every dream is just the culmination of a lot of tiny steps, after all."

She seemed to chew on her words a moment.

"Right now, MgRonald's giving me a pretty stable life. I've got talented people like you under me, and I'm notching some serious career achievements. Maybe a promotion's in my future. Who knows? But…" Her hand gripped the shoulder bag at her side.

"There's always going to be this dream alive in a corner of my mind. This idea that I can build my own history as an individual person. That I can take that step."

Her eyes seemed to twinkle like a little girl's as she revealed her heart. Not even people Chiho's age talked so frankly about their dreams like that too often, but here was their boss, a fast-track manager going everywhere in life, laying it all bare for them. She wanted to be a barman, an expert in every aspect of service. That was her dream, and the unexpected installation of a café in her Hatagaya location had helped kindle the flame a little. She had that dream because she knew her talents made her dissatisfied with the status quo. Her efforts in life granted her the right to dream.

"We might all dream in different ways, but depending on how we live and what we strive after, we can always have a new dream to pursue. Whether you make it happen or not is another matter, though."

Kisaki shrugged and pointed at the empty storefront in Sariel's condo.

"This place looked pretty fancy when it was open, didn't it?"

"I...think so, yes," Sariel said, trying to recall.

Kisaki nodded. "I thought it was a little cheap for what it offered," she sniffed. "Must be something else going on with it."

Something about the way she put it suggested that she was more than window shopping. She must've discussed the space with a real estate agent, at least.

"But why, though?" Maou asked. "I'd figure the condo residents would eat here, and I don't think there're many other restaurants around to provide competition. If the décor suited the location, you'd think it would attract a customer base..."

"One way of putting it, yes," Ashiya retorted. "But if you think about it another way, those could all be negatives as well."

"What makes you say that, sir?" Kisaki addressed the stranger politely.

Ashiya responded by timidly looking up at Sariel's building. "From what I can tell, this building is not that fully occupied. It might be nearby, yes, but no resident is going to stop here for lunch on a daily basis. The moment it grows old in their minds, they will stop coming. And being located in Hatagaya, I imagine the rent cannot be all that reasonable. A restauranteur would have to factor that into their prices. Perhaps you would have to charge 500 yen for a cup of coffee—but if you went *that* high, it would be difficult to ask that of customers without some sort of added value that goes beyond the quality of the drink."

He took a look around the street.

"However, have you noticed? We have been loitering here for quite some time now, but we have yet to see anyone so much as brush past us. On a straight two-lane road without any stoplights, cars are going to pass by without even a second glance, so despite the amount of traffic, there likely would not be too many drop-in customers. Those cars have a municipal road lined with stores and restaurants just a little way ahead as well."

Then he turned toward the condo's residential floors.

"We are far away from both the rail station and the local shopping district, and there are no other shops near us. You could frame that as having little competition to deal with, but having no stores here means there is nothing else to drive people into the neighborhood. That was likely why few people visited this café. Even if they were counting on work-commuter traffic, this area is wholly residential, and one would have to live here to even realize there was a café at all. They simply had a very limited audience to work with. And, I imagine, the killer blow was the convenience store right next door."

Kisaki listened on, impressed at this impromptu economics lesson.

"I have the impression that there are relatively few families around this neighborhood. Most of the apartments seem to be meant for singles, and you have to travel a fair distance before you begin to see any stand-alone housing. If you live by yourself, I think the choice between a café and a convenience store is fairly obvious. With most convenience stores, it's almost a given these days that you will find drinks from Moonbucks or Dully's Coffee on offer. Most single condo dwellers have visitors only on rare occasions, and even then, they would be unlikely to entertain them somewhere outside of the home. Along those lines, as well, a convenience store offers everything they need. …Those are my impressions, at least," he added to Kisaki, beginning to regret going on for so long.

Kisaki, who had been listening with eyes closed and a finger on her chin, turned to Maou.

"You've got a good brain on your side."

"Um, thank you."

Ashiya bowed at the indirect compliment.

"I completely agree with that. The only good things about this location are the exterior and the equipment. Beyond that, it doesn't offer any of the elements a restaurant needs. In terms of the locale, I'd guess it's better suited for a barber shop or beauty salon or something. I'm glad I figured *that* out, at least."

Kisaki nodded to herself with a smile.

"Well, sorry I stopped all you guys. I'm heading to MgRonald, but are you all going home?"

"Um, yeah, for today, anyway," Maou nodded.

Kisaki gave him a smile. "All right. Thanks for putting up with my rambling about my dreams. Next time you all show up at my store, I'll treat you all to a café au lait from upstairs, so stop on by when you're close."

Just as she was about to briskly saunter away, a tiny, withdrawn voice behind her back stopped her.

"……ah……"

It was soft enough that even the tapping of her heels could've concealed it, but Kisaki's ears noticed it nonetheless.

"I'm guessing the reason you're looking like that," she said, back still turned, "isn't because Sentucky's sales are hurting, is it?"

"N-no, um…erm…"

She was talking to Sariel, whose voice remained tiny and imploring. He stammered, knowing that telling her the real reason would only disenchant her even more. But it was too late for that.

"I heard that it's mainly because I banned you from my restaurant."

"Mngh!"

Kisaki must have known that from the start. Even Emi and Suzuno, originally hearing the story secondhand from Chiho, could see that.

"You're more sensible than I gave you credit for. I all but resigned myself to seeing those stupid red roses on the counter just like normal the next day."

"I-I figured that would go too far into stalker territory for your tastes," Sariel timidly stated.

Kisaki shrugged and chuckled to herself. "If I wasn't as generous to you as I was, what you were doing *before* then was stalker-ish enough. I don't know where you heard my age from, but giving a total stranger one rose for every year of her lifespan is grounds for a sexual harassment lawsuit these days."

"You…you did that?"

"Oh, man, you gotta be kidding me…"

"Duuuude. See, this is *exactly* why we got such a bad rep these days."

There was little Sariel could do to counter this criticism.

"I still believe I'm justified in banning you. *You're* the one acting creepy around all the women you see—it's completely your fault. … But." Kisaki turned just a little toward Sariel, eyebrows still lowered. "I feel like I'm using your whacked-out love to bring down Sentucky, and that doesn't make me feel good. No real barman would defeat their business competition with dirty tricks."

"Then…you'll…?"

With a hefty sigh, Kisaki turned her face away from him.

"If I have to watch you mope around on the street and have dogs piss on you, it'd be better for everyone if you're happy and sane inside my dining area instead. You can come back starting tomorrow."

It is difficult to describe the transformation in Sariel's facial expression. Imagine a penguin chick, surviving a brutal winter's blizzard, sighting the first blessed ray of sunshine spreading out from between the clouds. The very color of his soul had changed.

"*But!*" Kisaki snapped. "No more roses. *Please.* I have to get permission from my regional manager to put plants in the restaurant space, and I'm sure you do, too. It's a pain in the butt to deal with. Also, this is your final warning. If I ever catch you making trouble for my staff or customers again, you can expect a permanent ban and maybe a court summons if I'm in a bad mood."

Then she sauntered off into the Hatagaya evening cityscape, not bothering to wait for a response.

"...That sure worked out well, didn't it?"

"I suppose so," Maou blankly replied.

"Mm...? L-Lord Sariel?!"

"Sariel! Sariel, snap out of it! You're f-floating in the air!"

The happiness within Sariel, a dreamy, doll-like smile on his face as he watched Kisaki leave, must have been made of helium. His body was bathed in an angelic light as his feet left the sidewalk. The street was deserted, luckily, but it still took ten minutes to get him grounded again—emotionally and physically.

✳

Saturday. The day of the MgRonald Barista seminar was almost tragically beautiful.

As far as Maou could tell, Chiho's skill with holy force hadn't improved all that much in the few days since Kisaki had lifted the ban on Sariel. Work prevented Maou (and Emi, too) from being around her for very long, but that was the impression Ashiya and Suzuno gave him, at least. Farfarello and Erone remained incommunicado, so it appeared to everyone that this was going to be a drawn-out battle.

Maou sweated it out at nine AM as he waited for Chiho at Sasazuka station, cursing the sun for this final blast of summer heat but still finding himself oddly anticipating the upcoming seminar.

Even during summer break, the ever-diligent Chiho remained busy. Between her club activities, her part-time job, and her alien-world magic training, there wasn't much free time left. She more or less wrapped up all her summer school projects in mid-July—that was so classically Chiho of her—but considering all the trouble these visitors from Ente Isla had caused her this summer, Maou felt that he owed her a trip out somewhere after the workshop was over.

Then, inside a pocket of the tote bag he was using to bring writing materials and such along, his phone vibrated.

"Huh?" he said to himself as he brought it to his ear. "That's odd. Is she late or something?"

{"I'm right behind you, Maou."}

"Waggh?!"

The sudden voice in his head made Maou jump on the spot.

"Um, sorry if I scared you!"

She was right there, clad in a robin's-egg blue dress and hefting a large shoulder bag, looking a little despondent upon realizing that she gave Maou heart palpitations with her act. "Are you all right? I thought I'd surprise you a little, but...sorry."

"Oh, uh... No, it's fine, but...*that*, just now..." Maou blinked, noticing that Chiho had no cell phone in her hand.

"Uh-huh! That was an Idea Link."

"Y-you mastered that?"

She seemed completely serene, the act of activating her holy force not taxing her strength at all. The voice that spooked him had a direct link to his brain, no doubt about it.

"Not quite yet, actually. Your phone rang just now, didn't it?"

"Yeah." Maou peered at his phone's screen and bought up his call history. "...No caller ID? I thought I had anonymous calls blocked on this thing."

He didn't check before picking up, figuring it had to be Chiho calling him, but the only word in the call log was "Restricted."

"I still can't get it to work unless I have an amplifier to work with. I don't need to have anything on me, but I can't get other people to pick up on my messages unless they have a phone on them."

"Huh. Kind of a roundabout way of doing it, isn't it? That'd actually be harder for me than just linking up directly."

Chiho chuckled. "Suzuno and Sariel said the same thing."

"You're pretty much just making a phone call with holy magic, aren't you? That's kind of a convoluted way to keep from using up your minutes."

"Well, I just can't quite picture linking into someone's mind like that yet. But I know you can talk to someone by sending a message to a phone number at the right wavelength or whatever, so I tried memorizing Suzuno's number, and…it just kind of worked."

Chiho made it sound simple enough, but not even Emi could have come up with that idea, and she used a phone to Idea Link with Emeralda all the time. The way holy magic worked, it was the spell-caster, not the receiver, who needed to have an amplifier. What was the science, so to speak, behind *this* approach?

"…Wow. Even if I wanted to try doing it that way, I'm pretty limited in terms of dark power, so…"

Even now, Maou still had no idea how Emi and Suzuno were recharging their holy force. Urushihara seemed to be in on the secret, but he refused to tell him—"it wouldn't help us anyway," as he put it. If Chiho was tapping into the same supply as the other two, maybe Maou would have a chance to see that in action today.

"Well, either way, I'm glad you can send out an SOS when you need to now. What kind of range do you have?"

"As far as we could tell during practice yesterday, I can manage a radius of three hundred feet or so."

"Three hundred feet?" Maou's face soured a bit. "That's pretty damn good for a beginner, but it's hard to say if that's gonna be good enough or not. I guess phone signals can't break through Erone's barrier, either. I doubt your power's affected by that much, but I wouldn't rely too much on the maximum end of that range, either. 'Course, I guess we'll spend all day together anyway, so it doesn't matter too much."

"…!"

The way Maou said "all day together" so naturally made Chiho gasp a little.

"I…I guess it's been a while, hasn't it? You and I together, alone, for a while…"

Maou reflected thoughtfully on this for a moment. "Ummm…

yeah, you're right. Not since that whole deal underground at Shin-juku. Hard to believe that was only three months ago."

"............Yeah."

Chiho expected that tepid reply. But, inside, she wanted the topic to last at least a bit longer than *that*.

"Well, shall we, then?" Maou said as he took out the ticket he already bought and headed for the turnstile.

"...Sure," Chiho said glumly. "Oh, wait a sec, I need to go buy a ticket." Maou waited for her to buy a one-stop ticket before joining her through the gate.

Three pairs of eyes stared at them from behind a nearby column.

"Why do we have to stalk her like a bunch of Peeping Toms?"

"We must. Chiho may have acquired the knack for sending Idea Links, but the Devil King himself has practically no ability to fight."

"I am prepared to sacrifice everything I have to protect the crew of my goddess!"

"Oof. Talk about the leopard changing its spots. Are you cutting work today?"

"Say what you will. My goddess told us herself: No matter how old a man becomes, he must always keep sprinting toward his dreams! And I am not cutting work, thank you. I would never shame my goddess in such fashion! I took a vacation day!"

Emi, Suzuno, and Sariel all agreed long ago that they needed to tail Chiho today. What surprised the girls was how sincere Sariel was in his zest to keep the girl safe. They were concerned that Kisa-ki's softened stance toward him would make him break his promise to help with her training, but if anything, he was more passionate about it than ever before. The courtesy he now showed Maou and Emi was almost sickeningly cloying, and he even offered to cover all the training-space rental fees until Chiho mastered amplifier-based spellcasting. Now, even though nobody asked him—or even told him that Maou and Chiho were attending a MgRonald training seminar—here he was, following them around since morning.

"Well, as long as you don't get in our way... Let's go before we lose them."

The trio went through the gate and spoke in hushed voices as they watched Maou and Chiho line up for the front car of the next train to Shinjuku.

"You said, 'no matter how old a man becomes,'" Emi asked Sariel, "but are you guys really...just *people*, in the end?"

Gabriel had suggested as much to her. That "divinity," at least as it applied to the angels above Ente Isla, didn't really exist—that they were more human than not. She wanted confirmation, and now that Sariel was on friendly terms with her—who would've thought a MgRonald manager could've engineered *that* miracle? Truth really was stranger than fiction—she figured there was no time to waste.

"You must've made Gabriel confess to it, hm?"

Not only did Sariel not deny it, but he even knew the source of the leak.

"So you're not, like, immortal or...?"

"No. At least, *I* don't see myself as some sort of supernatural being. People call us angels, but really, we're just people, too. The only difference is that we live longer, we're more intelligent, we're stronger, we have more capacity for holy force, we're prettier, and we've got *scads* of holy charisma."

"God help me," Suzuno moaned behind them, "I can hear my faith disintegrating in my soul..."

"I didn't ask you to brag about it like that, but... Okay, one question."

"What? Wait. Before you say it, let me remind you: There's one woman in my life, and that shall forever be my goddess."

"I *know* that. She told you to knock that off, remember? I wish you wouldn't keep reminding me."

Emi wiped the sweat from her brow as she asked, "How is society, like, set up in heaven?"

"Hmm," Sariel replied, eyes turned upward. "Kind of a vague question, isn't it? We could take the next train from here to Hachiouji and back by the time I finished answering it."

The western Tokyo suburb of Hachiouji was the last stop on the opposite end of the Keio Line, thirty stops and a good twenty-five miles away. Not exactly a quick ride, in other words.

"Right," Suzuno said. "So how about the Heavenly Regiment?"

"Hmm?"

"They were equipped with shoddy weapons, mere toys compared to your scythe or Gabriel's Durandal sword. They are clearly different from angels or archangels, but what is their position in heaven, exactly?"

Inside a box in her apartment, Suzuno still kept a few broken pieces of the Regiment's weaponry she'd picked up from their battle at Dokodemo Tower in Yoyogi. They were of unusually poor make, forged from metal so brittle that a single kick of Suzuno's foot was enough to shatter them. Hardly weapons worthy of being wielded by an angel, in other words.

"Ah. Yeah, those are all originally Ente Islan, actually. I don't know about their weapons. Maybe they made 'em themselves? Or maybe they brought 'em with them."

"Whaat?!"

Emi couldn't help but exclaim in surprise as well.

"The Heavenly Regiment is all people from Ente Isla?!"

"Sure is," Sariel briskly replied, striking the two women dumb. "You know how there's all that scripture and mythology about people being called for by angels? Well, a lot of that's pretty true."

"B-but not even the loftiest of Church clerics... Some of them were canonized after death, yes, but summoned by the angels themselves? Not a one..."

The next train to Shinjuku chose that moment to arrive. The conversation continued inside the air-conditioned rail car.

"Hey, it's our choice to make, isn't it? What's the benefit to us, picking up some old geezer who spent the last X number of decades lusting after power, wasting his life on stupid Church politics, and cultivating a vast knowledge of things that matter to absolutely no one? Did you think *that's* the kind of person we'd welcome in? He'd rebel against us in half a second. We make *our* selections from the general public."

"The what…?"

"You know—tortured slaves, war orphans, that sort of thing. That's who we use to fill the Regiment ranks. They're really important to us! They take care of a lot of the little things for us in heaven, you know, and since these are people with a truly pure faith in the Church and all, they're never going to betray us. If *you* guys want to make it up there, I'd recommend going back to secular life, pronto."

He couldn't have been blunter. It was a complete damnation of the Church and all it stood for.

"It's not like the Church is totally useless to us, though. There's no more effective way out there to build faith in us, after all."

Even Suzuno, capable of compartmentalizing the Church's dual purposes as a beacon of faith and a de facto government, had trouble wrapping her mind around this.

"And plus, we sometimes pick people up from there if we think they'd be useful, even if there's a few skeletons in their closets. Not a lot, but some. I'm guessing that's the retirement Olba Meiyer's aiming for."

"That's crazy!" Emi exclaimed, face stiff. "What Olba's doing right now is making him accomplice to a completely new tragedy in Ente Isla. If *that's* the kind of person who's allowed into heaven, I'd say heaven's in sore need of a revolution!"

Sariel shrugged his shoulders. "Ooooh, you're a scary lady."

Their train, which started its journey on elevated rails, soon descended into a tunnel. Shinjuku was just a few moments away.

"Although…there's a pretty big information gap between the first-genners like Gabriel and the second-genners like me and Raguel. I guess you could say the first-genners aren't very big fans of keeping all of that on the down low."

"First-genner…?"

"Oh, didn't you notice? There's two types of angels you guys have seen."

"…Oh."

Suzuno clapped her hands in realization and looked into the eyes of Sariel, seated adjacent to him.

"Angels with purple eyes, and angels with red eyes..."

"Yeah, that. Red's the first generation, and purple's the second one. Ignoring the Heavenly Regiment, you can pretty much divide us into two groups like that."

"So Lucifer is in the second generation? And even then, he was equal in ranking to Gabriel?"

"Welllll..." Sariel shook his head. "There's a lot about Lucifer that not even I know about. He was always apparently kind of a lazy bum, though. Ever since I remember, he was always a fallen angel, out of heaven. But I'm one of the oldest of the second-genners, too, so who knows what's up with him?"

"What is the difference between the two generations, my lord? Do you see them as your parents or whatnot?"

Sariel nodded eagerly. "Ah, yeah, I better explain that first. The boundary's right when—"

Just then, the train shuddered loudly as it navigated the rail switches just before Shinjuku station.

"We're almost here."

The two women wanted to hear more, but they also needed to keep an eye on Maou and Chiho. The three of them sidled up to the door of the largely uncrowded car. And Sariel's last revelation, delivered alongside the conductor's station announcement, was something difficult for Emi and Suzuno to digest at the time.

"The boundary's right when the Cataclysm of the Devil Overlord took place. The first generation was born before it; the second generation afterward. That's how it was explained to me, anyway."

Ten shiny new coffee servers were lined up against one wall of a large conference room.

The part-time crew and salaried employees gathered here, at MgRonald's Japan headquarters near Shinjuku station's west exit, numbered about a hundred or so. The sight of all these employees looking to polish their MagCafé skills filled Maou with excited anticipation.

"Thank you all for taking time out of your busy schedules to attend this MgRonald Barista workshop. First off, I'd like everyone to make sure the number on their registration forms matches the one on their desks. After that, you'll want to go over your handouts to make sure everything's in order..."

The product-management staffer hosting the seminar politely guided the attendees through the preliminary paperwork.

"Now, to start out, we're going to watch a twenty-minute DVD that goes over what the MagCafé concept is all about. We'll get hands-on with the workshop after that."

The room lights dimmed as the video sprang to life on the large screen against another wall. Maou had seen more than a few training videos like this one. He always liked how detached from reality they always seemed, edited in such a different way from the corporate TV ad campaigns.

"...What's that?" came a voice from the side. Maou, distracted from his notetaking, looked in its direction—only to realize that he was now the only person in the conference room.

Chiho, seated a bit away from him thanks to drawing a later number, was gone. Next to him now, in the adjacent seat, was Erone in his samurai armor.

"...Farfarello is not here," he said calmly to assuage the agitated Maou. "He is monitoring me from a nearby building, but I am the only one in here."

"Were...were you sneaking around here under this barrier?"

"I was told to search for an opening we could use to kidnap you. But I can't. You're surrounded by too many people."

The reply was as unaffected as it was disturbing. The training DVD kept playing on-screen. The surrealness of the scene forced Maou to laugh a little.

"Farfarello told me to find out for sure what you're doing in order to conquer the world. What kind of...image is this we're seeing? Do you need it to conquer the world?"

The screen depicted a MgRonald crewmember from the United States or somewhere constructing a MagCafé menu in a location far larger than the Hatagaya one Maou darted around in. The MagCafé format was originally conceived in Australia, apparently, before being exported back to the American HQ and expanding out to Japan. Then it showed a brawny Anglo-Saxon man, one Maou had trouble picturing as an actual MgRonald part-timer, using latte bubbles to draw hearts and leaf designs on cups of cappuccino. Comical, but impressive.

"I totally do. In fact, everything I'm doing here right now…it's all completely required if I'm gonna take over this world."

"Huh. That's neat," Erone remarked, watching the screen.

"…Y'know, you're a lot friendlier than I thought," Maou replied. Erone's admiration was throwing him off his game.

"Farfarello and the others said the only right way to conquer the world is through power and fear. Is that man creating a potion to boost your powers?"

A lot chattier than he thought, too. Maou took that as a sign that Farfarello really wasn't nearby after all.

"Yeahhh…I guess that's what it is, if you get down to it. Um, do you know what 'industry' is? Industry is all about taking a whole bunch of different things and putting them together so they all work in unison. Making good coffee contributes to people's productivity, boosts their morale, and…um, creates higher-quality weapons for people to use, more or less."

"Industry…?" Erone raised an eyebrow. "I don't get it."

"Well, neither do I, really. That's why I'm here to study it."

"Study?" This seemed to confuse him even more. Understanding the concept of world domination but failing to know what studying was concerned Maou a little.

"Hummm…I don't know how to explain it. It's, like, too simple a concept."

Fishing for words, Maou watched the screen as it depicted a coffee field somewhere in South America.

"Uh, how about this? When you're studying, you're doing something in order to know something you didn't know before."

"So you study this…industry?" Erone said, piecing the unfamiliar words together like Alas Ramus. "And that lets you conquer the world?"

"Yeah. See, that's the thing about those of us in the Devil King's Army. We have no idea what it means for a country to rule over its people. So that's why I'm here in *this* country. I'm preparing myself to conquer the world, and this is part of that. The—"

The screen flashed over to a map depicting MgRonald's plans for MagCafé expansion in Japan.

"—the next step of my dream…to conquer the world in a whole new way."

"A new…dream?" Erone repeated the words slowly, sloshing them around in his mind. "Looks like fun." And with that, he disappeared, and a conference room full of focused screen viewers replaced him. Judging by Chiho's body language, she hadn't noticed any of it, and Maou certainly hadn't seen her inside the barrier.

"Um, hey…"

"Hmm? What is it?"

Maou turned around to look at the person who just tapped his shoulder. It was a crewmember from a different location, the pallor to his face clear even in the darkness.

"Were…were you always there, or…?"

Ah. Right. Chiho hadn't noticed, but to someone seated directly behind him, Erone's visit must have looked like Maou disappearing and reappearing like a ghost. Maou thought for a moment and whispered back.

"Uh, I dropped my pen and I was having trouble finding it…"

"…Oh. Yeah. All right. Sorry I'm acting all weird." The man settled back down, his face still more than a bit dubious.

"Yeah, not like I got a lot of say in it," Maou said to himself as he focused on the video.

"Oh! That must be them."

"Oof. *Finally* over. I was about to die of boredom."

"Uggh, we have to go outside again…?"

The Hero, the Church cleric, and the archangel were approaching hour four of their awkward kaffeeklatsch at a Moonbucks near MgRonald's Tokyo headquarters when they noticed a large crowd of people exiting the building. Given that most were in street clothes, it seemed safe to assume they were from the workshop.

"Where are Chiho and the Devil King?"

"Can't really tell from here..."

They were too far away to spot the pair out of the hundred-odd people streaming out, splitting into smaller groups and going each of their own ways.

"Is that him?" Sariel pointed out a lone figure by the front door—Maou, apparently. They could see him nervously eye his surroundings and bring his cell phone to his ear. The sight made Emi's and Suzuno's blood run cold. This wasn't just the face of someone wondering where his friend wandered off to.

"Devil King!!"

Emi, letting her worst fears dominate her mind, flew out and ran over to the dismayed-looking Maou.

"Oh! Um, Emi!"

He looked surprised at Emi's sudden appearance, but not enough to ask what she was doing there.

"Have you seen Chi at all?!"

She knew it. Emi gnashed her teeth internally.

"Chiho is gone?!"

"What on earth were you even doing in there?"

"Oh, all of *you* all with her, too?!"

"When did you get separated from her?!"

"It hasn't even been ten minutes. She was right next to me when we left the conference room!"

"And you are sure she's not in the bathroom or the like?"

"Ahhh, *damn* it! I wasn't paying attention! This is totally my fault! I should've pressed that bastard for more info when I had the chance..."

Maou looked honestly pained, but there would be time to assign blame later.

"Now is no time for that! If neither of us spotted her, then chances are she was taken in by Erone's barrier. And if she didn't send an Idea Link to either of us, they might have knocked her unconscious."

Maou started to panic. Emi's analysis seemed grimly accurate.

"Crap... What're we supposed to do now?!"

"Calm down!" Emi grabbed Maou by the shoulders. "If *you* start cracking on us, we aren't gonna accomplish anything!"

It didn't work at all. Maou was still in a panic.

What could have possibly happened in that conference room? If Maou hadn't been paying attention, did that mean he hadn't even noticed Erone approaching them?

"He was talking to me..."

"What?!" Emi's eyes burst open. She wasn't expecting *that* close of a contact. "What is your *problem*, Devil King?! That's totally not like you! He's our *enemy*, for God's sake!"

Maou covered his face with his hands. "...He was so *like her*. He made me put my guard down. We talked, he disappeared, and then..."

"So like whom?"

Maou, face contorted in pain, looked Emi in the eye. "Like...Alas Ramus. He wanted to know more about the world. That's what his face told me. ...He doesn't deserve to be used by people like us."

The sight of Erone smiling, saying *Looks like fun*, was the exact, same smile Alas Ramus displayed whenever a new surprise caught her eye. Maou had no basis for this, but seeing that smile convinced him that Erone was every bit the spawn of Sephirah Alas Ramus was. The moment he looked at his face, that was what he was instantly reminded of.

"Well, like or not, he's being used by those demons! It's your fault that you forgot about that, but whether you're right or not kind of depends on what we do next, okay?!"

"Emi..."

Her eyes were looking straight up at Maou. The straightforward encouragement, like nothing she ever gave to him before, helped calm his heart a little.

"Yeah… You're right." His shallow breathing returned to normal as he analyzed the situation. "The workshop ended nine minutes ago. Assuming they didn't run through a Gate, they've got to be somewhere in west Shinjuku, even if *he* was carrying her out."

"All right. Let me help you, then."

Sariel, of all people, nodded at Maou's analysis.

"Chiho Sasaki has a Yesod-fragment ring on her left hand, yes? Unless they've gone a fairly long distance away, I should be able to track that down."

"How?"

"Did you forget, Emilia?" Sariel smirked at her. "How did you think I managed to track you down in the first place? I had some intel from Olba, but as long as holy force or Sephirah fragments are involved, I can track 'em down faster than a GPS app."

Sariel squinted at the midafternoon sun, looking for something in the sky.

"Got it."

The rest of the group followed his gaze, using their hands to shade their eyes. There, amid the blue, they noticed something white and round floating in the air. It was the moon, just fading into sight in the late-summer afternoon.

"…Huh. Using an amplifier at long range isn't something your garden-variety spellcaster could ever do. With the right training, Chiho Sasaki could be one hell of a practitioner."

Sariel kept his eyes on the daylight moon in the sky.

"Not as good as me, though."

Then, at that instant, a ray of purple light shot out of his eyes. The next moment, the moon Maou and the rest had their eyes on turned the same color as Sariel's purple eyes and began to glow, eerily so.

"Wh-whoa, what're you doing?! People are gonna notice…"

It wasn't just a matter of Shinjuku. A purple moon was an event of international proportions. Emi couldn't be blamed for worrying about this ridiculously brash move, but Sariel merely brushed her away.

"The moon didn't really change color. It'll just look that way around Shinjuku for a bit."

"Oh," said Emi. "Well, that's fine, then—"

"No, it's not!!!"

Maou was forced to snap her back to reality. A midday moon wasn't something most people paid very close attention to, but in a district as densely populated as Shinjuku, *someone* had to spot it sooner or later. If that someone shot a pic and uploaded it to the Net, Maou couldn't imagine what kind of furor it'd cause.

"Ah, it won't make for anything more than a couple of viral videos," Sariel told the group. "Everybody knows there's no way the moon can turn purple in the middle of the day. No one's going to care *that* much about it. Now shut up for a second while I search around."

After completely failing to reassure his compatriots, Sariel raised a hand toward the moon and began to focus. Chiho's whereabouts were on everyone's mind, but the potential fallout they imagined if someone happened to pass by weighed even more heavily on them. Whether you knew what was going on or not, the sight of someone bringing a hand to the air and shooting light beams out of his eyes could easily earn them a free trip in the back of a cop car. Sariel, perhaps realizing this, took care to keep his voice down as he intoned a spell.

"Moon Mirror."

The spell remained in effect for just two or three seconds before he shut it down.

"Oh. Well, that was easy. They're right near us."

"R-really?!"

Sariel nodded at the frantic Maou and pointed up at a nearby building.

"Ironically enough, there's a barrier on that rooftop up there."

"Up...*there*?!"

Suzuno gasped.

"This is so annoying. I really wish they wouldn't steal my repertoire."

It was, of course, the Tokyo Metropolitan Government Building, a place all four of them were intimately familiar with.

"Well, what do you think? Because I think our demon friend's up there, too. If we storm the roof, it'll probably turn into a fight. A dimensional-phase barrier can keep people outside of it safe, but I can't speak for the building itself. I'm willing to bet all four of us could handle that Erone kid well enough, but we'll probably cause a hell of a lot of damage along the way."

"I don't care. If that's where Chi and Farfarello are, I'm on my way."

"What are you gonna do?" Emi asked, concerned that Maou was planning another haphazard, strategy-free assault.

The response went far beyond what she expected.

"Emi...Suzuno...sorry to put this on you, but I'm gonna need your help."

"Uh?"

"Wh-what?"

Both were taken aback by the request—really more of a plea, actually.

"Ashiya was right. Unless we can convince Farfarello to go back on his own volition, Chi's just gonna get taken again and again. I need your help to keep that from happening."

Then Maou did something even more out of character.

"Please."

He bowed his head to them. The king of all demons, bowing his head to the Hero and a Church cleric in order to protect a single human girl.

"...I swear..." Emi sighed as he glared at the whorl of hair on the top of Maou's head. "You don't care at all about us or what we feel, do you?" The words were harsh, but her tone was surprisingly gentle.

"Yeah, well, I'm the Devil King, remember. When it comes to not caring about what other people think, I'm pretty much world champion."

"Do *not* brag about it."

Suzuno found herself laughing at the way he put it.

"So, how do you like your chances? Do you think you can pull that off?"

"Yep," Maou replied, head still down. "But like I said, I'm gonna need both of you to help me."

Emi and Suzuno looked at each other.

"Don't have much time to mull over it, huh?"

"We have little choice. Chiho's life may be at stake."

"I *really* appreciate this," Maou said, raising his head and turning toward Sariel. "Can you put up another barrier on top of Erone's, like you did last time?"

"I could, but what are you trying to accomplish?"

"Great. Make it as huge as you can, all right? I'll take care of things after that."

With that, Maou took a jet-black ball out from his tote bag, gripping it tightly.

❋

"What is the meaning of this?" Farfarello asked the girl in front of him.

The girl, who introduced herself as Chiho Sasaki, was proving suspiciously cooperative, not showing any resistance to Erone's invitation. The boy managed to pull it off without attracting the Devil King's attention chiefly because his intended victim was being so agreeable with him.

"Well, I didn't want you beating me up or putting me to sleep if I resisted."

"I see. You're more collected than I thought you'd be."

"Oh, this isn't my first rodeo, if you know what I mean!"

The way Chiho chuckled to herself at this indicated exactly how collected she was. She would have to be, if she could take being carried by Erone's sticklike arms from the ground floor of the MgRonald building to the top of the Tokyo Metropolitan Government Building in a single leap without losing her mind or her lunch along the way.

"All right. How about this, then?"

Farfarello, still in his retro salaryman outfit, tapped a finger against Erone's armor. The moment he did, the armor disappeared into a black mist that descended upon him.

"Agh!"

Chiho unconsciously covered her eyes. In a single moment, the scrawny businessman transformed into an ominous, hideous demon. He had batlike wings and a single, gigantic talon curving out from each of his arms and legs, but his face remained unexpectedly humanlike.

She couldn't help but sneak a peek or two between her fingers. "...Oh," she said, relieved at the sight of the rough, hemp-fabric underwear Erone had on as she removed her hands. "You had clothes on the whole time?"

"...*That* was your concern? This demonic body of mine didn't terrify you?"

Having Chiho show more concern over his servant's modesty than his own ghastly, foreboding form made Farfarello feel like he was being toyed with. As a human, she should have been on her knees, begging for her life by this point. *This* reaction wasn't something they taught him in demon-chieftain college.

"Um...I'm sorry. I just thought you were gonna transform into something kind of...crazier than that?"

"......"

Now Chiho began to feel somewhat endangered. Farfarello clearly didn't enjoy that response.

"...Um, I didn't... I mean, it's not like I don't think you're scary or anything! You look really mean and intimidating and stuff! It's just that, like, I've already seen what Ma—um, what Satan and Alciel look like, so I think I'm just too accustomed to it."

"...Fine. Honestly, I'm starting to want to kill you now."

"Um, s-sorry?" Chiho tried to apologize honestly. She had her doubts over whether that would be enough, though.

"Did you see His Demonic Highness's visage...up close?"

"Uhh, from about the same distance we're at now."

"......"

His expression remained unchanged, but inside his heart, this greatly troubled Farfarello. He had heard secondhand that the Devil King Satan was capable of reattaining his cloven-hoofed form, but he found it impossible to believe that this…this mere *human* girl viewed his liege in all his glory. Most people would faint on the spot, overwhelmed by the sheer nature of his dark force.

"Wait…are you the one called Emeralda Etuva?"

"Huh?!"

Chiho's eyes shot open at this wholly unexpected case of mistaken identity.

"I understand that Etuva, assistant of the Hero Emilia and the most powerful of human spellcasters, is a woman of small size. Have you been living in this land of Japan, then, under the name Chiho Sasaki?"

"What? No! I mean, I've met Emeralda a couple times, but I'm not her, no."

She didn't appreciate being mistaken for her, but given that Farfarello couldn't have directly crossed swords with Emi and her crew, she couldn't blame him too much.

"Regardless, you have forged friendships with both her and Emilia, and you are capable of resisting my liege's demonic force. You are no rank-and-file soldier, no. I fear you must be one of the shackles that bind His Demonic Highness to this land, am I right?"

There was nothing she could do to convince him otherwise now. God forbid she mention that she was in the midst of holy-magic training. He'd probably think Chiho had been appointed Planetary Defender by the King of Earth.

"Well…I guess I might be, if you put it that way. Thanks to me, Satan and Yusa—I mean, Emilia—have had to go through a lot of bad stuff."

"…?"

"Um, Foulfellow?"

"It's Farfarello!!"

"I-I'm sorry, sir!" Chiho bowed in apology. "But Maou… Satan definitely hasn't given up his dream of conquering the world. That much I can guarantee to you. He's trying to learn a bunch of stuff in Japan that he can use to take everything over..."

"Ah, this 'studying,' yes?" Erone eagerly interjected.

"Um, yeah. That. He's studying lots of different things, and he's trying to *do* something with all of it. He doesn't have any money, so a lot of his time gets eaten up by work, but even so, Satan's always thinking about his people back home. I hope you'll believe that, at least."

This mere girl, completely unfazed, looked toward the demon with supreme dedication. Farfarello, growing up in a world where humans were supposed to fall into panicked insanity at the sight of a demon, never thought one would dare approach him with this sort of honest thoughtfulness. Her eyes were like nothing he had seen before.

"...I fervently wish that to be the case, yes. However—"

"So that's why I want to know..." Chiho interjected, "why did the Devil King's Army invade Ente Isla?"

"A ridiculous question," Farfarello bit back. "Of what value is Ente Isla if it is not in our hands and—"

"That's what I'm saying! *Why* did you have to invade it?!"

"......"

"I remember what you said earlier, Farfanilla. Something like, 'the more lives at stake, the longer the demon realms may yet survive.' Does that have something to do with it?"

"Far-fa-*rel-lo*!!" The demon lord wearily heaved his shoulders back. "What value would there be to *you* knowing?"

"Oh, that's obvious." Chiho resolutely stretched her back up high, her voice ringing out loudly. "I'd use that info to figure out what went wrong so I can help Satan make his dream come true!"

"Chi?!"

Maou's phone rang just as he was climbing the stairs leading up to the Tokyo Metropolitan Government Building. "Restricted," the screen said. It must have been Chiho's Idea Link.

"She's all right, guys! C'mon, move it! Let's show that Farfarello bastard what we're *really*—"

"Wait, Devil King!"

"Halt!"

"—What…?"

Maou's annoyance at being cut off dissipated quickly, as he noticed both women staring at their own phones. All three of them had "Restricted" on-screen. They took a look at each other and pressed their respective Answer buttons.

Chiho's voice boomed out from all three of them at once.

{"…so I can help Satan make his dream come true!"}

"What?"

Farfarello eyed Chiho quizzically, unsure what the girl meant.

"Satan's been telling me this all the time lately. That the way he did things before was all wrong. But I don't think he's really figured out what he should be doing instead yet. If I could, I'd do whatever it takes to help him out. I might be kind of a wimp; I might not be very useful in a fight, but there's got to be something I can do for him!"

"…Are you not human?"

"Of course I am!"

"Then why are you going on about helping us, the demons…?"

To Chiho, who believed beyond any doubt that Maou and Emi were both vital to her life, none of that mattered.

"It's all the same! Humans, demons…that doesn't factor into it!"

{"Humans, demons…that doesn't factor into it!"}

The thought broadcast itself not into their phones, but directly into their minds.

"Uh, is Chi dropping multiple Idea Links on each of us…?"

"Impossible." A clearly confused Suzuno shook her head. "That is a far more complex spell than one-on-one communication. She only just managed to link with me for several seconds yesterday."

"So do you think Chiho's doing this unconsciously, somehow?"

"That is all I can surmise…"

Suzuno swallowed nervously as the Idea Link continued.

{"We're making it work now…and if we can do that, I'm sure we can keep doing it!"}

"We're making it work now…and if we can do that, I'm sure we can keep doing it! We can conquer the world *and* have the Hero and Devil King at peace with each other!"

"…Perhaps I am not as well versed in the Japanese language as I should be. I am struggling to understand anything you say."

"Listen, Satan's definitely going to conquer the world, all right? He's working hard to make that happen every day. But it's not exactly the kind of conquering the 'Devil King Satan' was thinking of when he first came here…to Japan."

Chiho smiled cheerfully under the summer sun.

"He's working to create a world where the Devil King and the Hero…where demons and humans can work together to keep food on the table."

"…Absurd."

This girl's incomprehensible rantings were sorely testing Farfarello's patience. He began to wonder why he was bothering to humor her at all. But whether she knew that or not, Chiho kept going.

"Is it? 'Cause that's pretty much how it is right now. There's no reason why it can't stay that way!"

"You utter fool. The very idea of demons and humans living in harmony is absolutely prepost—"

"It's happening *right now!*"

Thus, for the first time in history, a teenage girl managed to shout down a Malebranche chieftain. The chastised Farfarello stared blankly downward.

"The Devil King and the Hero, two people who should be at each other's throats right now, are making it happen every day. They can even go out on playdates with the child they're taking care of. So why can *they* do it, but normal humans and normal demons can't?"

Because it came down to the individual people involved. Chiho knew that. But:

"And if they say they can't, I'll *make* them! I guess Maou and Yusa feel kind of bad for getting me wrapped up in all this Ente Isla drama, but there's no reason for them to think that way. Besides…"

Chiho smiled the boldest smile she could as she stared Farfarello in the eye.

"…I've got *every* intention of getting Maou and the others wrapped up in my own drama! I want all of them—Satan, Emilia, Alas Ramus, Crestia, Alciel, Lucifer—I want all of them to keep eating dinner with us, keep arguing with us, and keep saying 'see you tomorrow' after all is said and done. *That's* the kind of conquering *I* want to do, and *that's* what I'm going to help make happen!"

{"…And that's *what I'm going to help make happen!"}*
"……"

The three of them removed their ears from their phones, unable to withstand any more and too red in the face to look at each other.

"Jeez, Chiho," Emi muttered, trying to break the silence. "She's, like…even crazier than we thought."

"I can feel my faith being rebuilt into something far more twisted than before…"

"Ugh…for real? For real, Chi…?" Maou moaned.

"…Okay, so, what are we up to?" ventured Sariel, observing them from one side. "Are we doing this, or not? Judging by your reactions, am I to assume Chiho Sasaki is all right?"

"You were *there*?!" spat the blushing Maou as he stared up at the Tokyo Metropolitan Government Building. "…Get that barrier up for me. Emi, Suzuno…if you want to make this happen, you're both gonna have to be pretty damn persuasive up there."

"I-I'm not sure I'll be able to look Chiho in the face."

"I might start worshiping her, myself."

"…All right, all right," Maou grumbled, "let's just *do* this! Get moving!" Then, out of nowhere, he went down on all fours.

"I don't think I've ever seen a more pathetic way to give an order," laughed Sariel, as the daylight moon erected a barrier over the heart of downtown Tokyo for him.

"So that's why I want to know. Why did Satan have to sacrifice all those demons and humans in order to hurry along his world conquest...? If I knew that, I think we could maybe try a different direction next time."

Farfarello, chieftain for the Malebranche force, found himself averting his eyes, unable to withstand the forceful Chiho's gaze upon him. The concept was completely beyond him. He couldn't imagine even a sliver of the world Chiho pictured. There was no way a single, powerless girl could achieve that—but here he was, letting her overpower him.

Mentally beaten down, he slowly opened his mouth.

"...That..."

"Farfarello!" Erone shouted, looking upward. "The barrier!" Chiho, following his eyes, spotted a hazy, purple-tinted moon in the air.

"They're here...rather quicker than expected. How did they know...?"

Farfarello looked up as well, savoring the respite from Chiho's unrelenting stare. He was greeted with a sight unlike anything he expected.

"What on...?"

"Maou!" Chiho shouted, spotting the same thing in the air. "Yusa! Suzuno!"

She couldn't help but be reminded of the last time her prince came to her rescue here, with nothing but a mop and a pair of underpants. This time around, her prince—or king, perhaps—was flying in, his collar and belt being grabbed by a pair of women. Maybe not flying so much as hanging in the air, actually. Somehow, he still had the mental fortitude to glare at Farfarello. In one hand, he had his black sphere, the ball of concentrated dark force the demon had given him.

In Chiho's mind, she had accepted Erone's invitation in order to

clear up the questions she had about him. To Maou, she now realized, it must have looked like Farfarello had impulsively snatched
her away from him. *Oh, great. They aren't gonna fight up here now,
are they?* Alarmed by the very real possibility, Chiho shouted at
Maou.

"Wait! No! This is my fault, too! Fargobubble didn't do anything
to me!"

The demon she attempted to name-check rolled his eyes. "...Ah,
what does it matter?"

Keeping their eyes squarely upon the errant demon, Emi and
Suzuno dropped the hanging Maou onto the roof as they descended.
Maou made a nimble landing, then noticed his shirt. "Dahh," he
said, "the collar got all stretched out! Ashiya's gonna kill me."

Then, he turned to Chiho.

"...You okay?"

"Y-yeah, but...um...?"

Maou left his eyes on Farfarello in order to keep Chiho away from
his line of vision. Setting eyes on the massive, hulking body kept
his mind free of other distractions. "I guess Chi wants to defend
you," he said coldly, "but you're definitely here to kidnap her, aren't
you? Why?"

"Forgive me, Your Demonic Highness. I simply wanted to hear
about the time you spent in this world from a third party..."

Farfarello wound up hearing a lot more about Chiho's plans for
world domination than anyone else's, although neither he nor Chiho
knew that Maou had been listening in the whole time.

"So what about you, Chi? How is this 'your' fault?"

"Uh, um, I-I just wanted to know why you had to invade Ente Isla
in the first place, Maou. I kind of doubted you or Ashiya would tell
me, so—"

"Ughh...that's it?"

That topic wasn't part of the Idea Link the trio picked up. Perhaps
they covered it after he shut off the link out of pure embarrassment.
Maou scratched his head distractedly as he surveyed Chiho and
Farfarello.

"Listen, guys," he said as he thrust a thumb against his chest. "If you wanna ask about that stuff, ask *me*! I'm right here! I got nothing to hide from either of you!"

"Okay…I'm sorry." Chiho bowed despondently.

"Chi, there's…a few things I'd like to say to you. But for now…"

Maou recalled the Idea Link one more time as he approached Chiho and gave her a light, playful *bap* on the head.

"Ow!"

"I'll make time for the lecture later."

"Ooh, all right…"

Chiho ran over to Emi and Suzuno, hand covering the spot Maou had tapped. Maou, watching them each give Chiho chastizing *bap*s of their own from the corner of his eye, turned back toward Farfarello.

"Okay, now for you. Now that you've debriefed Chiho, what's your final take?"

"…To be honest with you, I find the evidence difficult to judge. A lot of what she said was quite a surprise to me. However, I cannot think this country has anything to offer my liege in terms of fulfilling his conquest."

"Yes, it does," Erone's childish voice warbled. "Satan is studying. About industry."

"You make it sound like I was taking some pretty damn shoddy notes," Maou chuckled. Then he reached into his pocket and took out his wallet. "But let me show you two. This country…this world, really, is full of things we can harness to save the demon realms from the mess it's currently in. Something you don't have to sacrifice blood or kill yourself for. And this is it."

He took out a single piece of paper from the plastic wallet he bought at the hundred-yen shop.

"…Could you at least buy a wallet where you don't have to wad up your bills to cram them in there?" Emi groaned, recalling when Maou used some of those pieces of paper to save her own hide once. "You could *try* to act like a grown-up sooner or later, you know."

"Do you know what this is? Here's a hint: They have this all over Ente Isla, too."

To Farfarello's eyes, all it looked like was a thin slip of paper with a portrait of some human being and a bunch of frilly characters written on it.

"What is it…?"

"All you need is some of this," Maou replied, "and you don't have to deal with crap like *this* any longer." Then he took his ball of demonic force, which he had tucked under an armpit in order to fetch his wallet, and halfheartedly tossed it at him.

"What? A single piece of paper that has more strength than dark magic itself?"

"It doesn't have it. People *give* it that strength."

Maou held the thousand-yen note up high, its portrait of turn-of-the-century bacteriologist Hideyo Noguchi shining proudly in the sun.

"If we have the will, we have the power to change the way the world works. And this is how we'll do it. With money. A valuable asset we can circulate around the demon realms in place of the dark force that'll dwindle away in the ensuing peace. If you change the way you look at things, the world and everything in it will change for you. *That's* what I've learned in this world."

"Money…I am aware of it, my liege. The paper and metal pieces humans use for commerce. But what meaning does it have in the face of power?"

"None right now. But we'll start to build meaning for it. And once we do, we could build anything. We can even have a world where the Hero helps me out instead of tries to kill me! We can create a dark, sinister force we can freely harness without having to kill anybody!"

Emi approached Maou from behind and put a hand on his shoulder. "Um, could you stop framing it like I'm helping you out because I need the money?"

"I know how human civilization runs on the core tenet that people need to be rewarded in order to take action," Suzuno said as she clutched his other shoulder, "but this is *not* the way I want it explained."

"Chi?"

Chiho remained behind him, unsure what was about to happen.

"Better start singing. Emi and Suzuno aren't gonna be able to cover for you, so you're gonna have to activate your own protection this time."

That was all the cuing she needed. Rubbing her eyes—still a bit teary at being scolded—she took a deep breath to calm herself down.

"It's time to earn your thousand yen, ladies."

"I really don't think we're getting market value for this...but I guess we have no choice."

"Indeed. This may not be quite what we imagined ourselves doing, once upon a time...but so be it. I want both of us to emerge from this alive, do you understand?"

With that, Emi and Suzuno began to transfer a vast quantity of holy force into Maou's body, through his shoulders.

"Wh-what are you doing?!" a dumbfounded Farfarello shouted. The amount of force flowing into Maou was completely uncapped, a torrent of holy wrath. In his current weakened human form, it could very well evaporate him.

"Stay there!!"

But he was stopped by Maou himself, the pain clearly evident on his face.

"Heh...heh-heh... Don't...don't get nervous. Wait'll you see what happens next."

"Are...are you sure about this?"

Maou seemed supremely confident, but he never got around to explaining what the point of it was to Emi or Suzuno. They reluctantly agreed to it, figuring he'd never do anything to put Chiho in danger. But all this looked like was them beating the tar out of Maou.

"Gaaahhhhh!!"

And before the magic torrent went on for very long...

"............!"

"Wh-whoa!"

"Hey!"

Maou's eyes rolled upward as he fainted.

No one watching him knew what the point of this torture was. No one except Chiho.

"Shining trees rustling under the new morning..."

Suddenly, she began singing the MHK radio-calisthenics theme. The effort started to activate the holy force in her own body just as Maou limply fell to his knees. Emi lifted him back up, her face clearly concerned for his safety.

"Open your heart up to the joy around youuuuu..."

Then, out of nowhere, things began to happen.

"And *reach for the stars!*"

Maou's body crumpled, as if someone had gone at him with a baseball bat.

"Agh!"

"Whoa!!"

Emi and Suzuno, trying to keep him upright, were blown away by the same force. A dark light began to glow from within Maou's body.

"Build a healthy body with MHK Radio 1..."

The light grew brighter and brighter, eventually cloaking Sadao Maou's whole body in inky blackness.

"Is that... It couldn't...!"

Farfarello shielded his eyes against the stream of dark light, but he still couldn't dare shy away from the sight.

"Open yourself to the fragrant wind—one!"

The first thing to emerge from the cloud was a pair of beastly legs.

"Two!"

Then his gigantic body.

"Three!"

Then a pair of horns, one notably blunted by Emi's sword.

"Daaaamn, that was close. Nearly lost it for a sec there."

Then a dopey remark that completely ruined the whole atmosphere he just built.

"What...what-what the hell?!"

Emi was the most surprised out of all of them. How could inject-ing him with a stream of holy force create the Devil King out of thin air? Suzuno remained dazed on the floor, incapable of anything but looking up at the monster looming above her.

"Jeez, guys, stop freaking out. ...You get what's going on, right, Chi?"

Even with her newfound skills in activating holy magic, it still pained Chiho to be near the Devil King's demonic force without any protection. Still, she flashed Satan a bold smile.

"I...think so."

Before their confrontation at Tokyo Tower, Chiho herself was poisoned by dark force created by her own body, a reaction to the holy-power overdose she'd received. So what would happen if you did that to Sadao Maou, everyday human? The answer, clad in a hid-eously overstretched UniClo T-shirt and pair of denim jeans, was right in front of them.

"Wow, you're big," Erone marveled, looking up at Satan with a light smile. Clearly he was the only one really enjoying the sight. ·

"My...my liege..."

Farfarello immediately fell to one knee. Having ascended to chieftain after the Devil King's Army was destroyed, he had never enjoyed a direct audience with Satan before. But having him, in all his gory glory, thrust upon him like this filled his heart with shame and regret. Satan, the Devil King, was alive and well, tapping into reserves of power completely beyond Farfarello's comprehension and preparing to seize the world for himself. And now he even had his old enemies on his side!

"Well? You got any more complaints now?"

The booming voice from on high immediately chided Farfarello's soul into obeisance. He fell prostrate before his lord.

"This...this is all due to my own imprudence. I am willing to accept any punishment you deem proper for ever doubting your heart, my liege."

A moment of silence ensued. Farfarello, on his hands and knees, was prepared to have his life snuffed out at any moment. But:

"Who the hell said anything about that?"

The reply was far more casual than he expected.

"It's just like I've been telling you this whole time. Just go back home, all right? I got my plan in action here, and I'm not gonna do anything stupid to mess it up. And get Barbariccia and his troops out of the Eastern Island already. I'm here in this new world, obtaining new power for myself, and paving a path to conquer the world with. As long as we're clear on that, it's all good."

"...I cherish your grace, my liege..."

"'Course, it's probably gonna take more than that to convince Barbariccia. Once you get home, I got a message I want you to give him. Tell him that I'll introduce him to the four Great Demon Generals of the *real* New Devil King's Army. I got 'em here on Earth."

"Uh?"

"Huh?"

"What?"

The existence of this force was news to all the humans in attendance.

"Alciel and Lucifer you probably remember. To that, you can add the Hero Emilia. She's an expert fighter, and she might even be stronger than I am."

"Hey!!"

"And over there is Crestia Bell, the 'Scythe of Death' from the Reconciliation Panel. She's a brilliant strategist with a background in Church diplomacy and an encyclopedic knowledge of the geopolitical situation in Ente Isla."

"What are you...!!"

"Finally, we have Chiho Sasaki, MgRonald barista and my personal assistant. Her mind-control skills are what it took to take these two former foes of mine and win them over to my side. These are the four Great Demon Generals of the new army I am assembling."

"That's *five!!*"

Emi and Suzuno couldn't help but shout it out in unison.

"Wait! That doesn't matter! You can't just make me a Great Demon General or whatever! I got a say in this, too!"

"Of all the nonsense I have ever heard from you... This is nothing short of defamation! I demand an immediate correction, retraction, and self-immolation!!"

"And what do you *mean* 'MgRonald barista'?! We can't put Chiho in any more danger than she already—"

"MgRonald...ballista...?"

"Huh?"

"Hmm?"

Maou made a point of introducing the Hero, the Reconciliation Panel enforcer, and the MgRonald barista as titles of apparently equal class. Farfarello actually bought it.

"A MgRonald ballista...a royal bishop defender? Are you a talented archer?"

"Where'd you get *that* from?!"

For reasons Emi couldn't fathom, he was mistaking a piece of résumé padding as some kind of elaborate military appellation.

"Wow...me, a general...?"

"Look!" Suzuno involuntarily exclaimed. "She is *enjoying* this!"

Chiho was ignoring them entirely, practically exuding holy force as she fell into reverie, the power of Satan's dark strength no longer any bother to her. Suzuno, at least, had a better idea of what was going on than Emi.

"*Magur on Alde...* A bishop in service of the King... Is his brain made of mush?!"

Farfarello ignored her. "I promise you," he proclaimed, "that I will join your new Devil King's Army and do whatever it takes to conquer both this world and the demon realms. From now on, I will never view the humans before me as my enemy!"

"Well said!"

"No, please *do*! 'Cause we *are*, all right?!"

Not even Emi screaming at Farfarello could snap him out of it. Maou nodded at him, convinced that he would no longer offer him any resistance.

"All right," he said, picking up the ball of dark magic on the ground with two gnarled fingers. "You can have this back. Oop!"

With a moment's concentration, Satan's body disappeared into a pyre of dark flame.

"My-my liege?!" Farfarello shouted in panic.

"...Take this with you."

In the blink of an eye, the Devil King Satan—his overwhelming power, his body, his royal majesty—was back in the form of a young man, his now completely stretched-out T-shirt hanging limply from halfway down his shoulders.

"This oughta help fill your coffers a little," Sadao Maou said. "Bring it back home and eat it, or pass it around, or whatever. Your choice." Then he tossed the ball of dark force at Farfarello.

It looked like little more than a cannonball, but the force imbued within was almost the entirety of the Devil King Satan's internal powers, reawakened by an overload of holy magic.

"But...but then, my liege..."

Now Satan was a weakling again, one with only the barest sliver of magic force. Farfarello failed to see how disposing of this power would help his liege on his conquest.

"Didn't you see?" Maou said. "I can pull that trick anytime I want to get that form back. Besides..." He chuckled as he turned toward Emi and Suzuno, seething silently at him from behind. "I better keep it cool around these ladies for a little while. You wouldn't like them when they're angry."

Farfarello could do little more than stare in mute amazement at the trio.

"Maaaaoooooouuuuu!!!!"

Then, with a shout that evoked memories of the Devil King of a moment ago, Maou's Great Demon Generals descended upon his back.

"Devil King! Take it back at once! You cannot have five Demon Generals!"

"Why not? Hell, how about I bring on two more? Then it could be Devil King and the Seven Demon Dwarfs."

"Oh, you want even *more*?! That's not even the *problem*!"

"A new set of Great Demon Generals, and a new civilization

engineered by His Demonic Highness… The people of the demon realms shall be very pleased to hear this!"

"I *told* you, that's *not* the friggin' *case*!!"

The voices of the frantic Emi and Suzuno, the emotionally overcome Farfarello, the holy-power-driven and practically airborne Chiho, and the artfully dodging Devil King Satan filled the Shinjuku air.

"Wow! Wowwwww…!"

Only Erone, witnessing the pandemonium from afar, was enjoying the scene, clapping in glee at it.

"…What're they even doing up there? If they don't need the barrier, I'm taking it down."

And finally there was Sariel, who had traveled up to the roof to find out why there was no to-the-death struggle going on. He found himself shrugging his shoulders at the casual bickering he encountered instead.

✳

"Look, I told you a thousand times! If we don't want to create any more enemies for ourselves, it's easiest for all of us if we acted like we were allies!"

Sadao Maou's shouting echoed across the Shinjuku evening.

Now back to human form, Maou was forced to sit down on the Tokyo Metropolitan Government Building roof and take a verbal beating from Emi and Suzuno, both enraged at their recent promotions to Great Demon General. The proclamation Maou had for Farfarello impacted everyone on the scene so much, his promise to lecture Chiho about trying to extract information from the demon was completely forgotten.

The thing that angered Emi the most was how he had appointed Chiho as a general, too. If Farfarello stepped through the Gate Erone had created to take him home and immediately reported *that* to Barbariccia, Chiho would no longer be a passing witness to events on Ente Isla—she'd be a full-fledged participant. Someone might see her as an enemy now; they might just pay her a visit, even. The whole point of teaching her holy magic was completely lost now, something the women nagged Maou about nonstop on the way home. But now he was sniping back at them, unable to withstand any more of it.

"Look, they aren't gonna mess with her *that* readily if she's one of my Great Demon Generals, all right? That'd be like one of your knight corps taking on Barbariccia by themselves, and he wasn't even a general in the first place."

"That's not the issue! Now everyone on Ente Isla might see Chiho as some kind of menace to them, you see? Plus, you made *her* a general instead of any of the demons in *your* realm! What if some would-be demon officer from your ranks gets jealous and decides to take her down?"

"My officers wouldn't do that! They're not *that* malicious!"

"Oh, so you only hired kind and benevolent demons for your army?"

"Oh, come on, Chi! Are you accusing *me* of being malicious here? You humans never believe a single word I tell you, but then you take my words out of context to make *me* the bad guy! If *that* isn't being malicious, what is?!"

"Well, if you *weren't* being malicious, then you were just being stupid, all right? And either way, now Chiho's in a completely *new* kind of danger thanks to you! You demonic moron!"

"Hey, you wanna go? 'Cause I'll go, man!"

"Oh, bring it on!"

"Will you *please* keep it down?!" Suzuno could bear it no longer. From the the Tokyo Metropolitan Government Building all the way to the Hatsudai station on the Keio New Line, Maou and Emi had been endlessly griping at each other. "There is no use crying over spilled milk like this. This is our fault for not fully solving the problem while Farfarello and Erone were still here. This is a defeat for us!"

"Suzu-Sis, don't be mad!"

Alas Ramus, sitting in Suzuno's arms, hit her on the head a few times. Suzuno childishly batted the pudgy arm away.

Just before Erone left with Farfarello, the child had sprung out from Emi's body, once again against the Hero's will.

"...Erone."

"Alas Ramus... It's been a long time."

"Mmm."

That conversation seemed to confirm it. Whatever Erone was, he was extremely close to Alas Ramus.

"Erone...are they okeh?"

"I'm sorry... I don't know. I'm fine, though."

"Mmm."

That was enough to make Alas Ramus beam brightly.

"Wanna play again later?"

"Sure."

And thus the short encounter between the two seeds of Sephirah ended. Alas Ramus never took her eyes off of him until he stepped through the Gate with Farfarello and out of Japan. Emi and Maou's arguing began immediately thereafter, and in the midst of it, the child was transferred over to Suzuno's arms.

"We failed to even ask where Erone came from before he left... You lose all of your brain power whenever Chiho is involved, do you not?"

"...Sorry, did you say something to me, Suzuno?"

Chiho, still half-floating in the air as she walked, was in a dream-like state.

"I did not. Chiho, let me remind you that *your* lecture awaits once we return."

"...All riiiiiiiight..."

It was difficult to tell whether that reply meant Chiho was listening or not.

"Dehhh! You people drive me to my wit's end!"

"Suzu-Sis! Don't get mad!"

"You may say that," Suzuno sternly replied, "but *someone* needs to stay serene and consider things rationally at a time like this! Otherwise, none of us would be thinking about anything at all!"

"Stay sreen an' consider things rasshon'ly?"

"…Ah. Little point telling you about it, I suppose."

There were still fairly severe limits on Alas Ramus's vocabulary skills. She tried her best to keep up, but there was only so much she could do.

"Ahh, let 'em gripe," said Sariel, himself almost floating in the air. "All's well that ends well. I've finally made up with my goddess. What more could anyone possibly ask for?"

"Is there *anyone* here willing to see things from my point of view?!" Suzuno snapped back.

"Ah! You scared me, Suzu-Sis!"

"Huh," Maou remarked as the cleric ran off in tears. "She's really putting herself through a lot, huh?"

"Whose fault do you think *that* is?" Emi replied. "And why'd you give that dark force to Farfarello anyway? Not that I mind, but…"

"Oh, like you were gonna let me keep the ability to turn into the Devil King anytime I want on the shelf or something?"

"Hey, I *said* I didn't mind!" Emi barked back.

"…Well, would you have, though? I mean, if I decided to stay Devil King, team up with Farfarello, and take over the world, that'd be a pretty darn good excuse for you to kill me."

"Do you think *that's* what I wanted this whole time?!"

"What do you mean, 'that'? Me taking over Japan, or you having an excuse to kill me?"

"……Are you just trying to rile me up, or what?"

Maou laughed a very deliberate laugh in Emi's face. "Haven't you been doing that all night to me? I deserve a turn, too."

Emi gnashed her teeth and turned her back to him.

"But to be serious for one second, considering Chi and all…"

The two of them turned back toward Chiho, still almost literally walking on air.

"Given everything she said to us, I wasn't stupid enough to leave anything for *you* guys to get in a big snit about. Oh, and before I forget, here's your fee."

Before she had the time to chew on that, Emi frowned at the ragged thousand-yen bill Maou dangled in front of her.

"What, don't you want it?"

"No."

"What?!"

She turned it down without any hesitation at all. Maou almost caught himself respecting her for that.

"If I take that, then it really *would* be like we've got a business relationship going. Don't get any weird ideas. I just helped you *this* time because I had to if we were gonna save Chiho."

"I wasn't really thinking along those lines…but, but if you don't need it, I seriously won't give it to you, okay? You sure about that?"

It was hard for Emi to imagine that Maou, sniveling to himself as he took back the money, was the same person as the Devil King who had just spoken regally about the future of the demon realms.

"Don't worry about it. But would you mind not telling Chiho that we heard her Idea Link, for me?"

"Huh? Why?" Maou asked as he wadded the bill back into his wallet.

"Well, I doubt she would've wanted us to hear that, and besides…"

"Besides?"

Emi's eyes narrowed against the light of the setting sun as they darted between Maou and Chiho.

"I don't know. It seems so…convincing. I hate it."

"What?"

The words from Emi's lips were so soft, they were all but drowned out by the sounds of western Shinjuku traffic.

"…Nothing. Just don't tell Chiho! All right?"

"Um, sure. Dunno why not, but…"

Maou nodded, confused. Emi was back to her usual grumpy self, but something about her didn't make sense. *Must be hung up on something still*, he supposed.

"Oh, right. Hey, Chi! Chi!"

"Yeahhh… Oh!" Chiho snapped out of her legal high. "Ummm, yeah?"

"Hey, so we can save the lecturing for later, but you mind coming along with me a little bit? There's a little side trip I wanna make."

"A side trip?"

"Where are you taking her?"

There was no way Emi would dare expose Chiho to more danger tonight. Depending on the location, she was prepared to tail them the entire way.

"Oh, yeah, you oughta know, too. I heard your birthday was coming up, Chi, but when is it?"

Chiho and Emi froze for a few moments.

"Birth...day?"

"Oh, um... Yeah, it's September tenth," Chiho replied meekly.

"Yeah? Well, I was just thinking...you know, I used to be Devil King and all, so I figure there's no way I could come up with a birthday present you'd like by myself, so...like, I thought it'd be safer to just ask what kinda stuff you like when I had a chance."

It wasn't exactly the smoothest move a man could make in a relationship. To Emi, the idea of a Devil King understanding the concept of celebrating birthdays seemed abhorrent in a way.

"Like, I still don't think I have much of an idea of what you're into, but I don't think you like all the cutesy girlie stuff Emi does, so..."

"I am *not* into 'girlie stuff'!"

"Hey, you can call it what you want, but you're still a grown woman carrying a Relax-a-Bear wallet around."

"That still beats your stupid hundred-yen-shop plastic thing! Plus, I'm only a year older than Chiho is!"

"Yeah, well, anyway...as you can probably guess, I can't spring for anything too fancy or expensive, but is there anything reasonably decent that you might like?"

It was almost too point-blank a question, as if Maou was asking her whether she wanted any sauce to go with her chicken nuggets. Chiho looked up at Maou for just a moment.

"I...I think I've already gotten it," she said, smiling.

"Oh? ...Wait, what? Did I give something to you?"

"You sure did. In fact, it might be the one thing I want the most right now."

"Um? Really?" Maou's confused face betrayed no memory of this. "Well, huh. What was it, though?"

Chiho was all but skipping down the sidewalk, a mysterious grin on her face.

"Pfft. Not a care in the world, huh? You two probably deserve each other."

"Huh? Do you know, Emi?"

"...I sure don't want to."

"Wh-what?"

"Hee-hee-hee! It's a secret until you figure it out!" Chiho brought a finger to her lips to emphasize her point. "Oh! But *your* birthday's in the fall too, isn't it, Yusa?"

"Me?" Emi blinked at the sudden subject change.

"Oh, is it?"

"I think Suzuno mentioned that to me one time or another..."

"......"

Emi glared dolefully at Maou as she nodded.

"Well, yeah, my birthday's in the early fall in the Western Island, but I don't really have one on Japan's calendar. It doesn't really matter anyway, I don't think."

"Aw, but you should!" Chiho excitedly grabbed Emi's arm. "Maybe we could exchange presents!"

"Oh, come onnnn, that's just embarrassing!" Emi's cheeks turned red at the extremely teenager-ish request.

"Well, I still have to repay you somehow, don't I? And you, too, Maou. If I don't do a favor for you guys, too, someone might really kill me next time!"

"Uh, jeez, Chiho..." Emi couldn't tell how serious she was being.

"But...yeah," Maou said. "Looking at it that way, I guess maybe I *do* owe you guys a little, huh?"

"Don't be so serious about it. And I *really* don't want you thinking about me like that anyway, all right?"

Emi couldn't bear the thought of, say, Chiho convincing Maou to buy her some sort of Relax-a-Bear merchandise. It would probably cause her to despise Relax-a-Bear forever.

"You wouldn't accept anything from me in the first place, would you?"

"Of course not. So don't think about it—"

"Okay, so how about this?"

"Huh?"

Suddenly, Maou clapped his hands in the middle of the sidewalk. It filled Emi with a sense of dark foreboding.

"I just named you one of my Great Demon Generals, right?" he began.

"If you're willing to let me resign as my present, I'd be willing to consider that a gift," Emi retorted.

"Not with Farfarello to worry about, I'm not. But instead of that, Emi, I want you to follow me around so you can keep watch over what I'm doing all the time."

Time stopped for a moment.

"What?" Emi and Chiho echoed, their voices cracking.

"Look, you're at an impasse, aren't you? Like, over whether you should keep treating me like your foe or not. So why don't you take the time to give me a second evaluation? You're in my inner circle of generals, you know; you could stab me in the back anytime you want. I'm not plannin' on going down that easy, but if you don't like what you see me getting up to, then let's settle it, right then. As Hero and Devil King. What do you think?"

"What do I—?"

"It'll be like starting with a blank slate. I'll show you with my actions that I'm not the kind of Devil King you think I am. I guess you're curious about what's driving me to conquer the world, too, huh, Chi? Well, I'll tell you everything from A to Z. And if you don't like that, let's duke it out one more time. So..."

Maou smiled, satisfied at the sheer genius of the proposal he thought up.

"...if you want to clear your mind, Emilia the Hero, then follow me. I've got a whole new world to show you. Once I conquer it, that is."

Chiho and Emi froze on the spot.

"Huh," observed Sariel, unaffected by this blip in the passage of time. "Quite the orator when you want to be, aren't you?"

Then:

"......——!!!!!!!"

"Huh? Wha? Huh?"

Emi's face burned red, as though someone had splashed gasoline on it and lit a match.

At the same moment, Suzuno, who had arrived at Hatsudai station ahead of them, marveled in shock as Alas Ramus disappeared from her arms. Simultaneously, the Better Half, and all the power it represented, settled into Emi's hand.

"Wh-whoa! Emi?! There's, there's kind of a lot of people around—"

She pointed it directly at Maou.

"Heavenly Storm Fang!!"

An unrelenting gale thrust its way toward him, plastering his all-too-human body against a nearby tree before dropping him into the bushes below.

"Do, do, do you have *any idea* what, what, what you're *saying* to me?!"

Emi had little idea what she herself was saying. Maou had even less.

"You *idiot*! You complete idiot! Forget it! You are my enemy! My mortal enemy! My nemesis! I was so stupid for doubting myself! I-I-I *dare* you to say anything weird like that ever again! I don't care what Alas Ramus and Chiho think—when that, that, *that* time comes, I'm gonna rip your neck off, you, you—"

Tears welled in Emi's eyes, her face flush with every emotion in the world.

"—you *thoughtless creep*!!!"

Then she stormed off, walking even faster than Suzuno before her.

"Wh-what's up with her...?" Maou mused as he crawled out from the bushes, still a little dazed as a shadow crossed his head.

"H-hey, Chi, give me a hand... Huh?"

In front of him, framed by the sunset behind her, Chiho grabbed Maou—not by the hand, but by his shirt collar.

"Chi…?"

"Maou, could you treat me to some cake, please?"

"Huh?!"

"You were going to celebrate my birthday, right? So treat me to some cake, *right now!*"

"What? Hey, c'mon, why are you kind of angry, too…?"

"I don't know!!"

"Um, um, Chi? I-I can walk just fine, so, uh, you can let go of my collar anytime you want, so…"

Maou found himself being dragged back the way he came by the teenager. Sariel, left to himself, chuckled as he pictured what kind of high-end Shinjuku sweet shop they would wind up in.

"Ah, friendship is a beautiful thing. I'd best think about dinner myself. My first trip to MagCafé!"

"What is *with* all you people…?"

Maou stared up at the setting sun as Chiho dragged him along. No matter how much he thought about it, he just couldn't figure out what had made Emi's face explode and cause Chiho to have such an outburst. "Too bad she couldn't always look like that," he said, smiling to himself. "That was kinda cute."

"What did you say?!"

"Nothing, nothing."

Then he stopped thinking. He knew what would happen if he riled Chiho any further, although he didn't know why it *was* riling her up. Turning around a little, he realized Chiho's ears were just a little reddened.

"Not exactly what I imagined," Maou whispered to himself as he watched the red Tokyo sky, "but I guess dreams never turn out exactly the way you want them to, huh?"

Kisaki had almost let her fantasies dupe her into committing to a bad property. Sariel had even more substantial obstacles in his way before he could have the kind of relationship with Kisaki that he wanted. Alas Ramus had finally reunited with one of her companions, but only for a few seconds. Ashiya was probably going to scream at him for tossing away his demonic power, and nothing about any-thing Urushihara did ever contributed in a positive fashion. And Suzuno, Chiho, and Emi—none of their realities were exactly what they wanted, but they were still trying to batter through those walls, trying to change it into the world of their respective dreams.

And Maou, too…

"Yeah, I kinda doubt a three-hour training session is gonna get me up to Ms. Kisaki's level…"

The MgRonald Barista workshop was a valuable experience for him, yes, but if he wanted the skills he needed to even approach Kisaki and her barman ethos, he would need to keep at it for a while to come.

Still, Maou and everyone around him had definitely taken another step toward their dreams compared to yesterday—no matter how small it was.

The heat still lingered after dark in late-summer Tokyo, but the evening sky was clearly beginning to show the telltale signs of autumn.

Well, huh, Maou thought to himself as his jeans dragged along the sidewalk. *Maybe a red sky ain't so bad after all. It just depends on how you look at it.*

"I'd like to have a shortcake, all right? One with looooooots of strawberries on it!"

"Um, strawberries are gonna be pretty expensive this time of year, aren't they? I, uh, I don't have that much to work with…"

The Devil King, the Hero, the demons, the angels, and the people around them. Their hearts, their goals, even their pathways home—they were all so dizzyingly different from one another.

EPILOGUE

On the wall by the order counter, there were now two more certificates next to Kisaki's indicating that the location was home to MgRonald Baristas, experts in the entire MagCafé menu. Most of the certificates were written in English text for some reason, but between the fancy white-and-gold lettering over the MgRonald red background describing the coursework completed and the frame it was inserted into, it looked quite a bit fancier than it had any right being. The names engraved on them—SADAO MAOU and CHIHO SASAKI—were visible across the entire restaurant space.

"Well, since we're all here, why don't we have Ms. Yusa try a taste test to see how much you guys have improved?"

Kisaki, as promised, was treating Emi and Suzuno to a free round of café au lait. They arrived just as Chiho began her shift.

"Oh, you're on!" Maou's eyes shined with confidence.

"I...I don't know," Chiho said, demonstrating just a tad of nervousness.

"Are you sure?" Emi politely asked.

"Well, I did promise you a free drink, and I'm sure Maou wants some revenge for his loss this morning."

"His loss?"

Chiho tittered a little. "I guess Ashiya and Urushihara came in earlier. They had a competition between Maou's and Ms. Kisaki's coffee, but..."

"Even Urushihara spotted the difference. Like, instantly. I was *so* pissed."

He looked the part. Kisaki laughed.

"Your coffee's consistent. You really understand what MgRonald is doing with their beans. You should be proud of that!"

"But both of them liked your coffee better..."

"Well, Mr. Ashiya looked a little tired, so I amped up the bitterness and body for him so he could kick back and relax a bit. And Mr. Urushihara didn't seem like a regular coffee drinker to me, so I kept it light and approachable, almost Americano level."

"......"

Maou fell silent as Kisaki perfectly described the preferences of his roommates, two people who had barely even ventured into a MgRonald.

"I guess I *was* cheating a little, though. After all, I wanted to reassure your friends that you're working under a talented manager."

"Indeed," Suzuno teased, "it sounds like this battle may be over before it begins."

"Not if I got a say in it!" Maou sniped back.

"Well, let's stop talking about it and get started, huh, Maou?"

Kisaki, Maou, and Chiho filled their small espresso cups with regular coffee and presented them to Emi and Suzuno. Both of them took a sip from all three cups.

"So from right to left... Chiho's, Ms. Kisaki's, and Sadao's, perhaps?"

"Yeah, I think Ms. Kisaki's is the middle one, too. But the other two...they didn't taste all *that* different to me."

"Geh..."

Chiho snickered. "There's just no beating her, is there?"

Just as they'd thought, the middle coffee was Kisaki's.

"Still," Kisaki said, "did you hear that? Your customers said there wasn't any big difference qualitywise. That shows how much better you've both gotten at this. Thanks to both of you for cooperating in this little game. I'd best return to work now, but feel free to stay for as long as you like. I'll bring both of you a full cup in a moment."

Maou and Chiho bowed to them, the former with extreme reluctance, as they went back to their posts. Watching them go, Emi took another look at the three cups in front of her.

"If anything, his is actually pretty delicious. It's *so* annoying."

Suzuno grinned. "He is nothing if not nimble with his hands. So is Ashiya, for that matter."

"So…what're we doing here, anyway? I wasn't expecting you to drag me into MagCafé like this."

Suzuno called Emi earlier to suggest they go out and see Maou and Chiho on the job. That was how Emi was here, but Suzuno had yet to reveal her motivations for this visit.

"I told you already. I simply wanted to see the Devil King and Chiho as they go about their duties."

"That's it? Really?"

"Well and truly, yes. In particular…" Suzuno picked up the middle cup. "I wanted to see how he acted under the watchful eye of Ms. Kisaki."

"…What do you mean?" Emi asked as she watched the trio handle a new customer.

"Well, everything still remains clear as mud, does it not? What drove, and what drives, the Devil King to conquer the world in the first place."

Emi fell silent.

"What is it? Your face is glowing red. Should we move out of the direct sunlight, perhaps?"

"N-no!" Emi brought a hand to her cheeks, embarrassed that Suzuno spotted her thinking about their trip back from the Tokyo Metropolitan Government Building a few days ago. "I'm fine, all right?"

Whenever she thought about that evening, she found herself exploding into a torrent of emotions, all beyond her comprehension. She was powerless to control it.

"We likely could have surmised this already, but the Devil King truly seems to have the utmost respect for his manager. Perhaps his statement about there always being someone you must bow your head to was from the heart after all."

"So…what?" Emi asked. "What're you trying to say?"

Suzuno silently took something out from her sleeve and put it on the table.

"That's...a piece of the Heavenly Regiment's weapons, isn't it?"

It was a small, jagged metal piece of obviously poor manufacture.

"The Regiment were all human beings...and the angels are not so far removed from us after all."

"Hmm...?"

"Everybody has someone they must bow their heads to. I can think of no other creature who can say that."

Emi gasped as she slowly began to grasp the point Suzuno was making.

"Bell, you...you aren't..."

"Now, I say that while being fully cognizant of the fact that the Devil King and Alciel and Lucifer remain our enemies. But...we have seen how they act here in Japan, and I thought it was time to reflect on these observations. To see what they mean to us."

The angels, which they had thought were sublimely supernatural, were just regular people all along.

The conclusion to derive from this was obvious.

The question that next came from Suzuno's lips was a literal "deal with the devil"—a sweet invitation not just for Emi, but for every man and woman on Ente Isla who was faced with the Devil King's invasion. But neither Emi Yusa nor Suzuno Kamazuki could dodge the question any longer:

"What...do you think the 'demons' *truly* are?"

THE AUTHOR, THE AFTERWORD, AND YOU!

I think that to a lot of people out there, coffee is an indispensable part of their daily work lives. I, Wagahara, am an ardent member of that group myself, and there's always a mug at the ready at a corner of my desk as I focus on my work.

That doesn't mean, however, that I have any deep philosophy about my coffee, any "*This* way or the highway!"–type requirements. My stance is that whether it's instant, brewed, or from a can out of the vending machine, the best coffee in the world is the one in my hand right now. Still, whenever I come across some coffee that matches my preferences perfectly...well, that's a rush I can never get enough of.

The original inspiration for this story came from a cup of coffee exactly like that. I encountered it at a certain café I stopped by once, and it was so perfect to my palate, I almost instinctively quoted the worlds of French Revolution–era politician Charles Maurice de Talleyrand, who once described coffee as "black as the devil, hot as hell, pure as an angel, sweet as love." A pity I couldn't have collaborated with Talleyrand on this book, in fact. We both seem to have preoccupations with demons and caffeine.

Sadly, this café is a good two hours down the freeway by car, so most of the time, it's good ol' instant coffee for me. You can't have everything in life.

Now, while I'm sure I don't have to remind anyone who's read this far, *The Devil is a Part-Timer!*, now in its second year of publication, is getting made into an anime series. I did a spit take with my coffee when my editor told me about it.

When 029 showed me the first visuals he was preparing for Volume 1 two years ago, and when both Akio Hiiragi and Kurone Mishima turned my work into two comic series a year ago, each of these talented creators used their own viewpoints to make the story even more attractive and engaging to readers. They helped me learn quite a bit about my own creation. Now, with this anime version, I'll have a chance to survey every nook and cranny of this world once again, a chance to rediscover all the charms it holds for me. That's something I think I can throw right back into these novels—it's the least I can do, after all, for all the many readers who've supported me thus far.

This volume depicted the story of a Devil King, a Hero, and a teenage girl taking one more step forward in the lives, as much as their budgets will allow. Whether they're in anime form or not, it's a beautiful thing to see.

One final note: Regular human beings are incapable of wielding holy magic, no matter how long they scream their heads off at the local public bath. Please be kind to your neighbors.

And with that, I hope to see you in the next volume.

Bye for now!!

HAVE YOU BEEN TURNED ON TO LIGHT NOVELS YET?

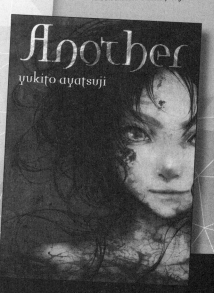